BACKWATER DIVA

A KURT HUNTER MYSTERY

STEVEN BECKER

Copyright © 2020 by Steven Becker
All rights reserved.
No part of this book may be reproduced in any form or by any electronic or mechanical means, including information storage and retrieval systems, without written permission from the author, except for the use of brief quotations in a book review.

This is a work of fiction. Names, characters, businesses, places, events, locales, and incidents are either the products of the author's imagination or used in a fictitious manner. Any resemblance to actual persons, living or dead, or actual events is purely coincidental.

Join my mailing list
and get a free copy of my starter library:
First Bite

Click the image or download here: http://eepurl.com/-obDj

MAPS

If you're interested in following along with the action or the locations it the book, please check out the Google map here:

*https://www.google.com/maps/d/u/1/edit?mid=
1APBzyefPpzoNrFNBCHzFYb85Coc&usp=sharing*

**Get my starter library First Bite for Free!
when you sign up for my newsletter**

http://eepurl.com/-obDj

First Bite contains the first book in several of Steven Becker's series:

Get them now (http://eepurl.com/-obDj)

BACKWATER DIVA

1

STEVEN BECKER
A KURT HUNTER MYSTERY
BACKWATER DIVA

The tottering stack of a half-dozen boxes sitting by the door was a pretty good clue my life was about to change. Packed inside was the household stuff I'd brought when I moved in, plus all my accumulated possessions for the three years I'd lived here, which had to make some kind of statement. My minimalist "inside" stuff was dwarfed by the "outside" stuff piled downstairs. There was every bit as much there and more—just in fishing gear.

Moving out of the Park Service house on Adams Key was probably the most difficult part of my reassignment. Even though I was relocating less than ten miles away to finally live full time in a new condo with Justine, my wife, and would still be working on the water much of the time, the island had become a part of me.

The light rain wasn't helping my mood any, either.

I picked up the first box and opened the door to take it downstairs. I made it halfway when Zero came barreling up the stairs. With my neighbor's pit bull mix plowing toward me, I had no choice but to retreat back up. Once those toenails started to click and claw on the wood treads, Zero had no choice but to go directly to the top. Between the narrow staircase and his stocky body, turning around would defy physics. I greeted him at the top and rubbed him behind his ears, wondering if he would miss me. I decided that he would, but certainly not as much as he would Justine and Allie.

"Hey, Kurt. He givin' you trouble?" Ray asked from the bottom of the stairs.

With only two residences on the island, my neighbor and I had grown close over the last few years. I'd watched his son, Jamie, grow from a toddler to a boy, and his younger sister from an infant to a toddler.

With my arms growing weary from the weight of the box in my hand after my encounter with Zero, I started back down the stairs. From behind I heard a loud *whomp* as an unhappy Zero flopped on the wooden landing, knowing he had made the trip up in vain. The ear rub had been a poor substitute for the treats he expected. I set my box down under the eaves to keep it out of the rain and took the offered beer.

I took a sip. "Always thought you would be the first to move." Becky had been beating her drum to relocate the family to the mainland. Ray knew it was inevitable, but this place was even more a part of him than it was of me. In charge of maintenance for Biscayne National Park's barrier islands, he spent most of his time along the skinny stretch of land that separated Biscayne Bay from the Atlantic Ocean. Once a week he and Becky made the eight-mile run to Homestead for groceries and supplies.

He drank. "Ain't beat yet. Mangrove's have been thick on the reef if you want to try your luck."

His invitation to go fishing made the move seem all the more real. Three years ago when relocating here, in a move I thought of as the National Park Service's witness protection program, I'd had no boating or saltwater fishing experience. With the help of Ray and one of the friendlier guides, Chico, I had learned both.

Adams Key had been a natural move for me. Ray had also taught me how to survive the eccentricities of both island life and my old boss.

Martinez had been kicked upstairs and now prowled the bars and golf courses in Atlanta. His old office had remained vacant the last few months while the division director did whatever division directors do to find a replacement. I was asked to apply, but declined, and ended up with a sideways promotion, which was what I preferred.

Being assigned to Biscayne National Park as a Special Agent had allowed me to get back on my feet after leaving—or rather, fleeing—California, where I'd become a target for a drug cartel. The job had been challenging, but had run its course, both professionally and domestically.

My story had become known over the years, but the condensed version was that I had found a pot grow in a national forest. My family had been targeted by the grower, a powerful cartel, whose focus was evenly split between making money and maintaining their reputation—which meant exacting revenge. That last bit had ended my marriage and estranged me from my teenage daughter. My life was back on track now thanks to my new wife, Justine, who's also an ace forensics tech and my attorney, Daniel J. Viscount. As they inevitably do, even bad custody situations end. Allie had turned eighteen and could now make her own decisions. She was a freshman at the University of Florida, and still called her mom's house "home," but spent every moment she could out here with me.

Ray drained the beer and crushed the can. "Daylight's burning."

Though he had essentially taught me how to fish these waters, we had seldom gone out together. Something in me wanted to keep it that way. "Thanks, though, but I've got to get this stuff over to the new place."

"See, you got to get control of this married thing."

Just as he said it, Becky called across the clearing of our two-house neighborhood.

He shook his head and called back to her, then turned to me. "Shit. Like I was sayin'. Often best to listen."

We both laughed and parted ways. I carried the boxes to the boat, where I placed them under a tarp I had rigged to try to keep things dry. At least the rain, the byproduct of some kind of tropical stew over the Florida Straits, was warm.

That wouldn't help me during the boat ride. Running at twenty knots across the bay would turn the mild hinderance into a painful pounding. Every benign drop became a projectile at that speed. If there was one thing I wouldn't miss about living out here, it was having to plan every trip around the weather and water conditions. There was something to be said for getting into a car and driving a few miles to the store.

I brought the last box down and set it under the tarp and had just secured the last corner when I felt my phone vibrate in my pocket. I ignored it while I finished checking the cargo, then stood under the protection of the T-top and pulled it out.

I was expecting Justine, but the text was from Grace Herrera. My sole ally in the Miami-Dade Police Department wanted me to call her back ASAP. Before I did, I figured I would query Justine. Since Justine was a forensic tech for the same department, I hoped to find out what was so important before returning Grace's call.

Justine was one of the two numbers in my favorites list, and I pressed connect.

"Hey. Got a hot one—or a cold one." I could hear a nasal laugh in the background that told me she was with the night and weekend medical examiner, Sid.

It sounded like they were on the road. There was enough

crime in Dade County that it might have been a coincidence, but I had a feeling. "Hey. Grace called."

She paused for a second. "Figured you might end up involved, but you better hear it from her first. Guess I'll be seeing you there."

Ordinarily, she would have shared the information. But I had already guessed that she was with Sid. I knew better than to ask, but I wanted to know where "there" was. It looked like it was going to be Grace who told me.

"OK, see ya in a bit."

I disconnected the call, found Grace's contact info, and sent her a text. She'd been promoted to captain recently, and I didn't want to endanger her standing by allowing her subordinates to hear her accept a call from the notorious Kurt Hunter. To most of the department I was like a red tide.

I didn't take it personally. There was some animosity with several of the detectives who I crossed paths with, but for the most part it was just the usual interdepartmental feuding. The National Park Service was badly underfunded and continually faced budget issues. Most of their revenue and funding went, as it should, to the maintenance and upkeep of the parks. But with fifty million acres under their umbrella, stuff was going to happen. There was going to be crime, but it was not a line item you could budget for. That left the investigative infrastructure lacking. We were reliant on local law enforcement for everything except vehicles and bullets.

Biscayne Bay National Park is located just south of Miami. Besides a harsh climate that eats infrastructure, the proximity to "civilization" makes it a catchall for everything and everyone flushed out of South Florida. That included more than our fair share of corpses. If Grace was calling, I suspected there was another one.

My phone rang, and I glanced at the display.

"Hey, Grace."

"Kurt. We've got one right on the line."

"Hope it's not Stiltsville." We'd done that dance before. Built a mile offshore of Cape Florida, the collection of structures was rich in history, both good and bad. The old community of "clubs" developed and thrived during Prohibition and later became the exclusive hangout of both presidents and gangsters. In 1985, the park's boundaries were adjusted to include what was left of the structures. Mostly fallen into disrepair, what remained after Hurricane Andrew had plowed through the area was the perfect meeting place for partiers and smugglers.

"The vessel in question is a large yacht on one of the mooring buoys at Fowey Light."

My first thought was, *Why would anyone be seven miles from land on a day like this*? "Why are you guys involved?"

"We got an anonymous call to stop a fishing vessel heading into Government Cut."

"And did you?" The light rain had now permeated the tarp and was dripping on me. It was an annoyance, but nothing compared to the perfect storm of bureaucracy this call was starting to sound like.

"Yeah, we stopped a fishing guide," Grace said.

"What are you holding him on?" She still hadn't told me what happened to make them stop the guy.

"We've got a body out there. The call said the guide was involved. Just covering our bases at this point."

"So, you've got him, and you want me to be a good ranger and run out to the light?"

"Yeah. I'm hoping that if we work together we can keep this clean. I need your permission to send Justine and Sid out."

It was an odd feeling to have Miami-Dade ask me if something was alright. This usually worked in reverse, where I uncovered a crime, or more typically a body, and needed their help to follow the case outside the park. "No problem. I can be there in thirty minutes."

"Something else you might want to know." She sounded reluctant to tell me. "The body is on a yacht registered to Alex Luna."

"Shit." I'd been involved with some cases with minor celebrities, but this was a big one.

"Yeah. Better dot your i's and cross your t's."

"Touch base with you later." I appreciated the warning. Not that I would treat the case any differently, but I had a few bad habits where protocol was involved. Martinez had been sure to always point them out to me, but I was on my own now and would have to watch my step.

Before leaving, I unloaded my worldly possessions from the boat and stacked the boxes under the covered porch, then threw the tarp back over them. The move was officially on hold. The sky was dark and the rain picked up the moment I stepped foot from under cover. I didn't have to look at the weather to know that if I had to take the small center-console offshore, it was going to be a miserable ride. My boat, a Park Service issue, was essentially a bay boat, designed for protected waters. For the majority of the park it was the right choice, but Fowey Light was several miles offshore on the tip of the famous reef that ran alongside the Keys. With the low freeboard and underpowered engine, it was going to be a wet ride.

I grabbed my foul weather gear, which in South Florida consisted of a light rain jacket, from the console and jammed a ball cap on my head. With the engine running, I released the lines and decided on my route.

The hard way, which was of course the route I chose, was to run on the outside of the barrier islands. It was a few miles shorter but generally more exposed to the elements. Since I was already wet, I figured the time savings would be worth the pounding.

Easing away from the dock at an idle, I moved into Caesar Creek. The short pass that allowed access to the Atlantic separated Elliott Key, the longest of the islands, from a smattering of smaller islands to the south. With the wind blowing in and the tide running out, I needed to power my way through the short channel. The first wave came over the bow, and I flinched as it crashed against the console, which did little to protect me. I was thirty seconds into my investigation and already drenched.

2

STEVEN BECKER

A KURT HUNTER MYSTERY

BACKWATER DIVA

The Miami skyline was barely visible on my port side as I approached the tower. That was only because of the weather. On a clear day, the cityscape stood out as a stark reminder of the fragility of the park. Biscayne Bay's tranquil aquamarine waters, emerald islands, and pristine coral reefs abutted the southern suburbs of the city, leaving the park as an easy place to dispose of all the bad things that happened just a few miles away.

On most summer afternoons it was possible to dodge the inevitable thunderstorms that were a side effect of the generally desirable subtropical climate. The anvil-shaped clouds grew high in the atmosphere as the day progressed. Backlit by the blue sky, the puffy clouds were often benign and a welcome relief from the sun. The active cells were distinct, with vertical lines connecting air to water. The darker the lines, the heavier the rain.

Today was different. A low-pressure ridge had settled over the area yesterday, and the sky was overcast. The squalls were only visible by their darker color. There was no avoiding them. I had already passed through several before the tower became visible. Mathematically, the 110-foot tower should have appeared from a little over twelve miles away. The storms had reduced the visibility and cut that distance in half.

The string of iconic lighthouses marking the reef had once been vital to navigating these waters. Just offshore, the Gulf Stream had been utilized by sailors since the days of the Spanish Main. Treasure-laden boats returning from the New World to Spain counted on the strong current to return home. Today, tankers and container ships plied the same routes. Fowey Rocks Lighthouse, as it was officially known, was the northernmost of the six lighthouses built in the 1800s with the purpose of marking the deadly reef. The advent of GPS and chartplotters had turned the structures into nothing more than landmarks for the white mooring balls set around them.

What struck me as odd was that as soon as the light came into view, a boat appeared as well. On a sunny day, there were boats scattered around the light like candles on a geriatric's birthday cake. But they usually weren't visible until you got much closer. That meant the yacht was at least fifty feet tall. As I approached the area, both the light and the yacht grew in size, but what surprised me, even as I gritted my teeth against the rain, were the dozen or so smaller boats swinging from the mooring balls.

Stars like Alex Luna meant nothing to me, but to most of the world she was a big deal. As I moved closer, I could see each of the smaller boats held at least one photographer with a telephoto lens longer than the boats' fish boxes. They weren't here for the reef. Several lenses swung my way, and I accelerated toward the empty balls away from the yacht. It didn't matter, as I soon heard the *thump thump* of a helicopter. As it circled around the light for a better view of the yacht, the logo of one of the local news networks came into view. There was once a distinction between the paparazzi and the media. Those lines had blurred lately. Both were attracted to a celebrity's death like snapper to Cheese Whiz. They were both undesirable and unavoidable, especially in a park where only an invisible line in the water marked three-quarters of its boundaries.

Many of the national parks have natural buffers around them—land indistinguishable from the park itself. Typically, the parks are in remote locations and accessed through a controlled network of roads and gates, places where what I was witnessing here would be avoidable. Biscayne National Park had no barriers or buffers.

For the first time I could remember, I was thankful to see two of Miami-Dade's boats tied off to the yacht. Another was cruising through the mooring field doing what they could to control the photographers. At least the police appeared to have a handle on the scene. There was always a downside when separate law-enforcement jurisdictions collided, but in this case, there was at least some initial value to it.

The two other Miami-Dade boats were rafted together off the transom of the yacht. They provided the only access point, which meant I would have to cross into enemy territory before I reached the scene. Fortunately, both boats were empty, proving that even a dead celebrity was a people magnet. I dropped my fenders over the port side and eased up to the outer boat, where I tied off to the bow and stern. I climbed aboard the first boat and crossed to the second before anyone saw me.

"Yo, Hunter. Someone call the Boy Scouts, or what?"

I grimaced at the sound of the voice. The officers around him ignored both the comment and me. Justine and I weren't the only ones who called the guy "Little Willy." William O'Roarke was every bit the stereotypical New York beat cop, South Florida style, though the demographics of the Miami-Dade Police Department had changed over the years. Once a refuge for northern cops to finish out their careers, Miami-Dade now had become as diverse as the community. That didn't make them any friendlier, though—just not as in your face.

Grace stepped out of the group. "Showtime's over. We've got incoming, so do your jobs."

She was smaller, thinner, and way prettier than the men surrounding the body, but her voice carried authority. After a snide comment from O'Roarke, the group disbursed. That left Sid, who was hunched over in what would have been an uncomfortable position for me—and I was thirty years his junior. Justine squatted next to him like she could stay there all day.

"Special Agent Hunter, where's your fishing pole?" Sid laughed.

It was no secret that I had "caught" several bodies while fishing the mangrove islands and channels of the park. I ignored the comment and glanced at the body. A large pool of blood spread out around the pop star, but was slowly being washed away by the rain. Under ideal circumstances, boats made for poor crime scenes. Justine's expression was intent, but worried. The weather was making this scene actually disappear.

"Cause of death?" I asked.

"To be determined," Sid answered.

I had the feeling that was a lead-in to an invitation to the autopsy. He always asked, mostly to enjoy my distress. It had taken the better part of three years, but I was finally almost comfortable with the procedure. Unfortunately for me, I considered attending the post-mortem a requirement to an investigation. Questions often arose just from my observation that the ME would never ask or notice.

Justine looked up from the deck, where she had been studying something invisible to me. "Autopsy at midnight." She shared a look with Sid, and they giggled like high school girls.

Sid and Justine were essentially the night shift for the Medical Examiner Department and the Forensic Services

Bureau. Sid had "retired" here from New Jersey, but quickly found out that he was lost outside of a morgue. The swing shift at the forensics lab suited Justine and allowed her to paddle most mornings.

I let their macabre humor go.

"Homicide?"

Sid peered over his reading glasses. "You're welcome to join us later."

That appeared to be all the information I was going to get. I turned to Grace and motioned her away from the scene. Justine ignored us. It was a theory of mine that Justine preferred a good-looking corpse to a live body. Most wives would have at least shot a look at their husbands if they walked away with an attractive woman. Justine didn't appear to notice.

"What do we have?" I asked.

Her answer was drowned out by the sound of a helicopter hovering above the deck. A cameraman, with only a harness to support him, leaned precariously out of the open door. Grace pulled her radio out. "Can someone get these idiots out of here?"

Those shouted words I could hear, but we had to wait several minutes for a police helicopter to clear the scene. When it finally did, another squall rolled over us. The rain pounding against the deck and water was distracting.

Grace raised her voice. "We're trying to get some answers from the guide we stopped in Government Cut. Even if the scene wasn't inside the park, I would have called you in. He asked for you."

No one asked for me. Ever.

She must have read my expression. "It's your fishing-guide friend, Chico."

"Shit." When I first had been assigned here, I had hoped to befriend the commercial fishermen and guides. My motivation was innocent. I didn't want their secret spots—I was just hoping to pick up a tip or two. But as I started to patrol, I realized that there was no way to cover the vast area of the park without utilizing additional eyes and ears. But the responses to my outreach efforts ranged from distaste to threats. I learned over the years that these were secretive people, often verging on paranoid. Most were aboveboard and good people, but their fishing holes were sacred ground. They would overlook most any indiscretions to keep it that way.

Chico was different. He had taught me how to fish these waters and was always receptive to a conversation. "You want me to talk to him?"

"I think that might help. Justine can handle what's left of the crime scene, and the boys can deal with whoever's aboard. I've spoken to the captain. As soon as we're finished, he'll bring the yacht to our impound dock on the river."

"Maybe better to get a pilot to run out and do it?"

"Good idea."

"I can run into Dodge Island. Can you get someone to pick me up?" The island housed the cruise-ship ports, the Miami pilots, and had a large industrial area on the back side. It was a convenient place to leave the boat.

"Sure. It's getting a little snotty out here. If you want, I can have one of the deputies run you in."

It was hard not to notice the weather had become worse, but I was already wet, and there was every chance the deputy would be as snotty as the weather. "I'll take my chances."

Moving back to where Justine was working, I stopped short. She was on all fours now, crab-walking across the deck. I'd seen this show before, and knew it was better not to interrupt.

Grace must have seen Justine as well. "I'll tell her goodbye for you."

I nodded my thanks and crossed both police boats to reach my center console. After starting the engine I cast the lines, and as the boats drifted apart I pulled the fenders. Ray had taught me about boating, and his three rules stuck with me—keep the water out of the boat, keep the people in the boat, and look good. Leaving fenders out while underway was like hanging out your dirty laundry.

I didn't even try and get on plane until I reached Cape Florida, where the landmass blocked some of the seas. Even then it wasn't comfortable, and I backed off the power and continued at ten knots until I was behind Key Biscayne. I started to accelerate, only to have the rain bite into me like a strand of fire coral, and slowed again. Part of boating was accepting what the seas gave you and what your boat was capable of. Neither were in my favor.

Almost an hour later I pulled up to the dock on the south side of Dodge Island. A police cruiser was waiting, its windows fogged up from condensation. I waved, figuring it was a fifty-fifty chance the driver saw me, and tied off the boat. Dodge Island had two distinct looks. The front, or north-facing side, housed the cruise-ship ports. The backside, where I was, was more industrial. The seawall was built for much larger boats, which forced me to scale a truck tire, hung over the concrete edge as a bumper, to reach the dock.

The weather had doubled my travel time. Initially, I had worried that the officer would be upset about having to wait for me. I knocked on the car window and waited a few long seconds until I heard the electronic locks pop. Opening the passenger door, I did my best to shed my rain jacket and water outside, then climbed in.

"You Hunter?"

I was about to ask, *Who else could it be?*, but thought better of it. "Yeah."

He pulled away from the seawall without another word, and I was thankful for the rain, which made a conversation neither of us wanted to have almost impossible. The weather hadn't discouraged anyone from driving, though, and as he turned onto the Rickenbacker Causeway, we were soon stuck behind a sea of brake lights.

I used to hate my phone, but for times like these it was a perfect diversion. That was, until I saw Alex Luna's face plastered across every site I opened.

3

STEVEN BECKER
A KURT HUNTER MYSTERY
BACKWATER DIVA

I'd never seen Chico like this. On the water he was the picture of calm. Watching him coach an angler fighting a trophy fish was a thing of beauty. The man sitting in front of me bore little resemblance to the man I knew.

"I got back to the yacht to drop the client off. The charter was covered in the online deal, but he wanted to tip me. Said his wallet was aboard, so I tied off my boat and followed him to a group of people by the foredeck. Man, they were all freaked out." He paused, a confused look coming over his face. "What happened, Kurt?"

"That's what we have to figure out." I said, trying to be careful with my tone. There was a distinct difference between an interview and an interrogation. I wanted to keep this the former. Playing the heavy was not a good role for me, and interrogation wasn't my specialty by any stretch. I felt even more out of place with someone I knew. But the little red light below the camera mounted in the corner near the ceiling was blinking. Deep in the bowels of Miami-Dade, I was under as much scrutiny as Chico. I needed to find some middle ground.

I pulled the legal pad one of the deputies had lent me closer. "Let's start at the beginning."

Chico rubbed his eyes. "All my bookings go through this website I use, so I don't screen clients like I used to. The request was for any guide in the area, not me personally. It's been slow lately, so I answered, and we agreed on a half-day charter for today."

"When did all this happen?"

"Yesterday. I was worried about the weather, but a paycheck's a paycheck."

"What was he after?" I asked, trying to humanize the discussion and find out a little about the client. Grace had told me it was Monte Luna, Alex's husband.

"He was more concerned with getting his beer on ice than with fishing. It's funny how sometimes they'll say they don't care about what they catch, but when it's time to pay, I know they better have some memories. Tides were for shit, so I talked him into tarpon. With the weather and all, I gave him the option to reschedule for a nicer day, but he was adamant that this was the only time he had."

I had heard many guides preferred beginners to experienced anglers. Expectations were lower and coaching was easier. Chico had the reputation as the guy you hired if you wanted a trophy or were after an IGFA record. It was surprising he even took the charter, but over the three years I had been here, I had noticed a large increase in personal recreational boats on the water. The old-timers told me it had started happening about ten years ago. I surmised that the charter business might be suffering.

A lot of fishermen dream of being guides or running charter boats. I'd been around long enough to see the reality of the situation. The illusion of spending your days on the water quickly turned to nightmares when you either weren't into it or the customers were difficult. On days where both were the case, it could be hell—and there was no escape until the time limit was up. I knew from experience that the best athletes rarely make the best coaches—it's the same with guides. Natural fishermen have little idea what they are doing right and can't express that to a novice. To be a successful guide takes a passion that most don't have.

The scenario didn't make sense. From Chico's description, Monte Luna was not a hard-core fisherman. I love to fish, but seeing the weather today, I would have canceled in a minute.

"He turned out to be pretty green, and he made a passing remark about his wife insisting he go."

"Any luck?"

He put his head down. "Rain makes fishing the flats a nightmare. Besides the wind, the visibility goes to shit. I figured if we went for tarpon, we could fish by one of the bridges and duck under if the weather got worse."

Chico seemed to have relaxed, so I decided to push for the full story. "Anything happen at the ramp?" I knew he met his clients at Bayfront Park in Homestead. The facility was right around the corner from park headquarters, and I passed by nearly every day.

"Had to go out to that big yacht parked on Fowey to pick him up."

I started to make notes. On the left-hand side of the page, I created a timeline; on the right, I listed questions and inconsistencies. "What time?"

"Seven when I picked him up. The yacht was pretty quiet. Just the client and some other guy waiting by the transom."

"He seemed OK then?"

"Had a hard time transferring to my boat, but he's a big guy."

I pictured the transom of the yacht and understood. Chico's flats boat had even less freeboard than my center console. It would have been a few feet down from the larger yacht to the guide's boat. In the heavy chop, even someone used to small boats would have found it awkward. "Then?"

"We had the discussion about what he was after. First thing he did was crack a beer. I got the feeling that if I put a worm on a hook, as long as he could hold his beer with the other hand, he'd be happy. I told him again that we could cancel, and he just glanced back at the yacht and shook his head. I've had customers who fished for all kinds of reasons. Drinking beer on a boat's high on the list. Some were there because their women wanted them out of the house, others wanted to ditch the family."

"Like he was forced?"

Chico shrugged. "You know how it goes. Might have been the weather. My boat was bobbing around like a cork behind the yacht. He almost seemed relieved when I headed toward downtown. I've always had good luck at the causeway."

"Rickenbacker?"

He nodded. "Good current there." He looked around the room. "I could use a smoke."

"I'll see what I can do, but we have to get through this first."

"Am I a suspect or something?"

I figured a little honesty might go a long way. In a high-profile case like this, Miami-Dade might have sweated him in an attempt to break him, but my gut told me not to. "You were aboard when whatever happened, happened. The cause of death was not apparent at the scene. Hopefully, the autopsy will reveal something."

"Bad goddamned luck."

"About what time did you get back?"

"Tide was bad when we got to the bridge, so I set him up with a Sabiki rig to catch bait. Took an hour or so until we anchored."

"Thought your specialty was fly fishing?" Chico had taken

me from being a freshwater stream fishermen to a pretty competent saltwater fishermen.

"No way that guy was going to handle a fly rod. I could tell pretty quick from the way he was getting off on catching pinfish that he was green."

Part of the appeal of fishing is that it is scalable. Out west, in the trout streams, I used a four-weight fly rod that made bringing in a six-inch trout a challenge and a twelve-incher an adventure. It was the same for bait fishing. Most hardcore anglers will deny it, but with a lightweight setup and the multi-hook rigs, catching bait could be as much fun as the target species.

"Any luck?"

"Had to sit through the tide change, but when it started to flow, his rod got hammered."

"How'd that go?"

"Once he put his beer down, we did OK. I had to release the anchor and chase him, but the channel was empty because of the weather, so we ended up landing it."

It was common and often necessary when fighting a hundred-pound fish to be able to move with it. Boats expecting that kind of fight were rigged with float balls that allowed the anchor to be jettisoned and easily retrieved after the fight.

I wrote down *beer* on the right-hand side of my page. It seemed to be a recurring subject.

"Got a shot of him and the fish. Didn't think he'd want to get that close to the water—or the fish—but he insisted. Turns out he was pretty excited." Chico pulled his phone out and scrolled through several screens before handing it to me to look at a picture.

"Can you send it to me?"

"You got AirDrop?"

I was surprised at his technological acumen. Offshore fishermen had long ago adopted fish finders and chartplotters. I'd never seen an inshore guy use more than a tide or weather radar app on his phone.

A second later my phone dinged, and I opened the picture. "Nice one." The silver-scaled fish would have been a trophy for most anglers. Monte was bent over in an awkward position that barely had him in the picture. It must have been a gymnastic feat for Chico to take the picture while holding the fish and still getting Monte in the frame. No one wanted a hundred-pound fish in the boat, so the pictures were usually taken with the fish in the water just before it was released.

"What happened next?" I asked.

"Released the fish. Started raining again, so we retrieved the anchor and sat under the bridge for a while. He drank a few beers while we waited."

"Fish anymore?"

"Nah, he kept looking at his watch. The rain let up and I ran him back to the yacht."

"How much did he have to drink?"

"Into his second six-pack, but he was a big guy."

"So, you ran him back to the yacht?"

"That's what the man wanted. Said he appreciated everything and wanted to tip me, but his wallet was aboard. Big goddamned boat."

Another sad fact of life, but I guess you didn't accumulate that much money by giving it away. "Anything happening when you reached the yacht?"

"Like I said, there was some kind of commotion on deck. Loud music, people freaking out and all."

"You took the tip and headed back?"

"Never got that far. Something wasn't right out there, so I bailed on it."

I paused for a few minutes. From my experience, Chico was

as honest as they came, but I probably had blinders on. I sat back and tried to play devil's advocate, but couldn't figure out how he was involved other than coming aboard for the tip he never got. I knew Chico, which was probably why he asked for me. He was no liar. I couldn't come up with any more questions.

"How about that cigarette?" he asked.

"Yeah, let's get you out of here." There was no ruling or any evidence that Monte, let alone Chico, had been involved in the death of Alex Luna. I wasn't even sure it was a murder yet. Trying not to glance at the blinking red light, I led Chico from the interrogation room. Catching several looks from the officers on duty, we left the building. Once outside, both of us realized we had no vehicle.

"I'd give you a ride, but I don't have my truck."

"No problem. I'll call my daughter. She goes to the U, so she should be around."

We sat on a low concrete wall, waiting together for his daughter to arrive. Chico nursed a cigarette he had bummed, and we were mostly lost in our own thoughts. Mine were about surviving the pending autopsy. A news van pulling into the lot brought me back to the present. I wasn't sure if it had anything to do with Chico or the death of Alex Luna, but I decided to play it safe.

"Come on, let's take a walk." It was time for some tough love. "Whatever the cause, this is going to be a high-profile case. Someone will figure out you were one of the last people to see her alive, and these guys—" I glanced over at the news van. "They have teeth. You might want to stay low until this blows over."

"I didn't see anything. It was getting all jiggy, so I took off. So do barracuda. I'll be alright."

I wasn't so sure, but I had warned him. The van had pulled past us and stopped in front of the building. The crew seemed to be doing whatever they do to prepare for a broadcast. There was some pointing and discussion. I got a bad feeling when they quickly loaded back up.

I thought we were out of their line of sight, and before I realized they were coming for the man in the Park Service uniform standing next to the fishing guide, a camera protruded from the passenger-side window. The door opened and the talent hopped out with a microphone in her hand.

"Agent Hunter!"

4

STEVEN BECKER
A KURT HUNTER MYSTERY
BACKWATER DIVA

THE MEDIA IS MY KRYPTONITE. I TRIED TO WALK AWAY—IT WOULD look really bad if I ran. Every press conference or interview I have done has gone badly. The only thing that I missed about Martinez since he had been kicked upstairs was his media savvy. My old boss lived for the podium.

"Agent Hunter?"

I knew the question was superfluous. If they didn't already know who I was, the khakis told them. But I couldn't stop the natural instinct to turn when I heard my name, and I glanced at the reporter. Her looks held my gaze for a second too long. In two strides of her longer-than-life legs, she was in front of me. The cameraman took four steps to catch up and stood just off to the side with the lens focused on both of us.

"Agent Hunter. Can you confirm that Alex Luna passed away earlier today?"

At least she didn't say the "M" word. "I can't comment on an ongoing investigation." I stopped short, knowing I had already blown it.

"An investigation implies foul play. Can you confirm?"

It's what they wanted. Dying by natural causes is boring—

homicide is news. I paused for a long second, knowing it would be used against me, but words mattered. "The cause of death will be determined by the medical examiner's office. Until then, there is *nothing* to comment on."

Before she could push further, a compact car pulled to the side of the road. Chico made a beeline for the passenger door.

"Any chance of a ride?" I asked.

He opened the back door before getting in and nodded. I forced myself to turn away from the model-slash-reporter, and dove into the open door. Seconds later, the car pulled away from the curb. Knowing the camera would be on us, I ducked until we were down the block.

"I owe you," I said.

Chico was watching the scene behind us in the side mirror. I risked a glance back and saw no pursuit, then realized they didn't need to follow us. They had the license plate number. Even before the COD was determined, Chico was a suspect in their eyes.

"Remember what I said about laying low. I'm sure they'll run your tag and figure out who you are."

"Thanks. The officer that escorted me in said they needed to keep my boat for a few days."

"I'll see what I can do about that. I might have an in with the forensics department." That got a laugh and broke the tension. We were several blocks away now, and his daughter relaxed her death grip on the wheel.

"Where can we drop you?" Chico's daughter asked.

My first thought was to grab my boat and run away to my island. Instead, I decided to be responsible and gave her Justine's address. Thankfully, instead of keying it into her phone while she was driving, she let me give directions. Fifteen minutes later we pulled up outside of the condo.

"I'll find out about the boat and keep you posted. Appreciate the ride."

"Sure thing. You got me out."

I left the car and walked down the path to the front door. Since keys and water didn't mix well, we had decided to use an electronic lock. I typed in my code. Every time I used the lock, I wondered what happened when the batteries ran out, but they didn't die this time and the bolt slid back. I opened the door, turned on the light, and found myself in the midst of another move in progress. Notably, there were about four times as many boxes as I had.

My dresser drawer remained intact, and after a quick shower and change of clothes, I was feeling better. The clock on the microwave told me it was T-minus six hours to the autopsy. I decided on a bite to eat and scavenged enough from the refrigerator for a sandwich. After I ate, I sat down with Justine's laptop.

I started with a search on Alex Luna. Not surprisingly, all the information was PR. There were a few results with clickbait headlines from the tabloids. I ignored those and started to dig deeper into her husband. The search results for Monte were even more generic, almost as if they had been scrubbed. After Google, I did the usual creeper stuff and checked out both their Facebook and Instagram accounts. As expected, they were vanilla. They looked like they were run by a publicist.

I found myself digging deeper, though at this point I had no reason to suspect foul play. All I had was a fishing trip and a death. Monte's excursion was well-timed. On the surface, it appeared he, or someone else, didn't want him to be on the yacht this morning—or he had manufactured a concrete alibi.

From the minute I got the call from Grace, there had been a sense of urgency about the case, or rather incident, as it would remain until Sid said otherwise. My gut told me something was wrong. Of course, everyone aboard appeared to be shocked and grief-stricken, but there was an additional vibe—a feeling of desperation aboard the yacht that was almost palpable. It took me a minute to figure out that losing Alex meant more to them. With her went their livelihoods.

Had the TV not been packed up, I might have bailed on the research to watch something, but with five hours until the autopsy, I needed something to do.

I pulled the folded sheet of legal paper from my pocket and laid it next to the computer. To the timeline, I added when I had been contacted, my arrival at the yacht, and the start and end times of my interview with Chico. I looked at my questions on the right side of the page, and acted on each.

I immediately saw a hole and texted Chico to ask which online booking company he used. That would reveal who paid for and booked the trip—not that it mattered at this point. The only other lead I had was the trophy picture. Opening it on my phone, I noticed two things. First, it was a really big fish, and second, Monte was stoked. Apparently, the trophy catch had changed his mind about fishing. He wouldn't be the first.

Tapping the pen on the pad, I started to think. Celebrities have the same issues as the rest of us, except they are amplified. Money and sex were the usual suspects. Even the clickbait results for Alex showed nothing in the way of marital affairs. She was known to be a driven performer, so I suspected that if there was foul play, it had to do with money.

I had access to credit reports and ran one on Alex and Monte. They were both voluminous and would take some time to wade through. I still had three hours to go, and with it near my bedtime, I was beat. Hoping some "light" reading would induce a nap, I started with Monte's file. I got through the basics when my phone rang.

This time of night, I usually only answered if it was Justine or Allie, and each had a distinctive ringtone. This was neither.

Tilting the screen toward me, I saw a 202 area code. When DC called, you answered. I picked up the phone and hit accept.

"Kurt Hunter."

"Agent, this is Ed Harris." He paused.

I had met the Deputy Director of Operations last year. "Hello, sir." There was little doubt why he was calling.

"There is a training video on the website about how to deal with the media, Agent Hunter. I suggest you watch it."

"Yes, sir." There was nothing else to say about that. "Autopsy will be conducted in a few hours. I've also interviewed the fishing guide the deceased's husband spent the morning with."

"I have no concerns about your investigative abilities. It's the media, Hunter. Just run the other way."

"You can count on that."

"And, about your status."

I had been a Special Agent for Biscayne Bay National Park under Martinez, who had been the Special Agent in Charge, a job I didn't want and had turned down because of exactly what this call was about. My successes did outnumber my failures, though it was a running joke that I created my own cases by hooking them. After Martinez was promoted, I retained my Special Agent designation, but instead of being officially relocated to another park, I was tagged as a roving national park troubleshooter. Aside from moving off the island, it was a dream job. Allie was away at college, and Justine didn't mind if I traveled.

"Sir?"

"It's your case."

I was waiting for the "Don't screw it up," which was implied, even if he didn't say it out loud.

"I'll be at the autopsy and keep you posted."

"Whatever you need. It's as high profile as it gets, so act accordingly."

I hated to ask for help, but I had been intimidated by the scope of the financial records. "Do we have a forensic accountant?"

"If and when you need it. I'll see what I can do."

I disconnected and went back to work, now fully awake. I waded through the documents, making notes. I would need tax returns to provide a picture of the couple's income, but the credit reports told me they had massive expenses. I finished Monte's report and was about to start on Alex's when my eyes started to close. Before I dozed off, I set the alarm on my phone for eleven thirty. There was no need to shower before the autopsy. From past experience, within a few minutes of the start of the procedure I would be a hot mess.

It took me a few seconds to realize it was the ringtone from an incoming call and not my alarm that woke me. Bleary-eyed, I glanced at the screen and saw Chico's name. By the fourth ring, I managed to sit upright, and answered.

"Hey, Kurt. There's a slew of the reporters sitting outside my house."

I got up and found the piece of paper I had left by the laptop. Turning it over, I wrote down his address. "You might as well call Miami-Dade, too. They'll send a cruiser to break up the party. I'll call someone I know as well."

"Thanks, Kurt. This is turning into a shit show."

"For both of us." I disconnected and got up. It was ten thirty and I knew that going back to sleep would be a mistake. On my way to the bathroom, it dawned on me that I hadn't heard from Justine, which wasn't unusual. She normally worked from two in the afternoon to whenever at night, and I was generally asleep by ten. If she called, it would be before that. I texted her to call me if she had a minute, and finished getting dressed.

My phone rang, this time with Justine's distinctive ringtone.

Smiling, I answered. "Hey! Almost autopsy time." I used my cheery voice.

"Figured you'd be asleep. Nice job on the news, by the way."

Though the comment was sarcastic, there was sympathy in her voice. "Yeah, got a call from DC already."

"How's Chico holding up?" she asked.

"Got a slew of reporters in front of his house right now. I was just about to call Grace to break up the party."

"No need. Text me the address. She's right here."

"Still on the yacht?"

"Sucker's Titanic-sized. She's about done interviewing the witnesses and I've done about all I can here."

I dreaded my next question, but her being onboard for going on six hours wasn't looking good. "Not natural causes, is it?"

"Let's wait for Sid. Mostly it's the rain that buggered things up. Took a boatload of time to gather the samples and document the site."

I figured I wasn't the only one who had gotten the "be careful" call from their superiors. If Grace was still there, she had gotten called as well. It wasn't fair, but that was life in the big city. There are about six thousand unsolved homicides in the US every year—Alex Luna was not going to be one of them.

5

STEVEN BECKER
A KURT HUNTER MYSTERY
BACKWATER DIVA

THE BODY ON THE EXAMINATION TABLE WAS DIFFERENT THAN I expected. I had figured that all performers, who these days were essentially models, were alike, but Alex Luna had the body of an athlete. She was well proportioned rather than thin. Her musculature was clearly visible. Sid prodded at one of her breasts, and it bounced back like rubber. He did it again, and I found myself transfixed by the unnatural phenomena.

"You boys having fun?" Justine asked.

"It's science, dear," Sid said, and winked at me. He did it again, and finally concluded that she'd had work done and moved on. Rattling my cage was one of his favorite activities. To that effect, he liked to fill in the gaps during the procedure with stories from his past life in New Jersey. "Concrete Boots" was one of my favorites. Working in Jersey, victims of gang-related violence were regular visitors to his table. They used every conceivable method to sink a corpse. In "Concrete Boots," he was tasked with jackhammering the concrete from a victim's feet.

He was in the middle of telling me about a victim who was so obese that he needed to be weighed on the freight scale when the door opened, interrupting him. Vance Able, the hipster-ish Chief Medical Examiner, entered the room. Though Sid had more experience, Vance was the boss and had probably gotten a similar call to the ones Grace and I had.

"Greetings, earthlings."

"I thought I heard that contraption of yours," Sid said.

Vance had mothballed the standard office drip coffeemaker. In its place was an espresso machine, which Sid did battle with on an hourly basis. Justine looked up at me and smiled. This might be an autopsy worth staying for.

"Roll with it, Sid. I'll assist," Vance said.

"I was working on high-profile corpses when you were in diapers."

The banter receded while Sid dictated his way through the external examination. Aside from the previously noted work, her anterior was clean.

With Vance hovering over Sid, Justine stepped back to take an observational role. Sid had gotten the message about the deceased and was being very thorough. With Vance present, he kept his usual comments to himself.

Without Sid's sidebars, my interest waned and I started to think of Alex and Monte as a couple. It almost seemed like a prearranged marriage. He was at least ten years older and in poor shape. During my research earlier, I had watched several YouTube videos of her performances, and though the music wasn't my thing, the woman could dance. Alex looked like someone who worked out every spare second she had. Money appeared to be the reason they were together—I didn't want to even try and imagine the sex. I made a mental note to look deeper into their relationship.

Four of the seven deadly sins can be interpreted to have something to do with money. Greed, lust, envy, and gluttony all pertain to an overabundance of, a lack of, or an attitude about wealth, among other things. The Lunas certainly appeared wealthy, but their credit reports showed some serious debt. They could very well be mortgaged to the hilt.

"Hunter, if you're still here..."

Sid motioned that we needed to turn the body. I stepped closer and on the count of three, we rolled the singer onto her stomach. As Sid and Vance started the examination of her posterior, I found myself staring at an ugly gash on her upper back.

"I thought you didn't know the cause of death?" On first glance, this certainly looked like a stab wound. It took all of two seconds to realize that Chico had been on the boat, and though I didn't suspect him, in the eyes of Miami-Dade I might have let a potential suspect go. The jurisdictional lines had yet to be established, but I had walked Chico out of the station.

"Agent Hunter," Vance said.

I took the scolding and moved a step closer. With a frustrated Justine by my side, we studied the wound. Between the rain destroying the crime scene and Vance's intrusion on her and Sid's usual gig, I could tell she wasn't happy.

Sid was right, of course. I had asked a doctor for a technical answer, which at the time he wasn't prepared to give. Alex may have died from internal injuries or maybe had simply bled out. The wound was a symptom and certainly related to her death—but was not the cause.

Sid moved carefully through the rest of the examination before returning to the wound. He prodded, measured, studied, and photographed it before commenting that it was a six-inch gash.

"Sloppy work if it is a stab wound. Could be an accident. She fell through a decorative glass screen."

I remembered seeing the glass on the deck. Thinking back, there was a railing constructed of glass panels inserted into steel stanchions running around the area where Alex had died. The panels separated a section of raised decking from a lower area. Etched with pictures of sea life, they were transparent enough not to block the view.

I shrugged, but before I could respond, Sid gave me the look. For me, the autopsy was over. The time of death was known, and it didn't matter to me whether she bled out or had internal injuries. From the evidence the ME's office had to work with, I wasn't sure they could make a determination. It was probably up to me to determine whether it was an accident or homicide.

"I'm out of here."

"I'm gonna stick around for a bit, but take a pass on the internals." Justine said.

I knew what was coming next and was happy to miss it. I had no interest in the process, just the results. Seen a few organs weighed and measured and you've seen them all.

"Tox screen?" I asked.

Vance looked up. "The whole shooting match for this one. Budget be damned for the Queen of Cuba."

That was an angle I hadn't considered. Alex Luna was a superstar, but to many Cubans she was also royalty, and there was no larger Cuban community than in Miami. If this turned into a homicide, things were going to get interesting.

"Thanks." I squeezed Justine's hand and made my way out of the room. Pulling off the mask, gloves, and face shield, I started for the exit, where I saw Grace Herrera sitting by the doors.

"The brass called you, too?"

She looked tired and just nodded. "Anything?"

I told her what I had seen. "Your people get the boat into impound and interview the crew?"

"Yeah. I stuck around and did the interviews myself. Justine's not going to be happy. Caught another squall on the run in. Might as well have pressure-washed the deck."

"Not her day."

A man came around the corner and approached us. From his snarky smile to the way he held his hand out, I smelled a politician.

"Greg Bittle, assistant district attorney."

He clamped my hand hard enough that I could see the exertion on his face. "Good to meet you."

I was tired and not in a friendly mood, but tried to be cordial. As soon as I saw the yacht, I knew the cockroaches were going to crawl out of the woodwork. I'd never met Bittle, but I knew him by reputation. Looking into his beady eyes, I wondered why the DA's office was involved in the case when it wasn't even classified as a homicide yet.

"He's bottom-feeding. Trying to run against his boss in November. Any scraps'll help," Grace whispered, as Bittle turned to answer a call that was obviously more important than we were.

Her remarks were out of character, but probably true. His political ambition explained why he was here. If you calculated the risk versus the reward for arriving in the middle of the night, it was a no-brainer. Worst case, he lost a little sleep. If the cause of death were released immediately post-autopsy, he would get the cameras on him. Knowing the medical examiner's office from Vance Able down, I suspected if there was foul play involved they would leak it tonight in order to avoid a press conference. Unfortunately, the press was not quite so naïve.

From what I had seen, Bittle was going to lose a night's sleep for no gain. There was no doubt in my mind the back wound was related to her death, but whether it was accidental or from an attack was not going to be decided before the morning news came on.

"If I were you, I'd go get some sleep. There's not going to be a ruling tonight."

"What do you know, Hunter?" Bittle was off the phone.

I glanced around the lobby in case a microphone was lurking. Bittle, for all of his ambition, was on the same side as Grace and me. Giving him the little I knew might even earn some goodwill.

"She's got a large laceration on her back. Could have died from internal injuries or might have bled out. I guess that doesn't matter. What does is that, at this point, there is no way to determine if it was an accident or not."

"Yet." His gaze moved from me to the interior lobby door.

My eyes followed his, and I saw Justine coming toward us. I wanted to warn her, but it was too late. The locks clicked open and she walked through the glass door.

Bittle was on her faster than a tarpon took a blue tip crab.

"Any news?" He introduced himself.

Grace was on her feet and we both approached him.

"If you'll excuse me, I've got some work to do." Justine pushed past Bittle and out the exterior door.

She handled him better than I had. Bittle started after her, but I got in front of him. "Look, if she had something, she'd have told you."

"I guess I'll leave that to you, then." Bittle pulled a business card from his pocket and handed it to me.

I thumbed the card. "No secrets," I said, hoping to get the same from him. If he was in this for himself, he needed to be my friend. There was no enmity between the DA's office and the Park Service. Since being relocated to Biscayne, I had been involved in every criminal investigation that had led to prosecution. There weren't many, though they were often homicides, and I tried to wrap up my cases neatly. Most of the infractions in the park were fishing related, which meant that they fell to the Florida Fish and Wildlife Conservation Commission, or FWC. Smuggling and drug running were handled by the ICE team led by Johnny Wells. My work was generally a quiet gig. I wrote some tickets, but with a few notable exceptions—mainly floaters—the park was not a hotbed of criminal activity.

I said a quick goodbye to Grace and pushed through the door after Justine. Abandoning Grace to the ADA was probably not my best decision of the day, but she had already shown that she could handle him.

"Hey." I reached Justine just as she got to her car.

"Hey back."

"Wanna grab a bite or something?" Though I should have slept, I was wide awake after the autopsy and confrontation with Bittle.

"Nah, feeling a little bummed."

I knew the day hadn't gone well for her. Crime scenes were her temples, but one of the most important cases of her career had just taken place aboard a boat that had been scoured clean by rain. If that wasn't bad enough, Vance's unscheduled appearance at the autopsy had relegated her to the sidelines.

"Anything I can do for you?" I asked.

"Take me home, Ranger."

I grabbed the keys and dropped into the driver's seat. Justine went around to the passenger side and opened the door.

"Hold on a minute. I want to check something," she said, turning around. Watching her walk toward the building, I noticed her body language had changed. She keyed in a code and entered.

A few minutes later, I saw someone exit the side door and start into a quick jog. Justine was running toward the truck with a folder tucked under her arm, a bag in her hand, and a smile on her face.

6

Justine opened the passenger door and got in. "Let's go before Kibble and Bits sees this."

"Is that what they call him?" Living in the boonies of Northern California when Allie was younger, I had spent hours driving her and her friends around. I naturally glanced over to see if Justine had fastened her seat belt.

She caught my look. "Really, Dad?"

There was no telltale sound, but I forced myself not to look over again. "Bittle and Grace left while you were inside." Finally, I heard the distinctive *click*. "Where to?"

"Depends if you want to have some fun or you want to go to sleep."

My body was begging for sleep, but she had my attention. "OK. I have to get up in a couple of hours anyway." I had tried to compartmentalize, meditate, and procrastinate, but nothing seemed to work. When I had a case, I was on it night and day.

"Crime lab, Kemosabe."

I was glad her mood had turned around, but I expected this was going to be more fun for her than me. Justine was a true science nerd. I hoped I wouldn't regret the answer to my question. "Whatcha got?"

"Pictures and a cast of the wound. We're gonna have some fun."

I couldn't imagine, but I was committed now. At this time of night—or morning—traffic was light. With the bars closing a few hours ago, there were more delivery trucks out than drunks. What would have been a forty-minute stop-and-go affair during the day took less than fifteen minutes.

The parking lot was deserted and the building quiet. Justine directed me to park by the side door. We were in her car, which helped. That Park Service truck would have been a beacon. There were a few vans nearby, probably from the cleaning crew. My goal when visiting the lab was to get in and out without a confrontation. The signs were good.

Justine swiped a card and the door buzzed open. She led me down the hall toward the lobby. We passed the interior security door there and continued to the other side of the building. A purplish glow from the combination of red, blue, and green LED lights on the equipment emanated from the floor-to-ceiling glass walls. Justine slid her card into another reader.

The door seemed stuck and it took an effort to pull it open. Justine had explained to me when they first opened the state-of-the-art facility that the lab was kept at negative pressure to contain anything that might be released into the air. It had a separate air filtration system as well.

We walked down the rows of idle equipment to her work station, where she opened the bag and produced the cast of the wound. Laying it on the desk, she opened the file. I saw the similarities immediately, but still wondered where the fun part was going to come into play.

"I'll be back," she said in her Terminator voice, and left me at her station.

I knew better than to touch anything, but I couldn't resist checking out the cast. I picked it up and rotated it in my hands, trying to imagine what had made the gruesome laceration that had killed Alex Luna. If we could figure out what caused the wound, we would be closer to determining if her death was an accident or homicide.

Justine arrived a moment later pushing a cart in front of her. On the top shelf was a large, square block of a Jell-O-like substance. I wasn't sure what the name of the material was, but I had seen it used on several TV shows. The rubbery material was thick enough to stop a bullet and had the ability to simulate the human body. It was certainly cleaner than the carcass of a pig, which was the next best thing. On the lower shelf of the cart was a tray with a variety of knives and other instruments.

Justine moved the block onto a large worktable and laid out the implements of destruction. "You first. Let's see if we can figure out what killed her."

I glanced around like we were doing something wrong. I'd had a hard time envisioning just what Justine had in mind "for fun" when she suggested we come here. The old lab, now a downstairs storeroom, actually had been the incubator for our relationship. We had spent many hours alone in the more private environment there. Even then, I always suspected there were surveillance cameras. I never determined if there were, but my paranoia about Miami-Dade was proven out more often than not. As a result, nothing too untoward—or fun—had happened.

I tried to create a picture in my mind of what the half-dozen knives of different sizes and blade types might do to a body. The wound looked too jagged for that, and I passed them by in favor of what appeared to be a shard of glass. When I picked it up, I realized it was plexiglass, but I didn't think it mattered. Justine handed me a glove. The blunt end of the shard didn't look like it could do much damage, but safety first.

"Good call. Let's see what you've got."

I measured the blow, then wound up and smashed the shard into the material. I've never stabbed anyone before, so it was a unique feeling when the plexiglass penetrated the material. I knew right away from the resistance that Alex's wound had been made by something thinner.

"Your turn," I said.

Justine paused, which I suspect was for drama. I had a feeling she had a pretty good idea what type of implement would match. She picked up a knife with a serrated edge and crouched into a position where she and the "victim" were on the same plane. I hadn't considered how important the angle of attack was. There had been no sign of any blunt-force trauma, meaning Luna was probably unaware when she had been struck. That realization alone moved the needle toward a homicide.

Justine moved back two steps and, remaining in her crouched position, took a long stride toward the ballistics material and slashed the knife across it. The blade came out cleanly and we both moved closer to inspect the result.

"It's not even close," I said.

"Fun, though, duh..."

We both laughed, breaking the tension of the last few hours. Now, instead of competing as usual, we worked together to carve out a section of the material in the shape of the wound's cast. When it was close, we tried each implement from different heights and angles of attack, until we narrowed the field of possibilities down to a claw hammer, a different glass shard, and a curved fillet knife. I wondered about the last, but Justine had picked it first.

Of course, she had the advantage of having reviewed the

scene and knew what had been found around the body, though she hadn't mentioned that they had found a weapon. In all likelihood, if it were a homicide, I thought the implement would have been thrown overboard.

She moved the knife around in the cut we had made, then set it aside. Standing over the implements, she pondered her next choice.

"Nothing found in the area?"

"Glass. She fell through a glass panel. It was tempered, so just tiny clusters. Nothing that could gouge out a wound like that."

"This storm hasn't made this any easier for you."

"That's an understatement. Forensically speaking, I don't have squat." The frustration was back in her voice.

"Try this." I handed her the other shard of plexiglass.

She took it and I saw the look in her eye. Her competitive nature got the best of her and she started to move the shard around in the cutout we had made. Suddenly, she pulled back and struck an underhand blow, which removed a surprisingly large chunk of material. We both studied the result. Though we were supposed to be impartial to the outcome of the investigation, the discovery was somewhat deflating. It wasn't perfect, although it was closer.

Justine stood back. "The glass could have held together in a similar shape. I've seen tempered glass shatter but not fall apart."

I again got the feeling that she was frustrated.

"But there would have been some glass remaining in the wound," she said.

Nice rebound. I thought about the wound. Tempered glass shatters rather than breaks. I knew something about it because my father had been a contractor, and I worked for him during several college summers. I liked the work and sometimes still had daydreams of my own workshop. Customers and building departments had turned me off the business, though. The building codes were voluminous and ever-changing. One inspector had told me that there were over three-thousand pages of codes, which made it impossible to know, never mind enforce, them all. It was generally up to each jurisdiction which code they would focus on. This makes a hard job even harder.

One of our jobs had involved a ton of glass work, and I still remember the inspector checking for the small etching in the corner of each pane that marked it as tempered. Standard glass shatters into pieces, with each one basically becoming a weapon. To protect the occupants from this, shower enclosures, glass doors, and any window within eighteen inches of the ground, floor, or doorway required the use of tempered glass.

A tempered pane shattered, but didn't break apart. Baking, or tempering, introduced a kind of resilience to the glass.

"This is it," Justine said.

She sounded convinced, but I wasn't.

"We're using this as a weapon to strike *at* something. She must have fallen through the panel. The force would have been exponentially greater."

"I get it, but like you said, there was no evidence of any glass in the wound. It was clean."

"Dammit, Batman. Foiled again."

"We're moving in the right direction." I paused. I had seen the body and gotten a quick glimpse of the scene.

"OK, so she fell—or was pushed. She hit the glass and it broke."

"Logical. That's the Special Agent I love."

Looking at her made it hard to focus, but the techno atmosphere of the crime lab didn't foster any romantic inclinations—at least in me. "I guess the question is, did she fall? And did the laceration occur before or after?"

"Duh, after."

This was moving along too well. I waited for the next stumbling block. "The fall put her on the deck. With our simulation, we were assuming she was struck while standing."

"Back to the drawing board, then. I told you this was going to be fun."

We rotated the cube to present a clean side and set it on the floor.

"Ladies first." I waited for her comeback, but it never came. Justine reached for a different knife. The first one she had used was a fixed blade. At six inches long, anyone using it would have had to wear a concealed sheath for it. She picked up a much smaller blade, similar to a paring knife.

"That's pretty small for the size wound."

"Sit back and watch. I got this."

Justine took two paces back and lunged at the block. With the blade facing upwards, she tore into the material. Novices used overhand grips, but an underhand grip was preferred by those with training or street-fighting experience. She landed awkwardly and dismissed my attempt to help her up. Instead, she crawled to the block.

"That's a match, Kemosabe."

I didn't need to compare it to the cast to concur. It was the viciousness of the strike that had caused the size of the wound. The characteristics of the blade had little to do with it. Whatever had happened on that deck was propagated by emotion—and that meant homicide.

7

STEVEN BECKER
A KURT HUNTER MYSTERY
BACKWATER DIVA

THE PIERCING RING FROM MY PHONE WOKE ME. GLANCING AROUND, I could see daylight fighting its way around the perimeter of the blackout shades. I rolled over to shut it off, surprised I had caught a little sleep. I got out of bed quickly, almost as if I were doing something wrong. Justine peered at me through one half-opened eye, then closed it, rolled over, and pulled the covers over her head. She didn't have to be at work until two; I obviously was expected now.

Grabbing the phone, I stumbled to the bathroom and closed the door.

"Hunter," I croaked, fighting cotton mouth.

"Nice job throwing me under the bus and disappearing."

It was Grace. It took me a minute to figure out what she was talking about. "Sorry, I hadn't planned on sleeping in. We didn't get back from the lab until almost five." Before we left, Justine had called Sid and told him the result of our experiment. He must have listed the death as a homicide. With any other case, it would have gone unnoticed until the scheduled 10:00 a.m. press conference, but I knew the more aggressive media outlets paid under the table for information. Someone from the lab must have leaked it, and the ever-eager media posted it as clickbait. We had been tired and left the evidence of our experiment in plain sight. By now, everyone in South Florida would have seen it come across one of their news feeds.

I had to squint surprisingly hard to make out the time on the phone's display. "Can we push the press conference up?" The sooner we could interrupt the media cycle, the better. She was ahead of me.

"I already did. This is your warning. Be here in thirty minutes."

I didn't have to do the math and just jumped in the shower. I was out before the water warmed, which in South Florida meant it went from lukewarm to hot. I left Justine a note that I borrowed her car, and in fifteen minutes I was heading toward Miami-Dade's Doral office. The department was decentralized, but the bigwigs were located there.

Rush hour ran in the opposite direction I was headed, allowing me a speed-limit ride west on 836. That changed when I turned onto 826 past the airport, but it was only a couple of hundred yards to the exit for the station. Media vans were parked everywhere. Their national logos told me the story was more than local—there must have been a dozen vehicles hovering around like predators swimming under bait fish, ready to pick off the weakest one. Staying to the perimeter of the parking lot, I circled the building until I could make my way to the back door without being seen. I was thankful I had Justine's car and not the Park Service truck.

Grace opened the door for me and led me down a hallway. After several turns we stopped at an unmarked door in the corridor, just to the side of a cluster of people at the briefing room's entrance. As we snuck in they saw us, but at the same time a voice over the PA system warned that the press conference would start in a few minutes. That didn't stop two of the more aggressive cameramen. Grace and I fought with the telephoto lenses that were jammed between the door and jamb. Teamwork prevailed, and she closed the door as I pushed the lenses away, all with my head turned to avoid some kind of macabre photo angle. The door slammed shut and we leaned against the hardwood slab, both panting. There was no shared sense of relief—we both knew it was probably going to get worse.

Nodding to each other, we stepped through the inner door to the briefing room. The reporters briefly turned on each other, each trying to be the loudest, as questions were hurled at us. Seeking whatever protection we could, we both crowded behind a podium made for a single person.

A shrill *squawk* stopped the questions as Grace turned on the microphone.

"Ground rules." She waited until the room settled down and then another long second for effect. She looked toward the door, where three officers stood. "Any outbursts and you will be escorted out by one of Miami's finest. Are we clear?"

Her tone was about the same as a kindergarten teacher talking to her class.

"We will cover the circumstances from the beginning, summarize our findings, and end with questions." She waited for the inevitable premature question, but the room remained quiet—they had succumbed to her threat.

I suspected they would be well behaved until we finished our summary. Once the floor was open to questions, it would be a free-for-all. With the advent of the internet and smartphones, the media landscape had changed. The old deadlines were gone. With news crawlers pervasive on most websites and TV networks, and social media having no time boundaries—or any kind of boundary, for that matter—few would stick around for the last questions. They would take what they could get in an effort to be the first to post the most outlandish, clickbait headline. In today's media, speed was as important as getting it right.

"Yesterday at fifteen hundred we got a call from a yacht moored at the Fowey Rocks Light. The call was answered by three police boats, along with Special Agent Hunter of the National Park Service. On arrival, we discovered Alexandra Luna was deceased."

Grace clicked a button and a picture of the late star appeared behind us. Cameras were raised above the heads of the people sitting in front, and the room became noisy.

"Do I have to make an example of someone?"

The kindergarten threat worked again, and I wondered when she was going to ask them if this was how they should treat their friends.

"We will release a press package containing photographs after the briefing."

The room quieted again.

"The medical examiner declared Alexandria Luna dead an hour later. The preliminary cause of death was related to a large laceration on her back. The actual cause of death was not determined at the scene. Last night, an autopsy confirmed that the laceration was a direct contributor to Ms. Luna's death."

This was where it was going to get dicey. Again Grace had it covered.

"Though there was broken glass around her, the wound appears to have been made by a knife similar to this."

She clicked the button again, and the knife Justine and I had experimented with appeared on the screen behind us. The room was dead quiet now. They were all waiting for the story.

"We will have updates available as progress is made on the case."

She didn't have to call for questions.

"So, is it a homicide?"

"As it is defined, yes. Though we don't know whether it was accidental or premeditated, another person contributed to her death."

A handful of reporters, sensing the real story was now at the medical examiner's office, made a beeline for the door. Much of the crowd, fearful that they would be left behind, followed. Within a minute, Grace and I were standing in a room with only a handful of reporters. One scantily dressed woman with eyelashes that almost reached the podium sat dead center in the nearly empty room. She held up her hand.

Grace shrugged.

"Does this mean the concert is going to be canceled?"

We looked at each other, trying to hide our expressions from the woman.

"You'll have to contact the arena for details."

Grace made eye contact with the few people remaining. None responded, and we walked toward the rear of the room. She already had her phone out and was calling for several units to head off the rampaging reporters headed for the medical examiner's office.

"Think we should get over there?"

"Yeah. Handling these SOBs is harder than locking up a three-timer."

We ran toward the back door. Grace pushed through first and led me to an unmarked car. A minute later, with lights flashing and siren blaring, we headed east toward Jackson Memorial, where the medical examiner's office was located in a nearby building.

Several news vans had already arrived when we pulled into the parking lot. They spotted us. Some headed out on foot, others followed in their vehicles as we continued past the main drive. Grace sped up and, with a determined look on her face, skidded into a smaller drive marked for deliveries. Instead of slowing, she accelerated toward a van. It looked like a game of chicken, and I tightened my hands on the arm rests, bracing myself in the seat. The van gave way and stopped before we reached it. Several more had entered the parking lot and there was soon a growing line backed into the street.

A police cruiser arrived, and Grace directed the officers to corral the vans in a corner of the parking lot. Leaving one officer at the entrance in case a creative reporter tried to slip by, she opened the trunk, grabbed a megaphone, and marched across the parking lot. I lingered by the car and pulled out my phone, thinking it might be a good idea to let Vance know what was happening.

Grace's voice boomed across the lot. She had changed her tone from kindergarten teacher to pissed-off coach. Her words were crystal clear.

"This crap is not going to cut it."

I waited for her to tell them all to run a lap around the lot.

I lost her next line as Vance picked up his phone. A minute later, he buzzed me into the side door. I texted Grace to tell her where I was and found him by the espresso machine.

"A little action out there?"

"Herrera has it under control. She should be about done scolding them."

"Justine sent me the pictures. I think she's correct. At this point, I agree with Sid's ruling that Ms. Luna's death was a homicide."

Grace walked into the room.

"The ball's in your court. I'll leave you to plot."

He turned his back and the espresso machine fired up.

With the official determination that this was a homicide, the playing field had changed. Grace and I looked at each other, although not with the calculating or threatening stare fighters give each other before a bout. The look was more shared concern about how we were going to survive this case.

"I think we ought to grab your fishing-guide friend before the vultures find him. He's going to be a person of interest anyway."

"Thought you had them handled out there?"

"If only. The best I can hope for is that they behave around the government employees. I can't stop them from cruising the county trying to out-scoop each other."

"And us."

"Yeah. I can have a cruiser pick Chico up, if you can locate him."

"I'll handle it. I've got a pretty good idea where to find him. Do you have the people who were aboard the yacht contained?"

"Preliminary interviews are completed, and I gave them the 'don't leave town' speech. I can start working that angle," she said.

"You don't have access to a forensic accountant, do you?" I summarized my research from last night.

"Think it's about money?"

"This looked like a setup from the start. Monte's no fisherman, and even if he just wanted to get out and drink beer, Chico offered to cancel because of the weather. I'll bet you right now that Chico is missing a knife that's pretty similar to the one Justine and I used on the ballistic jelly."

"Off to a running start. Sure, send me what you have on the financials. I know a guy."

The parking lot was empty of news vans when we left the building. Grace looked around, realizing she'd driven me here. "Drop you someplace?"

"Dodge Island. I'm going to find a fishing guide."

8

STEVEN BECKER
A KURT HUNTER MYSTERY
BACKWATER DIVA

Being on the water is like meditation. Running at twenty knots through the light chop leftover from yesterday's storms would usually put me in a good place. The ride was exhilarating, similar to riding in a convertible or driving a motorcycle. Speed takes on a different relationship when you are the dog, head out the window with your tongue hanging out of your mouth. Today I never reached my dog, er, Zen place.

I missed the feeling, but there was an underlying adrenaline rush that substituted for it. Even the direst of emergencies energize me. I had been in scenarios where Justine, Allie, and/or myself had been in trouble—often deadly trouble. No matter how bad the situations were, I knew I had it within me to rise up and take control. Call it my super power, but it was the one area I was confident about. This time it was different. Seeking out Chico was a morbid affair to me. After I found him and he was turned over to Miami-Dade, the outcome was out of my control —and I had a feeling it wasn't going to be good. I almost felt like warning him.

Compared to other bodies of water, tides in the Atlantic are fairly consistent. In South Florida, they're of no real consequence. With a predictable cycle, they change every six hours, advancing fifty minutes a day. The range was around two feet, not enough for anyone but a fisherman to notice. Justine and I had visited Bar Harbor, Maine, the month before and had to plan the water sports portion of our trip around the ten-foot swing in the tides. During low tide there, it wasn't uncommon to see boats sitting high and dry.

Being a fisherman and living on the water, I knew the state of the tides the same way I knew when the sun rose and set. The pattern was etched in my brain. There was no need to consult a tide chart or app to find Chico, though out of habit, I confirmed my calculations by checking out the piers of the Rickenbacker Causeway. About a foot of barnacle growth showed above the waterline and there was a noticeable wake pushing toward open water. Halfway into the outgoing tide, I expected Chico to be fishing the mangrove channels across from the Turkey Point Power Plant.

Fish like to use the cover of the interwoven roots to ambush prey during high water, but were forced to vacate the shallower water as the tide receded. That left them vulnerable to a properly placed fly. With the wind out of the southeast as was common this time of year, I expected Chico to be using the combination of the cover of the barrier islands and the tide.

Chico usually put in at Bayfront Park in Homestead, which was where I had first met him. The Park Service headquarters was tucked into a side canal off the channel leading to the park. Heading south, I followed the coast. Fowey Light was barely visible. *Diva* had been moved into the Miami River last night and Fowey's mooring balls appeared empty. I passed miles of mangrove-lined shores before reaching Black Point Park, one of the other large boat ramps for the bay. After cutting across the channels leading to Bayfront Park and the power plant, I crossed the bay just to the north of the shoals in front of West Arsincker and Arsincker Keys. Once clear of the hazards, I steered for Old Rhodes Key.

There were several flats boats working the channels, or creeks as they were called on this side of the bay. On the south side of Old Rhodes was a network of waterways where I suspected I might find Chico. I hoped he would be alone, as this was not a conversation I wanted to have in front of a client. Many charter captains worked only when there were paying customers. They were of the breed that the luster of being a guide had worn off, or they felt their bar stool was more important than time on the water.

Laypersons often thought that success catching fish was due to luck. This was far from the truth. Chico was on the water every day—with or without a paying customer. He knew if he was going to remain a top-notch guide that he had to put in the time. Knowing where the fish were inevitably led to catching them. There were intricacies, like the phase of the moon, water temperature and clarity, current, and bait, and the guy who knew where the fish were holding usually had a handle on those as well. That kind of knowledge developed instinct, which led to catching fish.

People often judge fisherman, classifying them as stereotypical worm-and-beer guys. They just didn't understand. One of my favorite quotes from the TV show *Scandal* summed it up better than I could:

You know, people who don't fish think that fishing is lazy or boring, but it is the complete opposite. There are a hundred little decisions to be made, variables to be considered. And you're never quite sure what made the difference. Did I cast too high, too far to the left? Did I reel it in too slow, or, or, or too fast? Is the lure too shiny or too dull? Do I stay here, or should I go over there? And you know it's not luck, but you do not know by how much. People are predictable, unchanging, monotonous. They use the same language, they offer the same excuses, they make the same mistakes. People are endlessly disappointing, because you hope they won't be.

As I approached, several boats pulled anchor, lifted their Power-Poles, or raised their GPS trolling motors and took off after spotting my forest-green T-top. It was the usual treatment I got from a number of guides. There were a slew of probable causes that permitted me to board and search a vessel, but fishing activity wasn't one of them. The enforcement of fish and wildlife regulations fell to the FWC. These were the kind of guys wary of any law enforcement, and unfortunately, usually the ones who knew what was going on.

Two boats were left and neither was Chico's. I recognized the guides and waved casually as I idled past, being careful to keep my distance and not spook the fish. I had thought this the most likely place to find Chico, but he was nowhere in sight. That left me two choices—I could wait, or run aimlessly around the bay. I chose to wait out the tide.

Some of my counterparts joked that if I fished without hooks it would decrease my chances of snagging a body. It was, unfortunately, partially true. There is an old saying that you never set foot in the same river twice. On the surface, that seems to mean the conditions will be different every day. If you dig a little deeper, it says something about the fisherman's psyche. Every day, the angler has different energy, ambition, and expectations. Today for me, all three were ebbing, but sometimes just going through the motions helps life make sense again.

Fishing is also an attention magnet. Hook a fish and every set of eyeballs within range suddenly find you. Somehow these far-off anglers know if you've snagged the bottom or are fighting a fish. I figured if I wanted to find Chico, the best thing I could do was my rendition of a fly fisherman.

I'd grown up fishing the streams in Northern California. As an adult patrolling the Plumas National Forest, a rod was never far from my hand. The ability of a ten-foot rod to break down into a backpack-sized two-foot tube made it all the easier. Stream and river fishing is about "matching the hatch"—copying the insects that are currently on or in the water. It takes a little investigative work, but once you know what you're looking for, it's not hard. Generally, casts are short and the current does the rest.

Transferring those skills to saltwater was harder than just up-sizing my equipment. With larger prey—many with razor-sharp teeth—rods, reels, lines, and leaders were bigger and heavier than their freshwater counterparts. There was a whole lot of difference between hooking a two- or three-foot trout and a hundred-pound tarpon. One of the challenges is the increased range the angler needs to cast. Forty to sixty feet is the minimum for some easily spooked species like bonefish. That's a whole lot of line whipping around in the air, especially when it's windy.

Casting that kind of distance in adverse conditions, and with any kind of accuracy, requires practice. That and learning to throw a cast net were always on my list, but rarely got done. As a result, I had resorted to fishing with more conventional spinning gear most of the time. I imagined if Chico were around, by demonstrating my poor casting ability, he would somehow sense it and come to my aid, if for nothing else than to appease the fishing gods.

I kept a broken-down, ten-weight, nine-foot rod in the console. After putting it together, I found the reel, which I attached to the base, and started to feed the line through the guides. Fly line is deceptively slippery and I had learned to double it so it didn't fall backwards through the guides. To the end, I tied a ten-foot section of twenty-pound leader material. A short section of heavier leader, known as a shock tippet, was often added between the leader and the fly, but I decided against it. I was trying to attract a guide, not land a tarpon.

I tied a loop knot to a Clouser minnow and took the rig to the bow of the boat. Fish seek out structure, either for ambush or protection. Casting toward open water might have been easier, but unless you were sight-fishing a flat and spotted tailing fish, it was a worthless exercise. If there were fish here, they would be around the mangroves. I estimated they were forty feet away and stripped about that much line from the reel onto the deck. Properly executed, a series of false casts would have the line airborne in short order.

Fly fishing can either put you in the zone or destroy your moral. I was surprised how today's Zen attribute of not caring worked in my favor—my casts were probing within a few feet of the mangroves. As I worked my way down the shoreline, I found myself caring more and more, and my casts in turn started to fall short or, in one case, snagged a branch. Frustrated, I started to pull the line with my hands. The boat moved within range of the offending branch, and just as I unhooked the fly from its restraint, I saw Chico's boat round the corner.

"Little trouble?" He idled to within a few feet of the Park Service boat.

I yanked harder and the fly came away. "You could say that."

"Any word on the case?"

"Kind of need to talk to you about that. Can we tie up over there?" I pointed the rod tip to a secluded creek.

"Sure thing. I'll follow you in."

I had no doubt that Chico was a pawn in a larger game, but it would do neither of us any good if I gave him a pass. He dropped his twin Power-Poles and I idled alongside. Reaching into the console, I grabbed two fenders and put them over the gunwales to protect the hulls. A single line tied the boats together.

"Serious, huh? I didn't think last night was going to be the last of it."

"You OK if I come aboard?"

"Sure thing." Chico stepped to the opposite side to counteract my weight.

"I need to see what knives you have aboard." I hoped he realized how I was skirting the rules. If I were to perform a search with anyone else, I would have restrained them first, then asked about weapons.

"Heard it was a homicide now. Didn't even get a tip to put up with this shit." He stepped over to a tool holder attached to his console. Instinctively, I moved the other way around the leaning post to help balance the boat.

"Not here. Usually have a four-inch bait knife right by the pliers and de-hooker."

I knew how organized Chico was and, unfortunately, I now knew where the murder weapon had come from.

9

STEVEN BECKER
A KURT HUNTER MYSTERY
BACKWATER DIVA

"My hands are tied here. I'm going to have to do a formal interview."

"I hear ya. Can I get my boat on the trailer at least?"

At some point I was going to have to treat Chico as a suspect, but I wasn't there yet. "Sure, I'll follow you to Bayfront. You can leave your truck and trailer in the headquarters lot."

"Appreciate it, Kurt. Too bad we gotta go now. Tide's about to turn."

Just as he said it, my line came taut. After pulling the fly from the brush, I had left it floating on the surface. The tide, though negligible, had given the fly enough action to entice a bite.

"You gonna get that?" Chico asked.

I applied pressure directly to the line with my left hand while I reeled in the slack lying on the deck. Once the line was all on the reel, I released it and let the reel take the pressure. I knew it was a jack from the way it ran. The practice of catch and release, and how species were given "gamefish" status, was a mystery to me. Jacks and ladyfish fought every bit as hard as bonefish and snook.

I tightened the drag and let the fish take what line it could.

While I waited for the pressure from the reel to tire the fish, I glanced back at Chico. He nodded, emphasizing the depth of the trust between us. Despite the bond, I sensed I was setting myself up for disaster. As usual, my hookup had attracted the attention of the other anglers in the area, and any one of them could have taken a video of me fishing.

I was OK if the fish cut me off in the mangroves, but instead of seeking the protection of the trees, it turned into open water. It was a matter of principle now, and I applied some pressure to the line with my left forefinger. Lifting the rod tip high, I pulled the fish closer, then released my finger and reeled. It took about a half-dozen revolutions before the fish was by the boat. I reached down and released it, then set my rod on the deck and moved to the helm.

"Nice job." Chico looked down at me from the tower on his boat. Remaining above, he started his engine and idled toward the creek's entrance.

I had been lucky to catch the fish. My mind had been on how to deal with Chico. By the book had to be the answer.

He nodded, and a few minutes we were running side by side across the bay. While I was fighting the fish he must have untied us and I wondered what else I had missed. I glanced across at him, expecting to see the same smile that was on my own face. Even with the circumstances, it was hard to hide the afterglow of catching a good-sized fish. If nothing else, it was the adrenaline rush. His facial expression showed fear, which puzzled me at first. When he accelerated and turned back toward the chain of barrier islands, I understood. He was going to run.

The Park Service center console was a utility boat. I'd often thought it underpowered with a 150-horsepower engine. With two people and gear aboard it had a hard time getting up on plane. Chico had a performance flats boat. With 300-horsepower, he could easily outrun me, and although the boats were the same length, his drew only a foot of water, while mine drew closer to two. The jack plate allowed him to raise the engine and run at the rated value. A foot might not seem like a lot, but on the flats it would allow him to cruise areas that I was forced to steer clear of.

After three years I knew the bay pretty well, but my knowledge was restricted to the waters I could run in. Chico took advantage of that and, immediately after crossing the channel between Swan and Broad Keys, cut into one of the creeks running through Palo Alto Key.

We were out of the park now, but I was well within my rights to chase him. The tower was an advantage while fishing, but now it was a detriment to Chico and allowed me to follow his boat while staying to deeper water. The area, a maze of keys and creeks too small to name, encompassed Crocodile Lake National Wildlife Refuge and was also the northern end of the John Pennekamp Coral Reef State Park. Even with the overlapping jurisdictions, there were no other boats within sight.

I followed on the outside as Chico moved through the creeks down to North Key Largo. Wondering what he thought he could gain, since I could still see the tower, I doggedly followed, wondering if I should call in backup. I decided against it, at least for the time being. Beside the embarrassment, I felt that Chico would declare his intentions before too long. We were reaching Card Sound, an area that was accessible to both our boats. I couldn't catch him, but he was heading for Monroe County, where I could call the sheriff for support without the baggage of dealing with Miami-Dade.

He was out in the open now, heading for Card Bank. With only two navigable passes through the flats there, it was easy to follow him into Barnes Sound. I was a quarter-mile behind and started to get worried when he crossed under the Card Sound Bridge. Not because of the water depth, but he appeared to be heading toward Manatee Bay, which had a canal accessing Everglades National Park.

Sensing he was headed there, it was time to call in backup. I slowed enough so that I could hear my phone and dialed Mariposa at headquarters. I could have called Everglades directly, but it would take too much time to explain, and I wanted to keep Chico in sight. Mariposa was also better than me at interdepartmental politics. After communicating to her where I thought Chico was heading, I set the phone faceup on the helm and accelerated after Chico. Once he reached the Glades, he would be gone in a hot second.

He had cut toward the west and the entrance to the canal. I slowed now, knowing this was as far as I could reasonably chase him. I could handle the canal, but I doubted he would stay within the manmade system for long. With hundreds of square miles of water, he could easily disappear into the unmarked and, in many cases, invisible channels running through the sawgrass. My counterparts at Everglades National Park had airboats, which were the perfect vehicle to find him.

I didn't want to turn back, but it was the right call. I intended to run back to headquarters and drive to Everglades park headquarters, where I could monitor the search. Chico's decision bothered me. He knew I had no choice but to take him in, but why run if he was innocent? We both knew it. I understood his fear, one shared by many minorities and anyone else having to deal with Miami-Dade. He knew I could help, but not completely protect him from those eager to make the death of Alex Luna go away—or promote their careers by having a hand in solving the high-profile case.

Thirty minutes later, I pulled into my slip in the small marina by the headquarters building. Mariposa tossed me the keys to one of the park's trucks, and I was on the road a few minutes later. Another half hour and I pulled up to the Everglades National Park building. Where Biscayne Park was in Miami's backyard, Everglades, though only twenty miles from the city, was another world. A man waved me over to an airboat and introduced himself.

"Roberto Conseco." He extended his right hand to shake and grabbed a pair of industrial grade headphones in his left.

He waited while I put them on. "Good on the com check?"

"Great. Any word on the boat?" I left Chico's name out of it. Conseco didn't need to know my relationship with the runaway guide.

"Chopper headed out a few minutes ago. Big area, though. Any idea where he's headed?"

I had thought about that on the drive over. Chico might be able to disappear for a couple of hours, but he wasn't going to escape in a flats boat. "My guess is that he's going to ditch the boat and have someone meet him in a vehicle."

"Makes sense." Roberto motioned me to the lower seat in the bow and climbed to the higher position at the helm. A second later, while the headphones muffled the sound, I felt the torque as the airboat's engine started. Conseco asked me to release the bow line and he idled away from the pier.

I'd been on an airboat once before, but it still took a few miles to get used to the feeling. The flat-bottomed hull made the ride feel as if the boat had a distinct lack of contact with the water. Rather than planing over the surface, it slid. The rudders were mounted behind the engine, rather than in the water, making turns feel like the boat was slipping sideways.

We were well away from the headquarters building when the helicopter pilot's voice came over the headset. "He's taking the back way into Florida City."

I had figured it out, but was in the wrong place. There was nothing I could do now except call Grace for help. Just as I pulled out my phone, I heard Roberto.

"No service out here—not even close. I can have the dispatcher patch you through to whoever you need."

I had hoped to keep the conversation, and my confession that I had lost Chico, between Grace and myself. "Miami-Dade. Captain Herrera, if you can find her."

A long moment later, she was on the radio. "What are you doing out there?"

It sounded like she was yelling, but I hoped it was just the radio connection through the headphones. "Chico was last seen heading toward Florida City. I expect he'll ditch his boat and have someone waiting." I paused. "It'll be his truck and trailer at a ramp." I gave her a description of his Suburban. That boat meant more to him than going to jail. I was willing to bet he'd had his wife or daughter grab his truck from Bayfront Park and bring it to a meeting place.

"That'll narrow it down."

Boat ramps were scarce on the bay, but there were numerous small parks and ramps in the canal system. Fortunately, most were along Alligator Alley and Highway 41. Finding the vehicle might be easier than the boat.

"Can you take me back?" I asked Roberto.

He gunned the engine to stop our forward progress, then reversed it. A second later, the boat spun in its own length. I expected to be swung around and gripped the handles tightly, only to find that, as I was in the center of the axis, I barely moved. Similar to crossing your own wake when you turn in a boat, reversing our course into the engine's old path covered us in a mist.

Minutes later, with my body tingling from the vibration of the airboat, I thanked Roberto and hopped into my truck. I called Mariposa and asked her to tell Grace that I was inbound to Florida City. Before I chased this fish into its hole, I asked Mariposa to take a ride to the Bayfront ramp and see if I was right. She called back five minutes later that the truck and trailer were gone.

That gave me some encouragement, and twelve miles later I was waiting for a light on US 1 to turn green. The intersection was a small side street with a longer than usual wait, which I took advantage of by looking up the closest boat ramps.

I found several close by and hit the left-turn signal to take me to the first one. Before the light changed, I got two texts. One from Allie and the other from Justine. Allie's explained everything. Justine had fallen victim to the paparazzi. An unflattering picture of my wife-slash-Miami-Dade forensics tech was making the rounds of social media and news sites. The caption below said it all: *Authorities have nothing on star's death.*

Before I could decide which message to respond to first, my phone rang. It was Grace.

10

STEVEN BECKER
A KURT HUNTER MYSTERY
BACKWATER DIVA

I pulled over to take Grace's call.

"Don't take it out on me. You can't judge how people are going to react when you put them in a corner," she said.

By this point I was beyond frustration, and I tried but failed to keep it out of my voice. "It was his knife that killed her."

"You haven't actually recovered it and forensics hasn't determined it was the weapon, right?" She didn't wait for me to answer. "So, he ran. What would you have done?"

"OK." I'd had time to think on the drive and realized there were more than a few holes in the "Chico killed Alex" story. Chico knew where everything was on that boat. "He didn't do it. I'm not sure why he ran, but it wasn't him."

"Your leaps of faith are rather extreme."

I explained about how Chico wasn't the kind of guy to lose an important piece of equipment and not replace it immediately. "If he did it, or even knew it was gone, there would have been a new knife in that holder today."

"I hear you. Listen, I wasn't calling to give you a hard time. I've got the crew and everyone that was aboard yesterday now confined to the yacht. Thought you might like to interview them."

"I thought you did?"

"It's your case too."

"Sorry. Yeah, let me know where and I'll head over. I've got an idea how to deal with Chico."

"OK. It's at the boat storage lot on the river."

We disconnected and I sat looking at my phone for a minute. Finally, I dialed Chico's number and waited for voicemail to take the call. I didn't expect him to answer, so I wasn't disappointed when a recorded version of his voice came over the line.

"Hey, it's Kurt. I'm sorry about how this went down." I laid out my theory about his innocence. "I need to meet you so I can call off the BOLO. Call me back." I ate my pride—he would need to as well.

I hadn't paid any attention to where I had pulled over and looked around the parking lot. US 1 in Florida City is a half-mile of primarily gas stations and fast food restaurants sprinkled with a few cheap hotels and liquor stores. I was in the parking lot of the Last Chance Saloon. I guess this was where you stopped if you needed a six-pack to handle the eighteen-mile death stretch to Key Largo.

I felt better after talking to Grace and laughed at my subconscious decision to pull into a liquor store's parking lot. I left as quickly as I'd arrived and was soon heading north on the Turnpike. The southbound lanes were moving slowly and I could see brake lights in my rearview mirror. Northbound was a speed-limit drive; at least the traffic gods were smiling on me.

It was past two, and I was surprised I hadn't heard again from Justine. I knew from experience that after being out of cell-phone range, turning the power off and on forced messages and voicemails to miraculously appear. I decided I didn't need that information dump and, instead of powering off, pressed the icon to call her.

"Hey. Took an Uber to get my car, thank you," she scolded me. Then her voice turned more sympathetic. "Heard you were having some trouble."

Efforts to cover my earlier ineptness had proven futile. Miami-Dade might not have the best reputation for solving crimes, but they already had figured out and spread the word that I'd screwed up.

"Got a handle on it now." I told her about the missing knife.

"I'm headed out to meet the dive team now. Figured with the murder weapon missing, the mooring site was a likely place. At least we know what we're looking for," she said.

Finding the four-inch knife was a long shot. The seas were calm, and the water was only about twenty feet deep where the yacht had been moored, but the reef below was good at hiding secrets. Countless wrecks and wealth lay around the lighthouse, and most never revealed themselves. I hoped because the knife was fresh in the water it might stand out.

"Wish I could join you. I'm heading to the yacht to do some interviews."

"Rather be diving. I'll check in later."

I disconnected the call just as I reached 836, which ran somewhat parallel to the river. Besides dividing the county diagonally, the Miami River reveals a cross-section of the city. Multi-million-dollar condos were the norm where the river met the bay. After moving through downtown, the real estate values dropped by the mile. By the time the river reached the airport, it was industrial. That was where the Miami-Dade lot was located.

I pulled into the open gate and parked by the trailer that served as an office. Grace's unmarked car was parked by the water, dwarfed by *Diva*. I pulled in next to her, left the truck, and walked toward the gangplank connecting the yacht to the seawall.

I walked up the aluminum plank to the main deck, which sat several feet above the seawall. Yesterday, I had boarded the yacht from the transom and went directly to what we now knew to be the scene of the murder. I had left the yacht quickly, with no time to explore.

The gangplank led directly into what could only be described as a well-appointed living room or on a yacht, a salon. There was little, besides some nautical decorations, that would tell you there was water under the floor.

Grace was in the center of a cluster of people. I immediately noticed three distinct groups. The first one that drew my eye, as they intended, was a group of women. They were fit-looking and dressed in Lulu-whatever workout wear. The men were off by themselves. From their dress and demeanor, some looked like dancers; the others were so bulked up I expected to find racks of weights somewhere aboard. The last group was a mix of men and women, and from their uniforms it was easy to tell they were the crew. My first inclination was to throw everyone together, but I knew each group had a hierarchy and I needed to discover it. The higher up the ladder someone rose in their respective group, the closer they would have been to the deceased—and the more likely they had a reason to kill her.

"We've got the names and pertinent information on everyone aboard. I thought it might be good to put the pieces in place," Grace said.

It sounded like a board game, but made perfect sense. Grace got the group's attention and instructed everyone to take their place where they were when the "murder" occurred. There was an immediate reaction to the word, one which I'm sure she had planned. I scanned the faces around the room, noting surprise on many. They quickly broke into smaller groups and started talking among themselves.

I caught Grace's eye and followed her gaze to a small, black globe mounted to the ceiling. Once I spotted the first camera, several others caught my eye. I'd have film to watch later. The reactions and interactions were important signs, but my interest waned knowing there was video.

Once the shock wore off, the crew, dancers, and muscle started to disperse. Watching their response had been worthwhile, but knowing there was surveillance footage was better than interviewing them. I watched the gangplank to see if anyone planned on taking off, but there was a uniformed officer sitting in a cruiser right next to it. I assumed Grace had taken similar precautions on the water, in case someone wanted to exit by a less conventional method.

"Care to take a walk, Special Agent?" Grace steered me toward a narrow stairway.

The yacht had four enclosed decks above water, and probably several more below. Deck space was surprisingly limited. There was probably a sun deck above, but as Grace and I walked to the top deck, it only had a narrow, open-air space toward the stern. Between the entourage and crew, there were about two dozen people aboard, which the ship had plenty of room for.

We climbed to the top deck, which was empty. It was open, but smaller than I expected. The only shade was from a radar arch above. Dropping down a level, we found several staterooms. A maid's cart was in the corridor. We checked each room and found two women crew members cleaning.

As we dropped to the main level, each deck became larger. The next deck contained the bridge and a large living space. We checked in to the bridge to find three crew members.

"Is the captain here?"

"Right here. Gerard." He introduced the other crew members.

I immediately noticed his French accent. "You were up here when the murder occurred?" I asked.

"We had planned to raise anchor about an hour after it happened."

"What was your destination?"

"Downtown there's a marina near the arena. This is kind of a tour bus. After that, Tampa."

"I heard about that," Grace said. She pulled out her phone and typed a query into the browser. A few seconds later she showed me the "Killin' It" tour schedule. Tomorrow night was scheduled to be the opening show in Miami. From there, Alex worked her way around and along the Gulf Coast. It was certainly a unique and slower way to travel.

"What's your cruising speed?" I asked the captain.

"Sixteen knots in good conditions."

I glanced at the schedule on Grace's phone and saw the shows were each several days apart. Making money didn't seem to be the primary motivator for this tour. Working on the road was a delicate balance of jamming in as many shows as possible while keeping your sanity. For Alex, dragging around this size of entourage on the boat was going to be very expensive. The limited number of appearances, though hers was a top-tier act, would ding the profits. Thinking back to the credit reports, I wondered about the planning of the tour. If you needed money, this was not how to make it. I made a note to follow up with the forensic accountant, as well as Alex's manager.

We left the bridge and started down to the main deck. Music was blaring and the dozen or so dancers were working through a routine. Several of the men who I had labeled as muscle hovered nearby, Monte among them. The dancers were working in the large room where we had boarded. I counted eighteen people—

a dozen dancers, five security guys, and Monte, who I easily recognized from the picture with the tarpon and from Chico's description. Most of the people aboard were here—and the murder scene was only a few steps away.

"That's a lot of people to rule out," Grace said.

"I don't know. The big guy might simplify this." Monte was walking toward us. A second later, one of the dancers left the practice and joined him. From their body language I could tell right away that these two were close.

"Monte Castro, no relation."

"Sorry for your loss," I said, wanting to gauge his reaction. If the missing knife from Chico's boat was indeed the murder weapon, then Monte was the most likely person to have removed it. That moved him to the top of my list. Being married to the star also generated plenty of opportunities for a motive.

"Thank you, yeah." His response seemed insincere. "This is Monika Diaz—she's Alex's number two. I have a feeling she's going to be the next big thing."

The comment was out of place and Monika lowered her head. Something was going on here. A love triangle, or maybe a partnership, were the most likely. Either would provide a motive for killing Alex. At least Monika seemed reluctant to accept the praise.

"So, the tour goes on?" I asked.

"Tomorrow night's going to be a memorial. Everyone agreed that we should do it for Alex. Miami loved her." Monte paused. "Monika has been doing the choreography and working with the dancers forever. With some good press, we can salvage this."

I glanced at Monika, who appeared upset with Monte's optimism. She seemed sincere, but she could easily be wearing a façade. This was her big opportunity, and I wondered if it was worth killing someone for a shot at fame.

11

STEVEN BECKER
A KURT HUNTER MYSTERY
BACKWATER DIVA

Detective work is a whole lot of sweat and, if you're lucky, a little glory. It takes all kinds to do this job. There are the grinders, the profilers, and the psychics, but those are styles. The work remains the same. It's similar to archeology. To solve a case, you simply have to dig deep enough. Patience is required to remove the dirt, and often some had to be replaced to shore up weak sections.

That was what I found myself doing now. Standing in front of me were the two prime suspects in Alex Luna's murder. There was a good chance they had acted together, which made things more difficult. Therefore, the structure of my questioning needed to be sound. I did have a few advantages. Neither knew that the murder weapon had been identified, or that I had a relationship with Chico, the man they had chosen as a patsy.

I held my cards close, knowing I would learn more from observation than from their responses. Even innocent people were wary of answering questions, and it took time to develop trust.

"If you're through, we have to get back to work," Monte said.

It was barely twenty-four hours since his wife had been

killed, and he was ready to get on with life—or rather, with Monika.

"We're through for now." I turned away as they left.

"What the hell was that about?" Grace asked.

I moved to the side so as not to interfere with the rehearsal. Monte walked away and called the group together. Monika took it from there and gave directions. There was no hesitation, making it clear to me she had done this before. Seconds later, a booming bass beat vibrated the deck, signaling the start of the gyrations, or rehearsal, depending on your point of view. I could tell that Grace was annoyed, but I wanted to observe the dynamics between Monika and the group. She was clearly comfortable being center stage. If I hadn't known that Alex was supposed to be the main attraction, Monika would have easily fit the bill.

The music business hides plenty of secrets. One was the seemingly random stardom of one person over another. You had to be naïve to think that the most talented performers were the ones who made it. There was a whole lot more to being a star than being good. From my layman's perspective, there was no difference between Alex and Monika. I needed to get a quick education.

"You going to tell me what's running through your sea-salt-ridden brain?"

Grace's words were clear, but we needed to move further away from the music to hold a conversation. Stepping around a bulkhead, where I hoped it would be quieter, I saw a man with a camera shooting pictures of the rehearsal.

"Hey," I said.

He glanced at me, or I should say, moved his camera toward me. His face was hidden behind the large lens projecting in our direction. Grace was having none of it and moved toward him. At the last second he lowered the camera, almost as if it were a weapon and he was surrendering. In the process, I could have sworn I heard the lens click several times.

"I thought we ran off all the press? Who are you?" Grace asked.

"Jake Reese. I work for . . ." He paused. "The production company."

"And your job is to sneak around and take pictures?" Grace asked.

"Pretty much. I find the shots are better if they don't know the camera's there."

"So, you worked directly for Ms. Luna?" I asked.

"For the company, yeah."

He was fidgety, but seemed amicable enough. Probably more comfortable with the camera in front of his face, he was caught in the open now. The name Jake brought to mind more of a badass than Jake Reese—CIA operatives are named Jake. This Jake tried to look like a badass hipster, but his shorts were too short, his arms too skinny, and his hair had too much product. The three-day beard seemed a little too perfect, and his sunglasses were just a little too big for his face.

"Get anything interesting yesterday?" I asked him.

"You mean like of the murder?"

Grace and I exchanged a look, each of us wondering if this guy was for real. She subverted the question.

"I'll need your pictures from the last two days."

"Got a warrant? The press has rights, you know."

Remembering the angle of the picture, I had guessed the one of Justine that had made its way through the social media circuit had been taken on the ship. A cell-phone shot had seemed the likely culprit, and with several dozen people aboard it could have been taken by anyone. That kind of footage is part of life now, and though I felt badly that Justine's first exposure in the press was less than flattering, I assumed there was nothing to be done about it. Now, with Mr. Telephoto Lens sneaking around taking pictures, I figured him for the odds-on favorite as Justine's picture source.

I'd had about enough of the pretty boy. If he had evidence that would clear Chico's name, I wanted it. If a bit of revenge for what he did to Justine could be exacted in the process, I was all for it. I took a step toward him, but felt a hand on my shoulder.

"Easy, tiger. That'll get you in more trouble than it's worth."

I snarled at Reese, but under Grace's restraint, backed away.

"You want a warrant, we can get one, but that'll include your nice camera and all your gear. Might be easier to just make a copy of the SD card." I was pretty sure we could get a warrant and including his equipment in it would be easy.

The decision came quickly. Somewhere in Paparazzi 101 there must have been a chapter on dealing with the authorities. "Give me a minute." Reese skulked away.

"That was nicely done. Might take him a few minutes to change his pants, too."

"As long as we get something."

"You know he can give us whatever he wants. It's not like the old days when you knew if a negative was missing. Now it's all digital files. Hit that trashcan symbol and it's gone."

I lived with a forensics tech. "Gone but not forgotten. The files are still there, you just can't see them."

"And if he doesn't give us the original card?"

"My guess is that he'll delete what he doesn't want us to see, save the rest to his computer, and give us the card out of the camera."

"Let's hope you're right."

Jake returned a few minutes later, wearing the same pants and holding an envelope. I took it and felt the hard outline of an SD card. It was all we were going to get from him now, and we walked away.

Music continued to blast as the rehearsal continued. I'd seen enough and wanted off the boat. Grace was feeling the same way, and we almost tripped over each other as we made our way to the gangplank.

"How long can you keep the boat here?" I asked, once we were onshore.

"At least a few days. Monte said they have a memorial show the day after tomorrow. It might not be the most glamorous spot, but the dock is free, and somehow they talked their way into shore power, so I don't think they'll be in a rush to leave."

I held up the envelope with the SD card. "I'm gonna take this to the crime lab."

"I can start running some of the names. The dive team is supposed to head out to the mooring site and have a look for the knife. I'll follow up on that, too."

I remembered that Justine had said something about heading out there this afternoon. "I got that."

"OK, lemme know what you find."

I walked to the truck, thinking that the contents of the SD card might be more important than taking a boat ride and checking on the dive team. That didn't stop me from heading out to check on the divers. The decision was one part procrastination and another part flexing my freedom muscles. Fowey Light was in the park, so I rationalized the need to supervise the team as part of my duty.

I drove back to headquarters and traded my truck for my boat. I immediately felt better just being on the water. Once I cleared the last channel marker, I smiled. Every day on the water is a different experience, and today proved that by being the opposite of yesterday. My center console is a bay boat. With its low freeboard, it's efficient and fun in calm, protected waters. In seas over a foot or so, it's more like Splash Mountain.

Today was a Miami postcard kind of day. Light clouds

streaked the deep blue sky. The effects of the rain were negligible. There were days following a storm when the usually clear bay waters were stained brown with tannin and sediment and covered in litter. Water bottles, trash bags, and lawn refuse were the main culprits. Along with the trash, the storms brought silt from every canal in South Florida into the bay. The timing of the influx was hard to predict, but with the light winds, only the frontrunners had reached open water. Justine and I would often stop to pick up trash when we paddled, but I ran through the garbage today. The tannin colored water was due to runoff and erosion, which had become hot topics over the last decade. Construction sites, another of the big culprits, were required to install catch and abatement systems. The mitigation had worked to some extent, but with a couple of million people less than a stone's throw away, the bay suffered.

The engine noise covered any notifications from my phone, and when I arrived thirty minutes later, I could only wish the ride had lasted longer. I pulled up to a vacant mooring ball, immediately noticing that, even with the better weather, there were fewer boats today than yesterday. The difference was the absence of the *Diva*. The parasites had relocated.

"Hey," I called over to a man on the dive boat which lay about twenty feet away.

"Ranger," he answered.

"Justine with you guys?"

"She's under with the team. You must be Hunter."

My reputation proceeded me. I only hoped it was the competent one that Justine cultivated, not my bumbling Miami-Dade alter ego. "When do you expect them up?"

Even the simplest recreational dives were planned. Any depth over thirty-three feet increased the risk of decompression sickness. Bottom times were calculated before any dive and a plan was made. Because of the choppy seas, Alex Luna's boat had been moored off one of the balls set in deeper water, where it would have been more comfortable. From there, the reef dropped off from a tame twenty feet to infinity. That left the divers in about fifty feet of water. I knew the dive tables well enough to recall this translated into about seventy minutes of bottom time. Few divers, especially when working underwater, could milk their tanks for that long, and I expected the man aboard the sheriff's boat knew that.

He glanced at his watch. "Thirty minutes tops."

I thanked him and checked the time, then moved back to the leaning post to see if any other untoward items had been posted to social media or broadcast by the news outlets.

The man called over. "I've got some ear issues and couldn't dive. If you're certified, you can use my gear."

I jumped at the chance.

STEVEN BECKER

A KURT HUNTER MYSTERY

BACKWATER DIVA

I RELEASED THE MOORING LINE AND, WATCHING TO STAY CLEAR OF the bubbles breaking the surface, idled carefully toward the dive boat. The man tossed a pair of fenders over the port-side gunwale and waited for me to approach. A dozen feet away and with the wind pushing me toward the police boat, I dropped to neutral and waited for the gap between the center consoles to close.

My boating skills had improved over my three years here. Where once this would have been a white-knuckle maneuver, now I casually looped a dock line over the midship cleat on the other boat and snugged the boats together. With the help of the officer aboard, the bow and stern lines were quickly secured. I shut down the engine and climbed over the gunwale.

I extended my hand, "Kurt. I appreciate this."

"Bruce. No problem. Justine's one of our favorites."

She had that effect. Bruce reached under a bench running along the starboard side, grabbed a large mesh bag, and pushed it toward me. Removing the gear, I checked each item like my life depended on it—which it did. There were many reasons for dive accidents. Malfunctions were far from the main reason people got into trouble, but were probably the most controllable. Once I had separated and inspected everything, I added eight pounds of weight to the belt and slipped the buoyancy compensator and first stage of the regulator onto the tank. With the buckles and fittings secured, I turned on the air. The tank was topped off with the gauge showing over three-thousand pounds of pressure. That would last me much longer than the fifteen minutes I figured the divers below had left.

I strapped into the gear and, with my fins in place, placed the mask over my head and swept my right hand around my back to retrieve the regulator. With the rubber mouthpiece clamped between my teeth, I breathed in my first breath of bottled air, nodded to Bruce, and moved my body forward to dislodge the tank from the rack. It pulled free, and I eased my butt onto the gunwale. After a final check, I gathered the hoses and gauges into my body, placed the palm of my right hand over my regulator and fingers over the mask, and fell backwards into the water.

As soon as I submerged, I spun over and quickly oriented myself to my new surroundings. As the boat ride had helped my mood before, being in the water purged my pent-up frustration. Releasing the small amount of air in my BC, I placed my fingers over my nose and squeezed the silicone part of the mask protecting it. The pressure in my ears released. I had to perform the same routine twice more while following the bubbles rising to the surface from the bottom and joining the other divers.

Justine didn't recognize me at first. Diving is a lot like skiing, where a person's features are covered in gear. It's the color and style that allows recognition. I saw her head turn toward me, but she probably thought Bruce was feeling better and had decided to join them.

It wasn't my intention to disturb the search. From the string lines forming a grid on the ocean floor, I figured this was their second dive. There would probably be one more. The fluorescent lines were stretched in a north-south and east-west pattern. The three divers were working through the ten-square-foot grids. Even if I didn't recognize Justine by her gear, I would have known her by her curves, accented by her wetsuit. I moved next to her.

Humans have a deep-seated instinct that tells them when someone is nearby. Without the sense that predators were lurking we as a race might not be here. Whatever the root, it works well in the water. She must have sensed me and spun around. Diver's faces are mostly hidden by gear, but I could see her eyes. It took a few seconds for her to recognize me, and then I could see, again from her eyes magnified by the mask, that she was smiling.

She held up a single finger and moved to the other divers. When she had their attention, she pointed at me and then herself. They understood that instead of the odd-man-out team of the three of them, we would split into the standard buddy groups. The two other divers moved into the next grid. Justine and I started on the adjacent one.

I'd dove several times to search for an old wreck in these waters and knew the difference between sightseeing and working underwater. It was still exhilarating for me, like being in your own world. I recognized that this might show something of my character that might not be flattering to the more experienced divers.

Justine and the two men used small plastic pieces to fan the sand. Even the smallest storms generate a storm surge. Yesterday's weather would have cast a thin layer of sand on anything on the bottom. Multiply that by years or centuries, and you have the need for the mailbox blowers and dredges the salvors use to recover treasure.

Without the tool, I fanned the sand with my hand. As the

knife had only been in the water for a day, it was a straightforward and easy process. We moved quickly to the next grid, which abutted the reef. The reefs in this area, and throughout the Keys, generally run north and south, which is a little deceiving because most people think the island chain runs in that same direction, where it actually runs east to west. Shallow reefs are usually patches, like oases in the desert of the ocean floor. In the deeper water, the reefs look like fingers. Ten or so feet in width, the coral rises several feet above the narrow, sandy strips between them. These are usually found in a group running parallel to each other.

The mooring was located in the sand just to the south, or the seaward side, of a group of these. Some reefs end in ledges, which can rise ten or twenty feet above the sand. In this grid, the ledges were just starting to appear. I moved onto the coral and started searching. Instead of using the fanning process, working the coral was more like lobster hunting. But instead searching for the telltale antennae sticking out from the small overhangs, we were looking for a glint of metal. With all the nooks and crannies, searching the sand was considerably easier, though this was more interesting.

Small groups of brightly colored tropical fish scattered as I used my hands to pull myself along the reef. In the distance I saw the flash of a large snapper. I shot a blast of air into my BC. It was fine to work on my knees while over the sand, but the coral would have shredded them. As I floated above the reef, it was even harder to keep my focus on the work. If Justine were able to call out, she would have yelled *Squirrel!* several times.

I checked my watch as we moved to the next section of the grid. I had plenty of bottom time remaining, but knew the rest of the team would ascend any minute. They had maybe five minutes remaining when one of the other two divers held up his hand. He'd found something. They had caught up to us and were working on the sand beside the finger reef. Justine moved toward them. The stream of bubbles from the trio of divers, whose heads were almost touching, was too much to see through, and there wasn't enough room between the coral for me in the group, leaving me no choice but to wait.

One of the divers left the group and started to ascend. I watched him, realizing that we were a good ways behind the mooring. I pictured the knife, floating from the boat to the bottom. There was always current of some kind, and no one expected the knife to be directly below the yacht. I just didn't expect it to be so far away.

With the find, this would be the last dive, and the divers were willing to milk every second from their bottom time. The diver who had ascended returned with a bulky camera and started to take pictures of what I guessed was the knife and the surrounding area. The other man removed a tape measure from the pocket of his BC. He anchored one end by the item and moved back to the mooring ball. I was wondering if he had the same thought as I did. Justine unclipped a reel from her BC and inflated the sausage-shaped end by purging her regulator into it. She held the reel as the bright yellow marker floated to the surface. Once it had broken through, she retrieved enough line that it was directly above the item in the sand. GPS devices don't work underwater, and this way the boat would be able to mark the coordinates of the find.

Once the item was documented, measured, and marked, I was allowed to inspect it. There was no doubt from the shiny metal that it was new in the water, and it certainly looked like the knife Chico had described. I nodded to the group, and one of the men removed a plastic bag from a pocket of his BC and with a gloved hand placed the knife inside.

We rose through the water as a single group. The other divers had been in much longer than I had, and were likely low on air, so I hung back and allowed them to board first. When I finally climbed aboard, the deck was littered with gear. I kicked off my fins and tossed them aboard before I climbed the dive ladder, adding them to the pile. Halfway up, I spat out my regulator and took a deep breath before climbing aboard. I moved to the same bench where I had geared up and dropped the tank into the retaining sleeve mounted to the gunwale.

I pulled off my mask. "Looks like that's it." I glanced at the knife. There were several rust spots, but no blood. I guessed that had probably washed off in the water. I knew from personal experience that even the best stainless steel rusted aboard a boat, so the marks were expected. "Matches the description that Chico gave me."

Justine held the bag up. She sealed it and placed it with her gear. "Let's call it then. I'll take it back to the lab and let you guys know."

I wondered what she could get off of it; fingerprints and blood would have washed away. But there might be a nick or some other microscopic DNA evidence on the knife. If it were there, she would find it.

"Back to the real world." I turned to Bruce. "Appreciate the loan."

He nodded back, and I kissed Justine before hopping over the gunwales and into the Park Service center console. After starting the engine, I released the lines and immediately idled away from the police boat. I would have preferred to float away, but the wind and current were against me.

I waved and pushed down the throttle. Another diver had found the knife, but that didn't dampen my spirits. The police boat circled back to mark the spot where the yellow sausage had broken the surface. It wasn't until several minutes later, when the police boat flew by me tossing my smaller boat with its wake, that I started to come back to the real world.

13

STEVEN BECKER
A KURT HUNTER MYSTERY
BACKWATER DIVA

JUSTINE HAD THE KNIFE, SO THERE WAS NOTHING TO DO BUT WAIT. She started her shift at two, but I doubted she'd wait until then to go in. Standing over her shoulder while she worked wasn't good for my health or our marriage. I was anxious for the result, but knew better than to get in her way.

While I waited for the results, I decided to work on the motive. I like to work cases methodically, like a jigsaw puzzle, instead of barreling through them to see what turns up. There is some merit to the latter tactic. Often suspects are rattled by this kind of approach and either run or inadvertently show their hand. But when there was a choice between playing good cop or bad cop, I chose the former.

Weird, random stuff often shows up in my Facebook feed, just after I think about it. With my search history, my feed is often cluttered with all kinds of crap that has nothing to do with my life. Somehow, one time, Facebook thought I was a jigsaw fan and placed an ad for an egg-shaped puzzle. Now, the thing about most jigsaw puzzles is that, although they may have a thousand pieces, they generally have four corners and straight borders.

The four corners are the key to putting together the puzzle. There is always a chance you'll find random pieces that fit together, but consistently working out from the corners, then filling in the field, is the best strategy. Just like in a puzzle, I match the corners of a case up to the main elements of a murder—motive, opportunity, and means are the standard three. To those, I add a trigger—the incident that allows the confluence of the other three.

Sometimes the trigger is evident, others not. In this case, I couldn't tell if the murder of Alex Luna appeared to have been orchestrated or was spontaneous. The activity on the yacht earlier and the witness interviews Grace had conducted that showed a rehearsal had been in progress when Alex was killed caused me to take note. The only thing that didn't sit right with this theory was that a setup scenario would have led to a less violent, more unemotional killing. The laceration appeared to have been made by an emotional, even angry, person—likely a male, although in this case the dancers were all physically strong enough to have committed the murder.

Opportunity seemed to fall into the same category. If the murder had been scripted to allow the killer opportunity, there was nothing to be gained by descending into this rabbit hole.

Means and motive. Chico had the knife and therefore the means, but he lacked motive. Even if I didn't know him so well, I would have ruled him out. Fishing guides, even catch-and-release ones, know how to use a knife. A killing blow from someone experienced with a knife would have looked different from the jagged wound I had seen at the autopsy.

Monte had the means and opportunity. He could have easily taken the knife from Chico's boat. He and Monika seemed to be the likely candidates, so I started to dig deeper. If they were in it together, chances were that Monte and she were having an affair.

I tried to call each of them. Both of their numbers went to voicemail. I left messages that I had some follow-up questions and stared at my notes. Money as motive was next on the list, so I called Grace.

"I was just about to call you. There's a YouTube video of the murder."

I placed the call on speaker as she guided me to the video. At first, the angle was such I thought it had been taken from one of the helicopters or even one of the other boats I had seen, but that wouldn't fit the timeline. It became obvious after a minute that it was from a security camera on the bridge.

Over the next half hour I watched, rewatched, panned, and zoomed in on the sequence. With my eyes burning and my brain spinning, I sat back, having only reinforced my theory that the murder was as choreographed as the rehearsal. I called Grace back.

"The only thing I can get out of it is pretty much what we already know, and that's the time of death. Alex's body isn't even visible for most of it."

"Yeah, just thought you'd be interested. It's all over social media," she said.

"That's not going to help anything." It did give me an idea. I hate to admit I watch much TV, especially reality TV, but there were a few shows I never missed. Their fishing and diving backdrop provided me with enough of an excuse to watch without guilt. "You ever watch *Deadliest Catch*?"

"Kurt?"

There was enough mockery in her voice that I knew she didn't. Justine laughed at me too. "They have cameras everywhere. Decks, galley, bridge, engine room."

"So, you think there's more footage than this?"

"It looks like it was shot from a stationary camera on the bridge."

"I'm in the process of getting a warrant," Grace said.

"No need. I met the captain earlier. I had some follow-up questions for Monika and Monte as well. Is the yacht still there?"

"For the time being. They want to move it to the Museum Park Marina for the memorial show."

I was familiar with the facility, though it was more a long, concrete dock than an actual marina, but it sat adjacent to American Airlines Arena, the concert venue. "The show's not until tomorrow night. Let them do it. We'll have access for another few days, and if we need to we can impound it again."

"I guess there's no harm. Might bring things back to normal for the cast and crew. Someone might make a mistake."

"Exactly." And I wouldn't have to deal with the officers at the Miami-Dade impound lot. "I'm still going to head over now."

"OK."

I had the feeling she was going to tell me not to do anything stupid, but let it go. Lacking transportation, I left my boat at Dodge Island and Ubered to the impound lot.

When I arrived, the focus of the officers and those aboard the yacht was on a sleek sports car. I was getting pretty good at identifying boats, but high-end cars eluded me. In any case, the custom-painted vehicle fell into the high-end of the high-end, no doubt the result of ill-gotten gains. The crew were the only ones visible aboard the ship. They were gathered along the starboard rail watching the new arrival.

"Know the story, Agent?" the captain asked.

"No, but I'm sure he didn't do it," I joked.

The captain laughed. "What can I help you with? We just got the OK from the police that we could move the boat."

"I was hoping to see the surveillance camera setup you have, and maybe talk to Monte and Monika."

"Think they went to the mall or something. They'll meet us at the marina."

"I'm happy to tag along." Spending some time on the murder scene with only the crew aboard might be a good thing. The captain broke up the party at the rail. I watched as he gave a few orders to the crew around him. They scattered to their positions, and a few minutes later I heard and felt the engines start. The lines were cast off, and the boat was underway. With the *Diva* being docked bow to the sea, there was no need to maneuver. The captain simply idled away from the seawall and downriver.

The Miami River's original flow had been altered. It was now fed by controlled canals upstream. Deprived of the natural outflow of the Glades, the waterway is generally placid. Not that it would have mattered with the power plant vibrating below my feet. I allowed the crew to finish their duties and made my way to the bridge.

"I guess you've seen the video?"

I pointed to a small black dome below us. "Yeah. That the camera?"

"Yeah. Before you ask, I'll tell you it's not one of my people."

"Who else has access?"

"We've got an electronics room. Used to be there was the VHF radios, single-sideband, autopilot, and plotter. Now there's interfaces for the interfaces. Engine room's too hot, so we use a closet by the crews' quarters."

I watched as he moved a joystick. The bow thrusters kicked in and the yacht reacted instantaneously, sliding almost sideways to starboard to give sea room to a barge coming upriver. The large, stainless-steel wheel was unused but still present and moved as the rudder was manipulated by the electronics. "Mind if I have a look?"

"We'll be out of the river in a few minutes. The dock's not far. I'll give you the tour if you can wait."

"That would be great." My interest was piqued both personally and professionally. I moved away from the "wheel" and felt my phone vibrate. Stepping further back, I exited the wheelhouse and accepted the call.

"Allie, how goes things?"

"Did you see the vid?" She was excited, thinking she had scooped me.

"Yeah, but someone else told me how to find it on YouTube."

"I follow Alex Luna on Instagram and saw it posted to her account."

That didn't surprise me. Everything was posted everywhere.

"Dad, I did a little investigative work and found out who posted it."

She had my attention now. I was proud that she'd been admitted to Florida, but also that she had chosen criminal science as her major.

"Who?"

"Jake Reese. Seems he's more than just a photographer."

"Met him. A bit creepy."

"So, he cross-posted it to his account, and I found a link in his bio that goes to his website. You're right about him being creepy."

It took a few minutes for Allie to guide me through the process of finding his site. It wasn't porn, but it was close. There was a montage of pictures of Alex Luna. She was clothed, but not by much. I felt almost embarrassed talking to my daughter while looking at them. "He's selling these pictures?"

"Yup."

I pressed the "See more" button and was directed to a page offering a subscription to the site for $9.99 per month. "A subscription?"

"It's the latest profit model. He wouldn't make as much up front, but you're gambling that most people won't cancel, or will forget to cancel, at least for a while. Keep them happy for a week and you'll have them for a year."

The yacht slowed. I felt the deck vibrate under my feet as the engines were put into reverse. A second later, I looked up to see our port side brush against the seawall. After another thrust, the pulse dropped as the speed fell. The crew were busy with the lines, but my eyes were drawn to the arena across the water.

"I gotta go. Call ya later." She said goodbye. I disconnected and entered the bridge. The captain was stepping away from the helm, and the first officer took control of the ship, which at this point meant little more than shutting the engines down. It seemed the captain was a bit of a control freak.

He motioned me back to the deck and started showing me the lifeboats and other features of the ship. As we went, I looked for cameras, finding three more before we reached the salon and main deck. We entered through a set of sliding glass doors and were immediately met by a blast of cold air. Moving through the main living areas, we dropped down a deck to what the captain said was the cast's area, and then another where the crew had their quarters.

"Funny," he commented as we approached the end of the corridor.

We were near the stern by an industrial-looking set of steel stairs that went down to the engine room. At the top of a landing, a door stood open. I glanced at the captain, sensing something was wrong.

"Electronics room?"

"Yeah, it's supposed to be locked when we're underway. You can damned near drive the ship from down here if you know what buttons to push."

14

The door blocked my view of the room. Just as I was about to step around it, my phone vibrated. I glanced at the display and saw it was Justine. I kept an eye on the corridor and answered.

"You're not going to believe this," she said.

"Try me."

"The knife is not the murder weapon."

"What?" It would be impossible to calculate the odds on that knife, found so close to the scene and fresh in the water, was not the murder weapon.

"No blood residue. No DNA. A couple of fish scales that are, like, glued to it."

"Couldn't the water erase all the evidence?"

"Saltwater's hard on stuff. Fingerprints and wet blood would have come off, maybe, on the straight edge, but one side was serrated. You stab someone that violently, there's going to be some skin or bone fragments left. The hilt was clean too."

The fish scales made sense and gave me an idea. "Maybe we should have the medical examiner check to see if there were any fish scales in the wound."

"He would have found them, but I'll call anyway." She paused. "Sorry."

"Crossing things off is better than adding them. I think this'll prove that Chico was set up, anyway."

"It should. I'll write it up and post it to the case portal. Tell Grace it's there."

"OK." I'd need to update her on the findings, anyway. Justine and I made plans for dinner later and I disconnected. My attention turned back to the electronics closet.

I heard the captain speaking to someone. The voice belonged to a man and, even if Allie hadn't told me who posted the video, I would have recognized the voice—Jake Reese. I stepped around the door and moved toward the two men.

"I'm just doing my job. Alex gave me permission to use any footage taken aboard the boat."

He was already on the defensive.

"I think the circumstances have changed," the captain said.

The captain nodded at me for support. I was an investigator, not a rules enforcer, and wasn't sure about the legal ground, but I took a chance. "In the present circumstances, I think the captain is in charge of the boat."

Reese's eyes told me he wanted to run, but his greed had him stand his ground. "I'll see what Mr. Luna has to say about that."

"You do that, but until then, this is off limits." He muttered something into a handheld radio.

We waited until Reese reached the stairs. He glanced back at us and started to climb to the crew deck.

"He cause any trouble?" I asked.

"Seems to be underfoot all the time, but I guess that's his job."

The room was nothing more than a walk-in closet with a set of wire shelves fastened to the deck and bulkheads. Dozens of LED lights blinked at me from different-sized boxes as I perused the equipment. The closet was well organized, and the captain knew what each was. It seemed like everything aboard had some kind of electronic component. He identified the ship's controls, communications, and finally the video equipment. I studied the boxes. Each camera appeared to have a module that interfaced with a larger box, which I suspected was the hard drive.

"How long do the tapes go back?"

"Nothing physical like tapes. Everything goes to the cloud now. I guess it just stays there. Never really thought about it. The only time I needed anything was when the dinghy got blown overboard in a storm. Came in handy for the insurance claim."

"Must have been quite a storm." I almost laughed at his use of the term "dinghy." The twin-engine center console mounted to the deck was bigger than my boat. "Any chance I can get access?"

"Leave me your email and I'll send you the link and a temporary password for the storage site."

I handed him a card and turned away, thinking I wouldn't have known how to create a temporary password if I was captain.

The visit to the electronics room and tour of the ship, though interesting, had turned into just something to do. I could have asked for the information over the phone, but then I wouldn't have seen Reese. That in itself hadn't raised any alarms, though. As he stated, he had permission to be there. Still, after Allie identified him as the mystery poster, I wondered if it were possible to manipulate the evidence using the equipment in that closet.

Thanking the captain when we reached the main deck, I disembarked and started to think about my next move.

Three large cruise ships across from the arena blocked the view of Dodge Island. It was less than a mile to my boat, so I did what no one in Miami does unless they are showing off on South Beach—I walked.

Fortunately, there is a wide shoulder on the bridge to Dodge Island, only a quarter mile long. I jogged it. About fifteen minutes after leaving the marina, I reached my boat and started the engine. I knew I was killing time, but with the *Diva* expected to remain in place until after the concert, I figured having my truck would be a benefit. Most people never thought twice about their mode of transportation. My situation living on an island was different, and it seemed every time I needed a boat, I had my truck, and when I had my truck, I needed a boat.

Running across the bay also gave me some time to think. Before leaving, I texted Grace that we were back at square one with the murder weapon. The only thing I knew was that Chico had been set up and someone had tossed his knife. That person had to be Monte. A picture formed in my mind of how the yacht was moored, and where Chico's boat would have been when he dropped Monte off. It had seemed a stretch that the knife was found so far from the murder scene. It wasn't surprising that the location where the knife was found matched my vision.

Martinez's old office was my destination. His idea of running the park had been to watch his dozens of security cameras on a bank of three oversized monitors placed next to his desk. All I needed was popcorn.

Being on the water clarified my thoughts. I would have preferred to be fishing, but the ride was all I was going to get today. There was a freedom to it. As you moved south through the park, cell reception faded, then disappeared at the southern end. Martinez had put a tracker on my boat, but I doubted anyone was watching now. That left me connected enough to place or receive a call if I wanted, or simply refuse it. My standard excuse of being on the water was never questioned.

I'd suspected Monte was involved from the beginning. The

fishing trip had been a setup. Then I remembered Chico saying that he used an online company to handle his bookings. Grace would likely remove him as a person of interest, but I doubted she would notify him. I knew he would be relieved. I decided to call Chico

I was just about to pass Cape Florida, which marked the end of Key Biscayne and the protected waters. From the cape, the bay was open to the Atlantic for a dozen miles. Various flats and shoals, several of which Stiltsville had been constructed on, offered some protection until Sand Key started the string of barrier islands that ran to North Key Largo. Reception was good here, and with Key Biscayne protecting me from the wind, I decided to make a quick stop and call.

Chico answered right away and I could hear the anxiety in his voice. His relief was evident when I gave him the good news about the knife.

"Where do you buy your gear?" I thought if someone went to the trouble to make it look like the murder weapon was his knife, they might have bought a similar one for the kill.

"Shoot. I just get 'em at the bait store. You know how it is on a boat. The water's like a magnet for stuff."

"Anywhere in particular?"

"I tie my own flies and order the material online. If I need anything I usually just buy it at the fuel dock at Bayfront."

That would be easy enough to check. I knew the attendant there. Those guys made most of their money on tips. Even though it came out of my own pocket, I always tossed a five at the attendants when I used the Park Service credit card. I knew most of the others didn't.

"What about the booking service?"

He started to rattle off a web address. I stopped him and grabbed a pencil and pad from my pocket and wrote down the website. Getting any kind of information from an online company like that was almost impossible. The chances were it was based in another state—or country—where a warrant wouldn't help.

"Any chance you could find out who booked and paid for Monte's charter?"

Chico readily agreed to help and I disconnected. I texted Justine that I was heading to the park headquarters and called Mariposa to give her a heads-up that I was coming.

Drifting on the outgoing tide had taken me past the point and close enough to the adjacent flats to see individual blades of seagrass breaking the surface of the water. It was getting dangerously shallow. My polarized sunglasses showed the white paths through the grass made by propellers. Some were healed, others new, but they all shared the same characteristic of ending in the middle of the flat.

To avoid that fate, I idled toward the west, checking the water behind me for the telltale brown muck in my wake. It seemed clear and I focused on the water ahead. It wouldn't look good for a Park Service boat to make the same rookie move, though I knew everyone grounds eventually—some just haven't yet.

Half an hour later, I entered the long channel to Bayfront Park and slowed at the fuel dock. The attendant saw me and waved. A minute later he dragged the heavy green hose and nozzle to the boat. I unscrewed the cap, placed the nozzle in the opening, and squeezed the lever. Marine pumps don't have the mechanism to stop the pump automatically, so we talked while I held the handle and waited for the tank to fill.

"Chico said he buys his tackle here?" I asked him.

"Not a lot."

I could hear the fuel gurgling and released the lever just before it hit the overflow port. Handing the nozzle back to the attendant, I replaced the cap, and stepped onto the dock. "I'll go in with you and have a look around."

The refrigerators and freezers holding beer and bait dwarfed the small tackle section.

"Got any bait knives?"

"On the counter here," the attendant called out from the register.

I walked to the counter and handed him the Park Service credit card. While he processed the payment, I reached into my wallet and pulled out a five-dollar bill, which I placed on the worn Formica surface. He snagged the bill and handed me the receipt to sign.

I handed him back the signed receipt and glanced at the plastic bin full of knives. Another needle in a haystack. "Sold any recently?"

"We move a lot of them. For five bucks, it's a steal."

There was some irony that a five-dollar bait knife had killed a superstar whose worth was in the millions. The store was old school, and instead of a barcode scanner the attendant manually entered the prices into an old register. Without being able to tie a purchase to a particular customer, it was another dead end. There was only one chance. "Do you have surveillance cameras?"

He glanced behind him and I smiled. There was going to be a lot of TV watching going on today.

15

STEVEN BECKER
A KURT HUNTER MYSTERY
BACKWATER
DIVA

Mariposa had been my ally since my arrival here. She had buffered me against the machinations of Martinez and my nemesis and co-agent, Susan McLeash, and become a friend. Justine and I never turned down a dinner invitation to her home. The flavor of her Caribbean recipes mixed with the "guests only" Appleton 21 rum she only allowed her husband to drink with company were intoxicating.

"You should come say hello more often," she said.

Since the departure of Martinez and McLeash, I had been in limbo for the past month or so. I'd been offered to interview for the Special Agent in Charge job, but didn't really want it. The small taste I'd had during the hunt for a contract killer had shown me how bad I was at administration and budgets. I preferred to be in the field. As a result, I'd made myself scarce in the office, especially not knowing when Martinez's replacement would arrive.

"Yeah."

"Maybe dinner soon? How's Allie?"

As I answered her, I eyed the computer monitor on her desk. Watching the surveillance video was important, but it was one of many things that I naturally procrastinated against doing. To his superiors Martinez had looked like a star, which was probably why he was promoted. His vigilance with his budget and my case closure rate were all in his favor. What they didn't know, or care about, was how he accomplished it.

Aging equipment, undersized boat motors, two-wheel-drive vehicles where the terrain required four-wheel drive, and skimping on everything except his own surveillance equipment were a few ways he stretched the meager budget.

For my part, I never counted work hours. My father had been a general contractor. Through some unknown and subconscious process of osmosis, I had inherited his work ethic. Working for him during my high school and college summers, I remember asking him how much he got paid an hour. His answer was probably the reason the business wasn't called Hunter and Son today.

"Get up and get the work done; when the work is done go home. Checks go in the bank, and expenses come out. If there's anything left, it's yours."

I really didn't understand it then, but I knew that was how I worked now. When the case was solved, I went home. Until then, I worked. But that didn't mean I couldn't work smart. The monitor on Mariposa's desk needed a serious upgrade and I knew just how to do it.

"I'll be right back." She shrugged and I walked upstairs. Entering Martinez's office, I checked for booby traps, then grabbed one of his monitors. Tucking it under my arm, I brought it downstairs and set it on Mariposa's desk. I then went back and brought another down. A few minutes of cable swapping and I had the dual monitors working with her computer.

She laughed. "That'd be right nice. Now I can watch a movie and work at the same time."

"Kind of what I had in mind." I pulled my phone out and

checked my email. The captain had sent the login info for the cloud service where the boat's videos were stored. Handing Mariposa the phone, I walked around the desk and stood behind her.

Mariposa logged into the site, and I directed her to the time frame I was interested in. She found the camera that gave the best angle of the rehearsal. The scene was erratic without the music, making it look almost contrived. To my surprise, it was Monika who was clearly in charge. That explained why the rehearsal I'd seen earlier seemed like a seamless transition, but it wasn't Monika who interested me. I had a list of suspects in my head, and they were who I watched.

I was careful to break our viewing session into scenes. The outcome was known. I wanted to see how the people aboard acted before and after, and be able to keep track of them. We started at the beginning of the rehearsal, which was about a half hour before the murder.

Body language is pretty easy to identify. I could tell after a few minutes who was into it and who wasn't. It came as a surprise that Alex appeared to be just going through the motions. Monika was running the show. Fearing my judgment might be clouded, I asked Mariposa her opinion.

"That one there, she doesn't want to be there."

Her finger pointed to Alex Luna, confirming my thoughts. We reviewed the footage a second time and then a third. As we got closer to the murder, I watched Alex closely, trying to find out where her attention was focused. It certainly wasn't the rehearsal. It was almost as if she wasn't interested. I had played enough sports to know that every practice wasn't perfect. I'd had my head in the clouds for more than a few. Instead of watching Monika, she seemed more concerned about watching the water. Again, far from conclusive. If I were on a boat sitting on a pristine reef, I would do the same.

Watching Monika's control over the rehearsals made her a larger player. I decided that a formal interview might be a good idea.

Next up was Reese. We watched the same footage again with him as the focus. He wove in and out of the dancers, taking pictures from every conceivable angle. As expected, he spent most of his time around Alex. Through the entire episode, his focus was on the rehearsal. Creepy, but not unusual.

"What's that business?" Mariposa clicked on the pause button. "Those two have something going on." She dragged the button on the bottom of the screen to the left, rewinding the scene about thirty seconds. "There." She stopped it.

It could have been a coincidence. Monika and Reese had turned their attention and, for a long second, held each other's gaze. Their eyes clearly locked.

"I raised a pair of girls. I know that look," she said,

I suddenly felt badly about removing her old monitor without grabbing the pictures of her grandchildren attached the sides.

"Advance it a frame at a time."

We watched as Monika moved her eyes from Reese to the stern area of the deck. My guess was that she was watching Monte as he came aboard. I noted the time stamp so I could check if there was a camera with another angle that could confirm. "OK, move it forward."

The song must have ended, and it appeared that Monika had called for a break. The dancers left their positions. Most moved to the side and grabbed water bottles. Monika, Reese, and several others gathered around Alex. Monte barged onto the scene with Chico right behind him. I could tell Monte was excited. Knowing that he was into his second six-pack and had landed a hundred-pound tarpon explained that.

The rest of the video was already all over social media.

Bodies blocked the camera's view, but it was evident that Alex fell to the ground, crashing through the glass panel as she did.

Chico was there, but not close enough to have killed her. That left five people present, six if you counted Alex. My suspect list had narrowed to Monte, Monika, Reese, and two others.

"Can you get a head shot and figure out who those two are?" I pointed to the backs of the two people.

"Sure thing."

I'd gotten what I needed from the videos. Questioning Monika was my next stop. I said goodbye to Mariposa, who scolded me again for being a stranger.

"Dinner?"

"Yes. I'll talk to the boss." Appleton 21 aside, we really did enjoy Mariposa and her family socially. "Hey. One other thing." I fished in my pocket for the receipt with the store manager's phone number and handed it to her.

"I'll cook you dinner, but I ain't your accountant."

"No, there's a number on the back." I asked her to call the manager to have him check their footage for anyone purchasing a knife in the past week. I knew it was a long shot, but hard work was often responsible for lucky breaks.

I avoided the upstairs, where my old office was located, and went out to the truck. Ensconced in the air-conditioned cab, I called Grace and asked her if she could set up an interview with Monika Diaz. I was on the road when she called back and said we could meet at the station in an hour.

The Turnpike construction between Florida City and the exit for 836 was nearing completion, but still buggered up traffic enough to slow what should have been a speed-limit ride. If there was any consolation, the rush hour traffic in the opposite lanes was much worse.

I reached the station about fifteen minutes early and decided to sit in the lot rather than chance a run-in with one of my fans from Miami-Dade. I noticed a group of reporters hanging around out front and then saw the reason.

Three black SUVs entered the lot and moved toward the circular driveway in front of the entrance to the building. The reporters swarmed them as doors opened and some of the muscle I had seen on the boat exited the vehicles. They quickly created a human corridor to allow Monika Diaz to exit the middle car.

A big, floppy hat covered her face. She stepped onto the sidewalk like it was the red carpet, removing her hat and waving it at the throng of media. She teased the reporters, who held cameras above their heads and stabbed microphones in her face. Where I would have been frustrated and run for the door, she sauntered toward the entrance, casually answering questions and posing for pictures. Her appearance gave me the opening for my questions.

A few minutes later we were in an interview room. A short, bald-headed man sat next to her. I wasn't sure if he was part of her entourage or had arrived separately. In either case, I probably wouldn't have noticed him during that grand entrance.

"Simon Wallace, attorney for Ms. Diaz." He handed me a card.

I introduced Grace and myself. Grace pressed a few buttons on a box sitting on the table and dictated the who, what, where, and whens into the device. Wallace started to speak for Monika, but Grace made the wannabe star do it for herself.

"Quite the crowd out there," I started. In response I got a smile.

"If you have more specific questions, Special Agent?" Wallace interrupted.

The online theory that had surfaced since the rehearsal video went viral was that Monika was plotting to supplant Alex

Luna as the show's star. With my first sortie shot down, I tried another tact.

"Some might say you stand to gain from Alex Luna's death?"

Wallace eyed me, but stayed quiet. He knew where I was going with this and whispered into his client's ear.

"That's show business. There's always a vacuum to fill somewhere," Wallace said.

"And you have your opportunity tomorrow night?" I directed my question to Monika.

"This is far from the sure thing, slam dunk, kill the boss and take her place thing you've got going on with me." She couldn't help herself and bent her raised right hand at the wrist and flexed the joint, mimicking a dunk.

"Word on the street is you'll be fine."

"Alex has, had, the best people. They're pros, and despite the circumstances they are still doing their jobs," said Monika.

I wanted to point out that she would be the beneficiary of those efforts, but left it alone. "There was a group of five people around Alex's body when she was killed. You were one of them." I figured I might as well get some confirmations out of the way.

"I saw her fall and ran right over."

I hadn't seen it that way and eyewitnesses were notoriously unreliable.

"Did you see anything suspicious?"

"It looked like she fell through that glass panel."

"Anyone push her?" The seas had been choppy, but on a boat that size I doubted it would have been noticeable.

She wiped a tear from her eye. "Can't say. I just saw her lying in a pool of blood."

16

Monika's confident veneer seemed to break, though her occupation made me doubt her sincerity. Performers were all actors. I had little doubt she was able to manipulate her emotions on demand.

"It's getting late, Detective," Wallace protested.

I glanced at Grace for help. Potential suspects dictating my timeline was a constant irritation. If it were up to me, I would work straight through until the case was solved.

"I've got all night."

Grace raised her eyebrows, and I discreetly checked my phone.

It was almost ten o'clock. "OK, just a few more questions. Otherwise we'll have to resume in the morning." As I suspected, they agreed.

"Ten minutes. Then we're leaving."

"OK." I slid my phone across the table, displaying a screenshot of a frame Mariposa had taken from the video. "Can you identify the two people?"

She was no fool. If there were other suspects, she would throw them under the bus in a hot second. "Rico and Suzanne."

"Last names?"

"Sorry. Monte might know. He takes care of the business end."

"When is your next show after tomorrow night?"

"If we can pull this off and they don't slaughter us, we've got Tampa this weekend."

Using tour buses for the crew and tractor-trailers for the equipment could have transported the show to the city in four hours. Taking the boat, which seemed to be the MO for the tour, would take a couple of days. Evidence needed to be overwhelming to stop the tour and detain key personnel in Miami. That gave me three days to solve the case. The additional time was a gift, and I again wondered why Alex had chosen to tour by boat.

"Thank you. We'll be in touch," Grace said, sliding a card toward both Monika and Wallace.

"One more question." I didn't wait for a refusal. "Why the tour-by-boat thing? Sounds like it'd cost a lot."

"One of those things Alex insisted on. She wanted to rest between shows."

The expression on her face showed she clearly disagreed.

Monika was about to add something, but her attorney, knowing the interview to this point had been more beneficial than harmful to his client, shuttled her out the door. We could have offered to escort them to the back door to avoid the press, but my feeling was that Monika wanted the attention.

"Rico and Suzanne." In a business of flashy names and unique spellings, those names were downright boring.

Grace interrupted me. "Leave it for the night and get some rest. You look like how I feel."

She was right. There was nothing more to be accomplished tonight. We left the building together and I walked her to her car. After agreeing to touch base in the morning, and with a stern reminder that the work day didn't start until eight, she pulled out. Walking back to my truck, I realized how tired I was.

Going to sleep hungry wasn't good for me, and Justine was still at the lab. I called her and asked if she wanted to meet for what she called her lunch. Half an hour later, we sat down in our favorite diner.

Midnight is an odd time of day in Miami. Anyone with a daytime job is in bed, and those out partying don't usually go looking for late-night food before last call. That left us more or less alone.

Justine put down the menu. "I'm having breakfast."

We'd been here often enough that I didn't need to look and concurred. Taking a "lunch" hour and eating breakfast at midnight was about right for how I felt. Usually, it's after a case is resolved that I experience a big letdown as the adrenaline wanes. I felt that way now and didn't even have a prime suspect. Justine picked up on my mood.

"How about we go dive in the morning and have another look?"

Something in my brain had written off any chance of the murder weapon being found. "Do you want to call in the dive team?"

"They have another case. A car wrecked in one of the canals off Highway 41 in the Glades. Just you and me."

I wasn't going to turn that down and didn't need to ask why she was passing on the team dive. Justine hated freshwater diving, mostly because of the alligators. The threat was enough to put me off as well. People are aware of the gators, but the American crocodile, which reside in the bay and the Keys, are nastier by multiples, but don't get the press for sightings on golf courses and in swimming pools that gators do. Instead they lurk, generally unseen, in canals and brackish water.

"Count me in."

Fortunately, I had already moved my gear into town. After checking one of my boating apps, I noticed a strong current was predicted for the early morning. With that in mind, we discussed logistics for getting air fills and dive time. I'm a get-up-and-go guy. It was a little frustrating for me to wait and go out late morning, but it worked for Justine. She would have time to get a paddle in earlier. I knew my girl—on the days she paddled, she was happy, and that made the world a better place.

Justine had a few more hours to work, so we split up after we ate. She went back to the crime lab, and I went back to her condo, maybe for the last time before we moved. Beat, I didn't make it past the couch and when I woke, it was with Justine's head hovering over me.

"Come on, lover boy. Time to roll."

I hoped she meant back to the bedroom, but when my eyes opened I saw that it was already light out. She was dressed to paddle and my hopes for an early morning tryst crashed. "I'm up."

"Yeah, right. When I see your feet on the ground, I'll believe it."

Slowly, I swung my body and rose.

"God, you move like an old man."

She easily evaded my grasp and grabbed her pre-workout smoothie from the counter. "Ten o'clock."

"Yes, ma'am." I watched her head out the door, wishing it was the other direction. Alone now, I rolled my legs onto the couch and laid back. Grabbing my phone, I was relieved to see that nothing had happened overnight. Somehow, my eyes closed again and it was nine when I woke.

I felt better, but was pressed for time. Justine was due back any minute, and it wouldn't go well for me if I were still here. Jogging to the bathroom, I did a quick evaluation and decided, though it was borderline, on waiving a shower until after we dove. After performing minimum maintenance, I dressed and was out the door.

As I rushed to the dive shop with four tanks clanking around in the back of my truck, I was grateful for the mid-morning lull in the never-ending traffic. I reached the shop and, after unloading the tanks and paying for the fills, sat down with my phone to wait.

There was still nothing new on the case. In many instances, this would have been alarming, but the major players were entertainers, their support staff, and the press that followed them. It was a late-night business and they were likely all still asleep.

With the tanks filled, I reached the marina before Justine. That gave me the upper hand in our ongoing punctuality battle and would gloss over my sleeping in—if it were discovered.

I loaded the tanks onto our twenty-four-foot center console and got everything ready. The boat had no tank rack, so I slid our BCs over two of the cylinders, secured the straps, and blew a few breaths into the manual inflation port. Placed this way, the partially inflated BCs protected the deck from the tanks slamming against it and would stop them from rolling. The spare tanks were placed between the others and the sides of the boat. These weren't secured either, and because of that, I left the regulators off. I'd seen more hoses burst and gear mangled from incidents above the water than below.

Just as I finished, Justine appeared with two cups of coffee in her hand. I took one, swearing to myself that it wouldn't gain her any points for being late. She hopped onto the gunwale and stepped down to the deck.

"Ready?"

"Just waiting for you. How was your paddle?"

"Good, thanks. How was your nap?"

Somehow she knew and my advantage was taken away.

Answering her would be an admission of guilt, so I decided to drop it. You had to lose a few battles to win the war.

I started the engine and Justine cast off the lines. A few minutes later, we were at the mouth of the river. As we passed the markers I checked the tide and current. Though only a few miles apart, there was almost an hour's difference in the tide from Adams Key in the park to here. The tides at my island, or rather my old island, were ingrained in my head, and I sometimes failed to make the adjustment when I was in Miami. The height of the water, and the speed it was streaming past the piling, told me I had been correct in waiting. By the time we were ready to get in the water, the tide would be slack.

The current didn't always follow the tide as there were other factors involved, but it was usually a good benchmark. Retracing the route I had taken yesterday I noticed the waves were tight and stacked, indicating the tide was running against the wind. It made for an uncomfortable ride out to the light, one of those times when it was smoother to go faster. If you were going to get beat up, you might as well get it over with. We reached the mooring field by the light about a half-hour later, and tied off to the same ball that Alex Luna's yacht had been on.

Yesterday, the sheriff's divers had determined the search area and set up their grid before I arrived. Today, it was up to me. Being in a small boat, we were within a few feet of the mooring ball. The yacht would have used lines to extend the short pennant attached to the ball to reach the deck cleats. Pulling a hundred-foot line out of the console, I attached it to the loop on the mooring line and let the boat drift back.

We appeared to be fortunate that the wind and seas were similar to the day Alex was killed, or it would have been a much more complicated procedure. With conditions as they were, I fed out line as the boat drifted backwards to estimate the position of the deck where Alex was murdered. The recovery of

Chico's knife had taught me that there was little current. The knife had been found directly under where his boat had been tied off to the yacht.

In theory, the murder weapon should be below our boat. Things didn't always work out as planned, though. Currents were fickle. A southeast wind, the prevailing direction in these waters, didn't always mean the deeper water flowed in the same direction. An outgoing tide, which we were experiencing now, would run against the grain. The interaction between tide and waves would have created something similar to the pounding waves that had smashed the boat on our way out. They weren't large, but the conditions made things uncomfortable to gear up.

The tinge of nausea I'd felt disappeared when I hit the water. Once submerged, I released the air in my BC and dropped to the bottom. In better circumstances, with a spotter aboard the boat, I might have chosen to go without fins, but stranger things had happened than a mooring line releasing and a boat drifting away. Fins would be cumbersome and stir up silt, but were a bit of insurance that I could at least swim to shore if needed.

Justine met me a second later. I looked up to check our position. We were directly below the boat. If I had calculated correctly and the weapon was indeed tossed overboard, it should be within fifty feet of our location. We didn't have the materials or manpower to set up a grid, but I did have a hundred-foot tape measure and a stake. Driving the stake in with a weight from my pocket, I hooked the end of the tape over the steel tip and, starting at the five-foot mark, we started searching in a circular pattern.

Two revolutions later, we were at the fifteen-foot mark. I heard a noise beside me. Communication underwater is difficult, but after I turned to her it wasn't hard to interpret Justine's expression. Magnified by her face mask, her wide eyes made it clear she had found something.

17

THE OBJECT GLITTERED IN THE FILTERED SUNLIGHT, BUT I COULD see from twenty feet away that it wasn't a knife, which was probably why it was ignored in the first search. Finning closer, an irregular shape appeared, almost like a shard of glass. My hopes plunged. We already knew the glass screen had shattered. I expected this was just a piece of it. As I swam next to Justine, I had no idea why she was so excited.

Every new diver is taught basic signals as part of their certification process. Well-known signals for OK, out of air, surface, descend, hold steady, boat, and the ways to express how much air you have remaining are commonly used. Justine trying to explain what the significance of her find was while underwater was impossible. Since I was of a different opinion, we were both frustrated. She gave me a thumbs-up to surface.

I allowed the regulator to drop from my mouth when my head broke the surface and waited for Justine, who was a second behind me. After shooting a blast of air into my BC, I floated on the surface while I waited for her.

She held out the piece of glass to show me. "This is it."

"What?" I thought we'd already established a knife as the murder weapon.

She swam toward the boat, carefully holding the glass shard above the water. I reached the ladder first and removed my fins, which I tossed into the engine well. Timing the waves to my advantage, I rocked as the crest came under the boat. The additional momentum allowed me to easily climb aboard. I dropped my tank on the deck and went to the ladder.

Justine handed me an evidence bag with the piece of glass. I set it on the bench seat at the helm while she took her fins off. Back at the ladder, I reached down and grabbed hold of her tank valve. We waited a brief second for the next wave, then I helped her aboard.

She spat out her mouthpiece. "This might be from the screen, but someone tossed it overboard. The incident happened almost a dozen feet from the rail."

If she was right, it was important.

"She was pushed through the screen of tempered glass, and then stabbed with this sharp piece. Then it was thrown overboard. We were supposed to find the knife, which would implicate Chico. Just finding this would be insignificant—unless you know the difference."

We both stripped off our gear and stood above the shard. Justine wrote the pertinent information on the outside of the bag with a Sharpie and, as we were directly over the position where she had found it, I recorded the coordinates of the boat with the GPS. Justine had me call them out and wrote them on the bag as well. Confirming the numbers, I glanced at the bag and now could see why she was excited. There was clearly a blood stain on the surface. I hoped that the fingerprints might be intact as well but, after finding none on the knife that we now knew was a decoy, doubted we would find any,

"Let's head in. I'll get this processed ASAP," Justine said.

She stowed the gear while I released us from the mooring ball. Within a few minutes we were underway, heading toward the Miami skyline. I always looked forward to the ride back. Not just because we were heading home, but with the wind behind us and the resulting following sea, the ride was much smoother than the beat-down we had suffered on the way out.

My usual smile eluded me, though. We had found an object that might be the murder weapon. Even so, my hopes weren't high for the discovery pointing me in the direction of the perpetrator. Justine was happy because it was evidence, and second to a dead body, it was a challenge for her. My focus was to find the killer, and I just didn't see that piece of glass helping. If anything, it made things more difficult.

The general consensus from Sid, Vance, and our experiment with the ballistic cube was that a man had committed the murder. Doing the kind of damage to Alex Luna with a short blade took strength not many women had. I wasn't sure if the shard we'd found would change that paradigm.

The best I could come up with was that the murder was opportunistic. Monte barged onto the scene, exuberant after catching the tarpon and somehow Alex had been pushed through the screen. Seeing this, the murderer grabbed a piece of broken glass and finished the job, then tossed it overboard. I knew there was a lot of ground to cover before I could call it anything but a theory.

I kept my thoughts to myself as we crossed under the Rickenbacker Causeway and reduced speed as we approached the entrance to the Miami River.

Back at the dock, we hosed off the boat and gear. I'm always hungry after diving and thought a quick lunch might be a good idea. With no breakfast my stomach was rumbling.

We didn't get to eat together during the day very often, and it took a stupid long time to choose a restaurant. After too much deliberation, we settled on a burger place and were soon sitting across from each other. I could tell Justine was anxious for a quick meal so she could get to the lab and do what she did best.

"You don't seem that excited?" she asked as we waited.

I took a long sip from my drink before answering. I couldn't help but think, as I parsed my words before responding, how maybe if I did the same before spouting off to the Miami-Dade people I'd have a better relationship with them. In the big picture they weren't worth the effort, but Justine was.

"It's great to have the murder weapon, but it doesn't get me closer unless there's an evidentiary link to the perp."

"You saw the blood on it. Might not all be Luna's. Then there might be fingerprints, or even DNA, stuck under one of the jagged edges."

She was right, but it still didn't improve my mood.

"Find out who shoved her through the glass screen and you'll have your killer," Justine pointed out.

"Mariposa and I watched the surveillance footage yesterday. We were able to narrow the field to five suspects—Monte, Monika, Suzanne, one of the dancers, and Rico."

"What about Camera Boy?"

I had forgotten about Reese. "He was in the video, shooting the rehearsal." From watching him, I was confident he worked harder during the break than during the actual rehearsal. The magazines and websites that supported the paparazzi loved the candid stuff. Reese had already shown he was in this for himself.

"I've got an SD card he gave me." I had been so excited about the video footage, I had forgotten about the still photos.

"You did sleep awhile," she said with a smirk.

I knew that was going to come back to haunt me. We both had something to get excited about now, and we dug into our meals. Our food vaporized as we inhaled it, and ten minutes later, we were walking to our vehicles.

"Catch you later," she called out as she pulled from her parking space.

I waved after her and climbed into the truck. Mariposa had helped look at the footage from the store at the fuel dock, and she had been a big help yesterday. I figured it would be worth the drive to check the SD card along with her.

Heading south to Homestead, I found myself driving in the after-lunch lull. I'd noticed that at grocery stores and in traffic there was a pattern. This time of year, everything was timed to the school schedule. Two o'clock was the witching hour when the soccer moms rushed to the grocery store before picking up their kids. By the time the clock hit the top of that hour, I was pulling into the small driveway leading to the headquarters building.

Mariposa had her nose buried in between Martinez's monitors when I walked in. "Hey." It wasn't often I got the drop on her.

She looked up. "I'm almost done with the fuel dock footage. Nothing so far."

I didn't want to tell her she had wasted her time. "Things have taken a turn."

"Good thing your buddy Martinez isn't upstairs anymore. He would not like that."

We shared a laugh at his expense. Martinez always wanted cases to be open and shut. Crime never worked that way, but when one's primary concern is the budget, that's the standard I was judged against.

"Got this card." I handed her the SD card from Reese's camera.

She took the card and inserted it into a slot on her computer. A minute later a screen showing thumbnails of the drive's contents appeared. I had to admit to being surprised at how many pictures there were—and how many looked the same.

"There're a lot of them."

"Never seen your daughter's phone? They all take ten pictures to get one good one."

Mariposa was a little older than me, and we reminisced about the good old days when you had to take a roll of film to the store and wait a few days for the pictures to come back. I still took pictures like they each cost something.

She clicked on the first picture and we quickly scrolled through them. It bugged me just looking at all the duplicates. I knew memory was cheap and reusable, but it seemed wasteful. From the time stamps, the pictures began at breakfast on the morning Alex died. Reese might have transferred the previous day's footage to his laptop and wiped the memory card.

We waded through them for close to an hour before we reached the ones around the murder. By the time we found the break before Alex was killed, I had a good idea of Reese's style and who his favorites were. Alex and Monika were featured prominently, as I would have guessed, but something was bugging me. The next go-round through them, I asked Mariposa to save the pictures that I thought might be helpful to her hard drive. I wanted the SD drive preserved as evidence.

After I transferred both the original envelope and SD card to the evidence bag, we went back to work on the pictures. It took two more times through them for me to realize that there were no shots of Suzanne or Rico. After having watched the surveillance video several times through, I recognized everyone I didn't have a name for by their clothes. The practice was informal, with the dancers wearing sports bras and either yoga pants or gym shorts. The muscle wore baggy basketball pants and t-shirts. We went through the pictures one more time to be sure. Neither of the two people standing over Alex in the frame from the video were pictured.

It was like buying a lottery ticket, but I hadn't won yet. There could be a number of reasons why neither was in Reese's montage of the rehearsal. Monika might know, but I'd had enough of her attitude. I hoped the head of security might be helpful, so I called Grace to arrange an interview. She called back that we could meet him onboard the yacht in an hour. I was glad we wouldn't have to go through the media circus at the station, although I knew the vultures would be watching the yacht as well.

The logical course of action—after a quick weather check—was to take the boat. I could pull along the blind side of the yacht and board without being seen from shore. The thought of evading the paparazzi was almost worth the additional time to get there. I didn't feel the least bit guilty playing games in the middle of a murder investigation. The press had done me no favors.

"I'm going to take the center console up to Miami and meet the head of security." I gave Mariposa instructions on how I wanted to document the pictures and asked her to review the video footage again to see if Rico or Suzanne appeared before the scene around the body.

I headed down to the docks and hopped aboard the center console feeling like I was making progress. After starting the engine, I released the lines and returned to the helm. As I set my phone on the console I saw a notification for a message. Justine had texted, asking me to call.

18

MY INVESTIGATION WAS STARTING TO FEEL LIKE GROUNDHOG DAY. The only difference was that today I was commuting by boat and the interview was being conducted on the yacht. Yesterday at this time I was driving to Doral to interview Monika.

A lot had changed in the last twenty-four hours. The run up from Bayfront Park to Miami was ingrained in my memory and I didn't need to think about the course, which left me time to think. With the steady drone of the 150-horsepower engine just loud enough that I couldn't hear my phone, I felt like I was in my own cocoon.

The find of the glass shard cleared Chico of any involvement. Suzanne and Rico had surfaced as persons of interest. Monika still had motive, but she was no mastermind. But, most significantly, the physical evidence of the shard of glass recovered this morning changed everything.

I allowed ideas and people to pop in and out of my head at random. There were two activities I had found to foster creative and analytical thinking—running the boat and fishing. Being on the boat let me think outside the box, without censure or judgment. Ideas flowed, although it took a far second to the analytical powers I found when fishing. There was a certain zone I was able to access when I hunted or fished. Attuned to nature, my mind saw different aspects of a problem. Unfortunately, I didn't always need that superpower—but it was always good to cast a line.

Thinking about the shard of glass, I stumbled onto something that I had missed. By pushing Alex through the glass divider and finishing her off with a piece of glass, the killer was trying to make the murder appear to be an accident. I let my mind wander along those lines, testing whether guilt bounced off or stuck to each of the players.

The realization that the murder had been staged to look like an accident hit me like a cast thrown back in my face by the wind. If someone wanted to make it look like an accident, then why steal Chico's knife? Occam's razor states that if two explanations account for the facts, the most likely solution is the simplest. Taking a look at the knife from that angle, I realized my bias stemmed from our experiment with the ballistic material. The knife could very well have been inadvertently tossed over.

Just because the knife damage to the block matched Alex's wound didn't mean that it was the weapon. Anyone fishing aboard a boat for long enough knows that things have a tendency to disappear or be lost overboard. What if Chico's knife had somehow suffered the same fate? Picturing the layout of his boat in my mind, his tool holder was on the same side of the boat where Monte had released the fish. His bulk easily could have dislodged the blade and it had fallen overboard when they tied off to the yacht.

By the time I reached the Intracoastal waterway, my theory had been refined once more. Now I needed a motive for someone who wanted Alex Luna dead from an accident. Collecting on life insurance was a likely motive. That went hand-in-hand with the financials, and I decided to follow up with Grace if Miami-Dade's forensic accountants had a chance to look at her finances.

I passed under the main span of the Rickenbacker Causeway and then underneath the bridge to Dodge Island. American Airlines Arena lay just ahead and beyond that the yacht was tied to the seawall. I slowed and steered toward a marina on the eastern side of the Intracoastal. I wanted a better look before going aboard. As I passed the *Diva*, I noticed a swarm of news vans and reporters kept at bay by a barricade and several muscle-bound guards. Another group of people was more sedate, leaving mementos and paying their respects to Alex. Seeing the obstacle, I was glad I had taken the boat. I would have had to face them if I'd driven.

Once I was across the Intracoastal, I headed west alongside the MacArthur Causeway. Turning to the south, I ran parallel to a palm-tree-lined walking trail with a museum behind it. The large green space of a park followed, and then I was at the boat.

I have a love-hate relationship with the Florida heat. During the winter months, otherwise known as summer to the snowbirds, it was wonderful. During the summer months, known locally as hell, it became an inferno. Those accustomed to the climate still respected the sun and avoided it when possible. It was often a way to tell the locals from the tourists. The reporters were a mixture, with about two-thirds hiding under any shade they could find and the rest looking up toward the bright orb.

They were several hundred feet away from where I crossed the narrow gap between the seawall and the yacht. I continued around the stern and tied off to the back of the monstrous swim deck. Unobserved, I shut down the engine, stepped over the gunwale of the center console, and crossed the teak platform. A small ladder was mounted to the transom, which I climbed to reach the main deck.

Just as my feet hit the teak, I heard a commotion from the paparazzi. Grace had not been so lucky to avoid them, and I immediately felt guilty for making her run the gauntlet instead of offering a ride. The reporters and photographers converged on her like a school of birds on bait, thrusting microphones in her face and snapping pictures.

The security guards quickly moved the crowd away and allowed her to pass. It was a rare occurrence for the media to treat the police with any form of respect, but Grace had tamed them. They knew that if they behaved, she would throw them some scraps.

We reached the salon at the same time and entered through the sliding glass door.

"Can we talk before we do the interview?"

She glanced at her watch out of habit and nodded. I led her to a small sitting area and we sat down. I explained about finding the glass shard by Fowey Light. She wasn't happy about Justine and I taking it upon ourselves to dive without the department's involvement, but there wasn't much she could do about it. I worked for the feds and, though she could technically make trouble with an interdepartmental complaint, I doubted she would.

"I really need that help from your accountants."

"Let me make a call and see what I can get going. I can check on what she had for life insurance, too."

Luna's head of security came over a few minutes later and introduced himself. I recognized him from the footage as Rico.

"Thanks for doing this here. As you can see, I've got my hands full." He glanced outside to the seawall. I followed his gaze to another group who had gathered and were placing flowers and mementos on a growing shrine.

If I thought he was a large man when he was standing a few feet away, after he sat down barely fitting in the chair, I realized how big he really was. The video didn't do Rico justice.

"Can you run down what you were doing before the murder?" I asked.

Grace stopped him, pulled out her phone, and introduced the interview. After the pertinent information was recorded, she nodded to him.

"We were on a break. There was a new dancer that I hadn't met, so I introduced myself."

"Name?"

"Suzanne. Have to check her file if you want the last name."

"And you spoke to her?"

"It's my job to know about Alex's people. A little conversation'll tell me a lot about who they are."

It was apparent he cared about his charge. Some investigators like to pepper their subjects with questions. I find it better to let them talk freely.

"She seemed the same as a lot of the others. Wanted a chance. Alex was good at mentoring her people."

"Kind of why Monika is continuing the tour, huh?" I wanted to hear more about his thoughts on that.

"Anyway. I always have an eye on Alex. Don't even think about it anymore. I saw her move to the side of the deck with Monika. That was all good, until Monte comes storming up. I'd seen those two tangle before and I started in their direction. I didn't realize it, but Suzanne was following me."

"Is Monte violent?"

"Nah, but he's got a mouth on him, though. I wasn't really expecting trouble, but I don't like that kind of vibe when everyone's around."

He paused for a minute and collected himself. "My purpose was to steer Monte away, but he was insistent he show Alex a picture of a fish he'd caught. I thought he was angry, but he was actually excited and maybe a little drunk. When I went to turn him away, I heard a crash and the next thing I knew, Alex was bleeding out on the deck."

Seeing a tear drop from his eye was a strange sight and I felt like stopping the interview. "I'd appreciate anything you could give us on Suzanne."

"Sure thing." He started to speak, but his focus turned to a fracas outside.

A bus had just pulled up. One at a time the dancers emerged. Some broke through the throng of reporters, but when Monika stepped off the bus and onto the sidewalk they mobbed her. I imagined it was choreographed, but I had to admit the woman had the ability to attract attention to herself. As I watched the scene, it made me doubt her motive to kill Alex. Dead or not, her time would have come.

"I gotta handle this," Rico got up. "They just got back from the dress rehearsal."

I had forgotten the concert was tonight. "No problem. If Suzanne's out there, we'd like to talk to her."

He nodded and left the salon. In a half-dozen strides he was on the dock and moving quickly toward the reporters. Rico dispersed the crowd like a big grouper clears a coral head. In seconds, the dancers were past the barricade near the four security men. Rico marched proudly behind them.

"What's your take on him?" I asked Grace. I'd pretty much made up my mind that he was a good guy.

"Military, maybe LEO background. Seems pretty straight up."

A second later he led a woman I assumed to be Suzanne into the salon.

"Special Agent Hunter and Captain Herrera, this is Suzanne."

I was surprised that he not only remembered our names, but also our titles. He was a pro.

"Please sit down, we've got a few questions," Grace said.

I let her start the inquiry, thinking it might be better to have a woman asking the questions. I quickly found out I was wrong.

She glanced at Rico, who looked away. "Why are you singling me out? Do I need a lawyer or something?"

With the large population of transplants and snowbirds here, I'd become accustomed to "Northern" accents. Personally, I preferred the honey-coated Southern drawl, though I knew that sweetness could hide venom. Let's just say that I could tell right away that she wasn't hired as a backup singer. Her body was also different than the other women. They were generally muscular, while she was rail thin.

"Where'd you work before you started here?" I asked.

"What? You want my resume or something?"

I was having less luck than Grace. "Just trying to get some background."

She looked up at Rico. "Do I have to answer these questions?"

"You were in the group around Alex when she fell. I would recommend cooperating. They could take you to the station—"

"Monika got all bitched up about that. I'm good here."

I glanced at Rico, thanking him with a tilt of my head. He nodded back.

Now that we had her agreement to cooperate, or whatever that meant to her, Grace went through the formalities again. I nodded to her to start the questions. Her skin was thicker than mine.

19

Suzanne was charismatic, intelligent, and obnoxious at the same time. After our initial failures and the threat of a visit to the station, Grace seemed to have better luck than I did, so I sat back and watched. This tactic allowed me to distance myself from the questioning and observe. It was an interesting perspective. Within a few minutes, I decided that she was capable of planning the murder, and that she and Rico were involved in some way. With every question, she glanced at him before answering. I couldn't establish any kind of communication system between them other than the personal connection which was strange as I remember Rico saying that he barely knew her.

Grace started by establishing that Suzanne had been with the group around the fallen star. She moved Suzanne backwards in time, trying to establish why and how she came to be there. Suzanne answered that she had approached Alex with suggestions for the act. After observing her pushy personality, I could believe it. Monika clearly could have taken offense and acted rashly.

The interview provided some background information that needed checking. When we were finished, all I got out of it was that I liked Rico and disliked Suzanne. My instincts were usually good, but I knew this personal reaction was a form of arrogance that led to mistakes.

Grace and I were alone again. Her phone rang and she stepped aside. I picked up mine to see if Justine had discovered anything about the piece of glass we had found. I was surprised to see no notifications. I had gotten so used to Martinez's continuous flurry of messages that seeing nothing actually worried me, so I texted Justine while I waited.

Grace came back and I could tell from her expression that something was wrong. She sat down and released her breath. "Bad news?"

She shook her head and placed it in her hands. I averted my gaze to give her some space.

Finally she turned to me. "Monte's been in an accident."

"What happened?"

She explained something had happened at the arena.

"That's not your fault." I tried to comfort her.

"Glad you think so, but there's more. They've assigned an Internal Affairs investigator."

I wondered if it was because of my mishandling of Chico. "But we had nothing to hold him on, or any reason to believe anything."

"I don't know, Kurt. I've accumulated some enemies since my promotion."

That I understood. One of my main beefs with the Miami-Dade power structure was the people at the top had climbed the ladder while backstabbing and throwing others to the sharks. Grace deserved every promotion she had gotten. She worked hard and had the respect of her troops. But I had always suspected that her recent promotion had benefited those above her more than Grace herself. By hiring a Latino woman, they had checked two boxes on the social justice card.

It was pretty common practice, though most of the women did deserve the promotions. The power structure was often an old boys network, and they didn't want a woman to infringe on their power. The promotions got good publicity, then they all shook hands and smiled for the cameras. Once things calmed down, it was often a simple matter to undermine the newly advanced, who then would be neglected, demoted, or fired without fanfare. The woman or minorities suffering this fate were powerless. Any dispute would be a black mark on their resume. Unless the slight was worth betting on a drawn-out lawsuit, there was no choice but to seek other employment. These cases rarely reached a courtroom, and then it was a gamble if a jury would be sympathetic.

"What can I do?" I asked.

Her expression turned hard. "We've got to do our jobs."

"What were the circumstances?"

"We might as well go see for ourselves. It happened at the arena."

Before we left the boat, I asked Rico to keep everyone aboard and also for an accounting of the whereabouts of the tour personnel for the last few hours—who was on the boat, who was on the bus, and who was unaccounted for. A group of the dancers were sitting around the lounge staring at their phones. One of them shrieked and showed her phone to another, who started crying. I hadn't planned on telling Rico the news, but social media gave me no choice.

"Whatever you need. Hope he pulls through. He's a good guy," Rico said.

"Thanks. Just get me the names and keep everyone aboard." I was starting to wonder if my first impression of Rico was wrong. He seemed as much a peacemaker as an enforcer.

"What about the show?"

"Give me an hour or so to sort things out."

He nodded and went over to the dancers. I left the group, found Grace by the ramp, and together we left the boat. I would have liked to leave on the center console to avoid what was about to happen, but the arena was less than a hundred yards away. We had no choice and there would be no escape.

"No comment!" Grace repeated over and over as the four security guards cleared a path for us.

I kept my head down, avoiding the microphones and cameras. Two of the guards stayed with us as we made our way across the park to the arena. Once there, I saw several cruisers and an ambulance. Thankfully, the medical examiner's van was absent. We were handed off to a uniformed officer, who chased off the press that had tagged along, and entered the arena through a side door. He led us through a long, wide corridor that ran underneath the seating area. Ahead I could see the arena itself and an area ringed with the first responders.

We reached the group, where Grace checked in with a sergeant, the highest-ranking uniform she could see. We stood on a concrete floor. The wooden court for the Heat and the ice rink for the Panthers were placed on top of this concrete substrate. Ahead was a steel stairway that led to the stage. The activity at the base of the stairs told me that was where Monte was.

Several paramedics hovered over the body. Another wheeled a gurney toward the scene. A sense of urgency prevailed that was uncommon to the crime scenes I was used to. It meant Monte was alive.

"What happened?" I asked one of the paramedics when they turned toward me.

"Head wound." He must have seen my expression. "Won't know until we get him back if there was a struggle or he just fell."

"Any witnesses? When did it happen?" My mind was racing.

"Have to ask security." Grace glanced up at the stage.

I followed her gaze and saw two of Luna's security guys talking to a man in a rumpled suit. His back was turned so I couldn't get a good look, but I knew who it was. It didn't appear that I was going to get anything else from the paramedics, so I climbed the dozen steps to the stage.

I reached the top and stopped, as my eyes were drawn not to the discussion but to the arena itself. I could only imagine what it felt like to stand here with thousands of screaming fans. Arenas appeared to have evolved since my college days, when I went to the occasional game or concert in California. The biggest difference were the luxury suites that circled the midlevel.

The arena was quiet, with only the murmur of the air conditioning running in the background, but the lights hanging on trusses over and in front of the stage were flashing in some kind of sequence. The show must go on.

It was bad enough that I wished I had my sunglasses as I approached Grace and Little Willy.

"Hunter." He glared at me. "This one's mine, understand?"

I'd been here before and wouldn't be surprised if he walked over to one of the stanchions holding a speaker and pissed on it to mark his territory. This wasn't the first time we'd worked related cases—one happening in the park, the other outside its boundaries. I had the authority to pursue my case wherever it led, as did he, which put us on a collision course. We'd both been around the block and knew coincidence usually weren't. Neither me or Willy thought this was an accident. With Grace's current problems, I didn't want her in the middle, but for now it was unavoidable.

"Got anything?" These kinds of guys only respected what they called strength, but what was really posturing.

We were glaring at each other like two marlin after the same baitfish when his phone rang. When he turned away to take the call, Grace glanced at me, caught my eye, and directed it to the opposite side of the stage.

"Internal Affairs is here," she said.

"Over there? In a bad suit?" I asked.

"Yeah."

"Is that Moses?" I got few lucky breaks when Miami-Dade was concerned. This was one.

As I started toward him, she looked like she was going to throw up. I walked up to my favorite detective. "Still alive, huh?"

"Could ask you the same."

"What do you have?"

"A freakin' headache. I hate this shit. Nobody likes the IA guy. Grace is a good officer, but the brass is on some kind of witch hunt."

"But how?" The last time we had met, Moses had been a detective.

"Shit. Got old is what happened. The choice of early retirement or IA came down from the top." He looked down and shook his head. "I got family, man."

Grace and Little Willy had wandered over, probably curious about our exchange.

"Nothing personal, Hunter, but the next thing you know the guys in the windbreakers with the three letters on the back'll be showing up to babysit you," Willy said.

"I'm happy to share what I've got. You can have the arrest." That seemed to soften him up. I cared little for the credit, and as far as the media was concerned, they could show the perp being escorted by Miami-Dade officers to one of their own facilities.

"Thinkin' it's the same perp?" he asked.

"You think this was an accident?"

"Jury's out, but I'm proceeding as such."

Of course he was being contrary. We were distracted by a

flurry of activity around Monte as the paramedics loaded him onto a gurney. They secured him, then hooked up an IV line before wheeling him out the wide corridor to the waiting ambulance.

Moses motioned me to the first row of seats. "Might as well take a load off." We climbed down the stairs on the opposite side of the stage. He moved toward the center of the front row. "Always wanted to sit here."

I was surprised how high the stage rose in front of me. Even in the empty arena with a potential crime scene only fifty feet away, there was still an electric feeling. I tried to focus on the case and recounted to Moses everything that I knew. As I talked, he took notes on an old-school flip-top notepad, interrupting several times for me to clarify something. I didn't mind—it meant he was paying attention.

"Anything from Doey on the piece of glass?" he asked.

He used Justine's nickname, a shortened form of her maiden name, Doezinski, which she had kept for professional reasons.

"Haven't heard." I checked my phone again, surprised that she hadn't responded.

"Too bad," Moses said. "Who you got for it?"

"Depends. What do we need to do to get the heat off Grace?"

"Our jobs. I'll just be tagging along. You know, make sure everything stays on the up and up."

I knew he was asking for my opinion. In most cases I would be careful before offering it, but I trusted him. "I'm still waiting on the forensic accountant to confirm that the Lunas were pretty much broke. If I'm right about that, it means that unless there's a whole lot of life insurance at stake, this mess is about the future, not the past. Monika has the most to gain, but I don't think she has it in her."

"And that leaves who?" He shook his head.

"We'll see. Rico, the security guy, agreed to help out with the whereabouts of the cast and crew at the time of the accident. That should help pin it down."

We sat and watched the action going on around us. Roadies swarmed the stage and rigging like land crabs at sunset. Arena employees were busy checking seats, and vendors were stocking their supplies. At least a hundred people were in plain sight, which according to the cockroach theory, meant that there were probably a thousand more somewhere in the arena. If this wasn't an accident, that added up to a lot of suspects.

Moses must have calculated it too. "Lot of people around here. Any one of them could have pushed Monte down the stairs."

"If he didn't fall, that means both victims were pushed. That's the common link. Alex was pushed into a glass panel."

Moses looked up at the ceiling. I followed his gaze to a black dome. "I'm going to see about the security footage."

It dawned on me that more crimes were probably solved by techs sitting in dark rooms watching surveillance footage than by actual detective work. The realization nagged at me as I left the seats and went over to where Grace and Willy stood.

20

Before I reached them, I saw Justine. She was hunched over, sniffing around the stairs where Monte had fallen, like a parrot fish pecking at coral. She must have sensed me, and lifted her head. I waved and walked over to her.

"No dead bodies. We're not even sure it's a crime scene."

"Tell that to the brass. Word is, the show must go on. Guess they're covering their bases. Once the show starts, any evidence'll be long gone," she said.

That was a repeat of the scene on the yacht, when the rain removed much-needed evidence. "Anything interesting?"

"Looks pretty straightforward. He definitely fell. Whether he was pushed or not is another matter."

"Moses is checking to see if there are any cameras on the stage."

She looked up. "Moses?"

I explained about the IA investigation and his involvement.

"Hell of a way to make your exit. He's one of the good ones." She turned back to her study of the steel stairs. "Wound is consistent with a fall. Looks like he hit the railing."

"You'll let me know if you find anything to the contrary?"

I was interested in the tox report, but that would come from the hospital.

"Did you have any time to check out the piece of glass?"

"No. Got it logged in and then the call came. I'll get it done tonight." She looked around the scene. "Steel and concrete, not much to do."

"OK. I'm heading back to the yacht to see who was there at the time of the accident and if anyone saw anything."

"Yeah, those dancers are hot, huh?"

"I interview the hotter ones first," I teased her.

"OK, Ranger Rick, let me know how that works for you." She leaned in and kissed me. "Call ya later."

I looked around for Moses and, not seeing him, left through the same tunnel that I had entered. On my way out, I noticed the theatrical lighting had been shut down and the roadies had disappeared. With the setup complete, people had been filtering out through the gates and exits. The arena was quieter now—the calm before the storm. That made me think I didn't have much time to conduct any interviews. I picked up my pace and crashed through the steel door, only to find myself surrounded by the media.

"Agent Hunter!"

My name was repeated multiple times by at least a dozen reporters. The microphone-toting vultures made up about half the group. The rest shoved cameras in my face. I fought my way through the crowd, throwing out a few "No comments."

I crossed the no man's land between the arena and the dock, then faced a similar throng of paparazzi. This time, security guards were there to usher me through to the yacht. By the time I reached the salon, I was exhausted and crashed into a chair.

"Looks like you could use a drink," Rico said.

"Water would be good." He brought me a bottle and sat across from me. He tore off the top page from a legal pad and handed it to me. The sheet was divided into three columns: *On the boat*, *At the rehearsal*, and *Not accounted for*. The last column was empty, which made things a bit more straightforward. I scanned the page looking for Suzanne's name and found it in the rehearsal group. I mentally placed another mark against her, though there was absolutely no proof.

"I don't see your name?"

"Oh, crap. Didn't think about it. I was headed over there to bring the crew back. Media likes a pretty face."

I got that. Thinking about it, I might have done the same. Before we could go through the list, my phone vibrated. It was Moses.

"Got a camera, but it shows just the bottom of the stairs. You can see the last bit, but not what happened. The incident happened at four-oh-four."

"Nothing from the stage?"

"From what the guy said, all the acts insist there be no cameras on the stage other than their own to stop the bootleg streams and videos."

"Good luck with that, with everyone having a cell phone." Justine had dragged me to just one concert in our three years together. I wasn't normally a fan of old-man rock, but she talked me into seeing one of her favorite bands. When Allie was around I would gladly pay for both their tickets. What did stick in my memory from that concert was the lead singer had actually asked people to take pictures and videos and post them, despite the legal warnings that anyone doing so would be prosecuted.

"There's a screen above the stage. Maybe the crew took some video."

The only other people present had been either actively participating in the rehearsal or were employees of the arena. There were probably clauses in the employment contracts of both groups clearly stating that making recordings or taking photographs and videos would lead to dismissal and possible prosecution.

"Good idea. I'll check on that."

It was refreshing to be dealing with someone from Miami-Dade who actually understood that working as a team would benefit us both. We could have been dealt a much worse hand by IA, which led me to think maybe this wasn't a witch hunt against Grace, but someone making sure all the i's were dotted and t's crossed, in case procedural mistakes were made and the investigation went south.

"Let me know. I'm about to start interviews here." I disconnected, and noticed a sour look on Rico's face.

"Showtime, boss. It's going to have to wait until later. I can get you and your girl tickets and backstage passes, though." He turned to the buffet table being setup at the end of the salon. "Help yourself."

I never thought my investigation would be derailed by a meal, and during the minute while I pondered my options they evaporated entirely. The salon quickly filled with the dancers, who started to line up and work their way through the buffet.

Rico smiled and walked to the end of the line. I followed him. "I can wait until later, but you'll need to hold the boat here until we complete the investigation."

"No worries. We can charter a plane if we run short on time."

He was worth every penny they were paying him. In one sentence he had told me that yes, he would cooperate—but not to the point of stopping the show. I was sure I had the authority to stop him from leaving, but I had the feeling that Monte's "accident" was a failed attempt at murder, which meant the killer was scared, and that meant I was close.

Just as I thought it, I glanced forward and caught Suzanne's eye. She looked away immediately, but it was enough to cast more doubt on her recent hiring. Whether it was justified or not, she was my prime suspect. While I was watching her, the line had steadily crept forward and I found myself with a plate in my hand.

It was an awkward position to be in, kind of like sleeping with the enemy. Perspective was critical to a good investigation and that meant staying aloof—something I was quite good at.

Deciding on the path of least resistance and caving to my grumbling stomach, I grabbed the fixings for a ham sandwich and walked back to the corner where I had been camped out. Rico with his loaded down plate joined me.

"So, what about the show?" he asked.

I knew Justine would go in a hot second, and I justified it as being part of the investigation. I had to admit using the backstage passes intrigued me. I was always curious about the way things worked. When watching sports, I was more interested in the coaching and logistical decisions than the actual players. "Let me check with my wife."

"She the hot forensics tech?"

I glanced at him, then down at my phone as I called Justine, wondering how he knew who she was. In a way, I was a public figure, but aside from her now-abandoned career as a professional paddleboard racer, Justine's life was private. At one point, she had placed in every race she entered and had several sponsors. The decision had been made over traveling. Her schedule permitted her time to train, but in order to make a living racing, she would be on the road most of the year. It came down to both age and passion. Dead bodies had won.

"Hey. I was just about to call you," Justine answered.

"Cool. If you're close, I got invited to the show with backstage passes." I turned away from Rico, who was so engrossed in his plate of food that he didn't notice. "We can call it research."

"Interesting. I'll bite. So, if you're done being the social director, I got a print."

"Match?"

"I'm running it through every database I can access. It'll take a while, but I'm guessing Luna's people screen their crew." She paused. "Maybe we can do more than research."

I had to be careful. Justine took evidence and analyzed it. How it was obtained wasn't an issue for her. Her world was polar—yes or no—positive or negative. Mine was everything in the middle, and I had to worry about what was admissible in court. That said, I wasn't opposed to her plan. Even if the fingerprints were illegally obtained, if I knew who the perp was, I was confident I could find something else.

"Why don't you head over here? I've got some calls to make."

"Roger, Kemosabe. I'll bring my kit."

I finished my sandwich and set my plate on the side table. The list Rico had given me lay there and I picked it up. Scanning the names, I prioritized our work for the evening.

Unless Justine got lucky with the print, we might be able to figure out who the killer was through obtaining inadmissible evidence, but I needed something hard, plus a motive, to convict them. I still hadn't heard anything from Grace about her accounting people. Money certainly seemed to be at the root of this, and it would help to know if my theory was correct.

I picked up my phone to text Grace, but it vibrated while still in my hand.

"No luck on the video. Cameras were everywhere else. We've got nothing," Moses said.

"Are you still over there?"

"Yeah. About to leave."

I wondered if I should enlist Moses in our enterprise, deciding against it because of his employer. We had an ally with him, and if Miami-Dade sniffed out what we were planning, he would be fired. That realization in itself should have warned me that I was going rogue by accepting the concert tickets. This outing would have to stay between Justine and me.

"Alright." I updated him on Justine's find and told him I would check back in the morning.

"Don't be shy if something breaks tonight."

I really liked this guy. After we disconnected, I texted Grace. She called back a minute later.

"Heard Justine got a partial."

"Yeah, she said she's running it now. No luck so far."

"Takes time. Anything else?"

I had an idea. "How can we print the crew here?"

"All of them?" She was quiet for a minute. "Without some kind of reasonable cause, I think it would take a warrant."

It was a long shot. "Anything from the money guys?"

"Ever check your email, Special Agent?"

Of course I hadn't. "I'm on it." We disconnected and I went right to my email app. Four hours' worth of emails waited for me, of which I deleted most, then opened the accountant's report.

Somehow I lost a half hour and didn't look up until Justine stood in front of me. I glanced around to find that we were the only people in the salon.

"Busy?"

"Financials came in."

"Anything helpful?"

"Maybe if I could make heads or tails of it." I explained what I could. "They were in debt, but that's about all I got. No life insurance, so that motive's off the table. I'm not sure if there's anything helpful."

"You'd think that money poured out of the faucets around here."

"It does, but the drains work really well."

"Well, let's go have some fun."

21

STEVEN BECKER
A KURT HUNTER MYSTERY
BACKWATER DIVA

BEFORE WE EVEN ENTERED THE ARENA I FELT A STRANGE VIBE. IT was crowded, but not with the usual energetic optimism of seeing one's favorite performer. Alex's fans were dressed and ready to party, but the overall mood was tempered. This show and the subsequent dates had been billed as a memorial tour in the hopes that, though they were offered, few people would request refunds. It had worked. The electronic signs announced the arena was sold out. Brilliance comes in many forms.

Women out-numbered men by about a two-to-one ratio as far as I could tell. Many of the women were in groups, while the men were mostly with their wives or dates. A large majority carried stuffed animals, flowers, or other tokens to leave.

Justine and I reached the stage entrance and ducked out of the crowd. I recognized one of the guards at the door and he admitted us, though he looked skeptically at Justine's bag. I explained that she was a forensics tech working with me and he waved us through.

The backstage area was in a controlled frenzy. Several large digital displays ticked off the minutes until the show, and even as we stood there I could see the anxious faces of the cast.

"Where do you want to start?" I asked Justine.

She glanced over at a small bar set up in a corner, where a man and woman were pouring champagne into plastic flutes. Thinking back to the rock and roll shows I had seen, I expected a rowdier group, although the bartenders working the portable bars were doing a brisk business. There had to be some serious nerves running through the troupe. Being part of Alex Luna's touring ensemble was a good gig, with little to worry about as long as you did your job. What was about to happen tonight was a crap shoot and they all knew it—especially Monika.

The new star emerged from her dressing room and called out for everyone's attention. She certainly had the timing of a performer and found the moment when the group quieted.

"Thank you for all the hard work you guys have put in. This is all for Alex and Monte, so let's go do it."

Short and sweet. Then I caught an elbow in my ribs.

"Watch who leaves their glasses where," Justine whispered.

"I'll take the left side," I said.

"Roger, Kemosabe, I'll take the right."

There was a flurry of activity around the bar. I glanced up and saw the countdown was at five minutes—just enough time for some liquid courage. I found Suzanne and watched her carefully. Rico was on Justine's side of the room, and I expected she was doing the same to him. The display ticked down to one minute, the dancers left their drinks and assembled by the stage door.

My imagined picture of what backstage at a concert looked like and what I was watching differed dramatically. I expected groupies and stoned musicians. Although this group had indulged in the champagne, they more closely resembled what I guessed a Broadway show looked like.

They lined up in what I assumed was a prearranged order, with Monika several paces behind, Motown style. I imagined the band would start, then the dancers appear, and when the crowd was whipped into a frenzy, Monika would make her entrance.

She glanced behind her, as if she were expecting Alex to be there, and in that instant I felt sorry for her. She'd fallen off my suspect list after the interview and that simple act before taking the stage reaffirmed my feeling. The digital timer hit zero and the procession moved through the door and onto the stage. The arena went dark, and after a few seconds a deep bass boom vibrated the walls as the music started. Monika was just about to step onto the stage when I saw her glance to the sky and silently offer a prayer. A long second later, the crowd erupted and the first number began.

Justine had a Sharpie in her hand and was writing the names or some kind of description on the plastic flutes as she dumped them into her bag. She should have been wearing gloves and bagging each cup individually, but we had decided that would be too much of a red flag. Her fingerprints would have to be eliminated, making the job a little harder. We were after a match and, knowing the evidence was inadmissible, sacrificed procedure and protocol.

She reached my position and I pointed out the flutes I had identities for, starting with Suzanne's. Just as we bagged the last flute, Grace walked through the security door.

"Hmmm. Eyes up," Justine whispered.

I was used to seeing Herrera in her business casuals. Even in those clothes, she was a good-looking woman. Tonight, she looked ready to party.

"Sounds like the show's started. What are you two doing lurking around here?" She had to scream to be heard.

Justine slung the bag over her shoulder, using her body to shield it from view. Not that Grace cared. She walked right to the stage entrance, showed her pass to the guard, and disappeared.

I glanced at Justine, motioning my head toward the exit. She went for the same door Grace had just entered and we were outside. It was a welcome relief to my ringing ears when the door slammed behind us.

"Didn't take her for a fan girl," Justine said, as we walked away from the arena. "Sure you don't want to stick around for the show?"

"You're all the show I need." That earned me a punch in the arm. "I've got my boat tied up to the yacht. Can you pick me up at the marina and we'll see if we have a match?"

"Sure thing."

Holding hands, we walked toward the yacht. The walkway to the gangplank was deserted, and the steel barricades looked out of place if you didn't know the scene from an hour ago. The boat was quiet as well, with only a few lights on.

I walked Justine to her car and kissed her, then waited while she drove away before starting up the gangplank. I had to enter the ship in order to reach the swim platform of my boat. Just as I was about to step onto the ladder leading to the center console, I sensed someone behind me. It hadn't dawned on me that stepping aboard a dark ship in the middle of Miami unannounced, especially this one, wasn't a good idea. When I heard the slide pull back on a pistol, I knew it wasn't.

"Something I can help you with?"

I recognized the voice as the captain's and slowly raised my hands. "It's Kurt Hunter from the Park Service." I had my uniform on, but in the dark, I could see how he was suspect.

"Sorry, Hunter. Little spooky with what's been going on here." He lowered the weapon and pointed the barrel at the deck.

"No worries. I should have announced myself. You the only one aboard?"

"The rest of them went to see the show. I don't care much for all that."

"Me either. Just taking my boat back to the marina."

"Have a good night then, and be careful out there."

He watched as I climbed aboard the center console and started the engine. I released the lines and waved to him as I pulled away. The Intracoastal was a hundred yards away, and before I turned, I glanced back and saw the outline of his frame silhouetted by the glow from the cabin behind him. I thought it a little strange, especially with one murder and another suspicious death, that boat wasn't lit any better or made more secure.

Already running behind, I turned into the Intracoastal and idled under the bridge to the port. The waterway opened up after that. I increased speed and headed toward the Miami River. Turning to starboard as I passed the multi-million-dollar condos, I entered the wider channel. The riverwalk was lit up in blue and green neon, making it difficult to see any boat traffic. On a weekend evening it was not anywhere I wanted to be, but tonight, it was quiet and kind of cool to pass through downtown.

Justine was waiting when I reached the marina and helped me secure the boat. We left in her car and were at the crime lab fifteen minutes later.

"You want me to scout it out?" she asked.

The new, state-of-the-art lab was wide open in design. Anyone still working would see that Kurt Hunter was there—not that anyone cared.

Justine swiped her ID through the reader at the main entrance, then the interior door, and finally the lab itself. We navigated our way through the maze of LED lights to her desk.

"You dust 'em, I'll scan 'em." She pulled out a brush and some powder, then reached into her bag and laid the flutes out on the work surface.

Apparently greasy fingerprints adhere very well to plastic and within a few minutes the distinctive swirls were clearly visible. One at a time, Justine took them and scanned them with a handheld reader. "No Match" displayed a dozen times on the screen and we were down to two flutes. As if I could influence the results by some kind of telepathic communication, I hadn't looked at which cups Justine had scanned, and had to admit when I glanced at the remaining pair that neither was Suzanne's. At this point, it was no surprise when neither matched the print on the shard of glass.

"Crap. I thought that would do it."

"You and me," Justine said, sitting back in the chair. "You have the list of who was aboard?"

"Yeah." I pulled it out of my pocket.

Justine took it and struck through the names that matched the cups. We were left with a half-dozen names, none of whom I suspected.

"Not good?" she asked.

"The captain, Reese, and not sure I know the others, are all that are left."

"Reese is the camera guy?" Justine asked.

"'Publicist' I think he calls himself."

"Surprising he wasn't backstage before the show."

He was. "I saw him floating around taking pictures. Greasy little prick. Probably so busy trying to catch that one-in-a-million shot that he didn't drink anything."

"I think he's hot for her," Justine said.

I gave her a questioning look. "Who's hot for what?"

"I know. You don't pick up on that kind of stuff. I watched him around Monika. I'm telling you."

"Reese and Monika? No way."

"We need his fingerprints."

She sounded frustrated, but I didn't see the connection. We were out of options, though, so I thought about the fingerprints and realized that I already had them. "I've got the SD card back at headquarters. Wanna take a ride?"

"Like a date? Maybe sneak in a quickie in Martinez's old office?"

"I'd put ten-to-one he still has a camera in there to spy on his successor."

"Probably right. If that's off the table, I've got some real work to do here."

She tossed me her keys, an evidence bag, and a pair of gloves. The SD card had been given to me freely, and Grace had witnessed it. The prints on it would be real evidence.

Though it seems like a different world, the park headquarters was only thirty miles away, although doubled with a return trip, and the ride was interminable. A further delay due to the construction on the Turnpike had me back just short of midnight.

Justine met me at the side door. "Yes?"

"Got it." I handed her the bag and followed her to the lab.

She waved me away as she logged in the card and extracted it from the baggie.

"Mariposa and I handled it, also."

"I can pull her prints from the database. Yours, I've got up here." She tapped her temple.

Instead of the old-school brush-and-dust, she took the card to a machine with a plastic dome and placed it inside. At the press of a button, a substance clouded the chamber, and a second later a vacuum removed it. My heart dropped as I saw the messy smudge of fingerprints on the small surface of the card.

22

"Not as bad as it looks," Justine said, as she removed the card from the enclosure. "Digital imaging will separate them."

The smudge of fingerprints on the card looked pretty bad to me. I turned and watched the monitor as the computer analyzed the swirls on the small piece of plastic. We were so intently focused on the screen that we didn't notice the two men standing behind us. I recognized Moses, but not the other man. Justine did.

"Major?"

"Those cups on your desk over there. How were they obtained?" he asked.

Justine studied the floor. She was almost incapable of telling a lie. I decided to take the fall.

"I collected them from the dressing room before the show," I told him.

Moses stepped up. "That could be called fabricating evidence."

I knew he had no choice but to be the bad guy. "I'd call it research. I apologize for bringing Ms. Doezinski into this."

"Come on, Hunter, we know you're married," the major said.

Moses stood behind him, looking uncomfortable. I raised my hands with palms up in surrender. I didn't know how they found out, but I imagined they had already decided what to do with us, or at least to Justine. They could make things difficult for me, but any disciplinary action would have to come from the Park Service—not to say that wouldn't happen. But the end of my career was not in the forefront of my mind. I was concerned more for Justine. She was a valued tech with a clean record. I would fall on my sword to protect her.

The bigger concern was, how did they find out—or who turned us in? Grace had been in the dressing room, but unless she had x-ray vision, she wouldn't know what had happened. Moses hadn't been there, either. It wasn't a question I could now ask outright, but I had to find out.

"The collection of evidence is part of my investigation. I needed the samples to compare to the partial on the glass shard." I hoped if they understood we were trying to identify a suspect and not bring false or illegally obtained evidence to court, they would minimize the infraction.

"You know we have a rule just for you," the major said.

"The Hunter Rule. I've heard." It was a protocol that kicked in when it seemed I was exceeding my authority. Of course, my name wasn't formally written into it, but everyone knew it was because of my cases. Now, whenever an outside agency requests assistance, they are required to get approval from the ivory tower. Before I had "exceeded my authority," the techs would simply enter the agency they were working for on their time sheets, with no question.

The major turned toward Justine. "You're suspended until we can perform an investigation. I'll need your ID and keys."

Justine was crestfallen. She dug into her purse for her ID and handed it to him. There were no keys. The major took the key card and snapped the corner in his fingers, like he was deciding if he should really take it.

I was facing the monitor and saw the screen suddenly change. A picture and description appeared, and everything came into focus.

The major was saying something to Justine about contacting her union representative, but my mind was elsewhere. I caught her eye and motioned to the exit. There was nothing else we could do here. The best defense was to solve the case, and I thought I had the answer.

"We'll do that." I reached for her arm and turned her toward the door. We made it to the exit and I released my breath.

"Did you see the screen?"

"Was it Reese?"

I was surprised she was so engaged after being suspended. "Are you OK with this?"

"I had my eyes open when we did it. Actually, it was my idea."

I was proud of her, but knew what the possibility of losing her job meant. "We'll deal with this."

"When we solve the case we will. You know they'll cave if we get results. Now, let's get a drink and figure this out."

I was all for that and realized as we drove to our favorite Mexican restaurant that it was kind of liberating that neither of us had anyone looking over our shoulder. After pulling into the near-empty parking lot, we entered the restaurant and were shown to our favorite table on the terrace overlooking the river.

With margaritas and chips and salsa on the way, we took a minute to unwind and silently process what just happened. The drinks came and were half-gone before we started talking.

"That little creeper was taking pictures in the dressing room," Justine said.

"You think he figured out what we were doing and turned us in?"

"In a hot second."

I sipped my drink, realizing it was almost gone, and thought back on the scene before the show. I recalled seeing him several times weaving in and out of the crowd snapping pictures. I'd assumed we had accounted for everyone by their flutes. He was working.

When I hunted or fished, I entered a zone where my attention was totally focused on the task at hand. I imagined it was the same for a good photographer. From a predatory perspective, Reese could have figured out what we were up to.

"But he wasn't in the group from the frame in the video. How could he have killed her?"

"He's got two strikes—one for his print on the murder weapon, the other for turning us in. One more and we've got him."

"Unless he has an accomplice," Justine said.

"Doesn't explain the print. At some point, he had that piece of glass in his hand."

I sat back and watched a sailboat cruising upriver.

Justine leaned forward. "Wait. Do you have a copy of the pictures on the memory card?"

"On Mariposa's computer."

"We need to go get them."

That would involve a trip to Homestead, but neither of us had any time obligations now that Justine had been suspended.

"Should we take the boat?"

"No. I'll drive, but you might want to bring your truck back up. Wherever this is going, it'll finish here."

She was probably right. So far, nothing had happened south of Fowey Light.

Leaving what remained in our drinks, we grabbed a handful

of chips each, paid the check, and were quickly heading west on 836 toward the Turnpike. The traffic I had suffered through only a few hours ago had dissipated, giving us a speed-limit ride.

"What are you thinking?" I asked, as I pulled in front of the headquarters building.

"It'll wait. That way, if I'm wrong, you'll never know."

We were only minutes from an answer, so I didn't press. In spite of my patience, Justine was like a puffer fish about to blow.

"The picture had five people, right?" Justine asked.

"Alex, Monte, Monika, Rico, and Suzanne."

"But the fingerprint says otherwise," she said.

I unlocked the door, thinking I should make a copy of the pictures in case Internal Affairs filed a complaint with my boss. Solving the case was probably the only path to redemption for either of us.

A minute later we were sitting behind Mariposa's computer that fortunately, due to Martinez's paranoia and probably against the rules of the IT department, wasn't password protected. I scrolled through the images on the screen.

"What are we looking for?"

"Timestamps. Find the murder."

I pulled up on the second screen the still image taken from the surveillance video to verify the time of death as 15:41:22. One at a time, I scrolled through the pictures taken from the SD card, until I found one stamped 15:38 and the next 15:47. The timestamps didn't include seconds, but that didn't matter. From the quantity of pictures on the card, Reese didn't take nine-minute breaks—especially when there was something as newsworthy as a murder to shoot.

"Suspicious?" Justine asked.

"I'd say so. Good thinking."

"It's for the team, Hoss." She kissed my forehead.

She was so passionate about her work that despite the very

real possibility of losing her job, she was more concerned with justice.

"So, we need to account for Reese's movements during those nine minutes." I closed the image on the right screen and opened the video link. Moving through it, I stopped at 15:40, a good minute before Reese stopped taking pictures.

"OK. Here we go." We both studied the screen. He was moving around quickly and in the general direction of the glass screen that Alex had been pushed through. Twenty seconds before the screen shattered, he was gone.

"Keep it going."

We watched the aftermath. The general panic. Monte was very visible and appeared to call 911. I'd not watched this far into the video and now realized it was Monte who took control. I'd expected Rico to be the person to organize things. Instead, it appeared he was only interested in comforting Monika.

I was about to stop it at the 15:40 mark, but Monte entered the screen and walked up to Rico. There was no audio, but I didn't need any to see the argument. Monte jabbed his finger into Rico's chest. Monte certainly appeared to be the accuser. That also gave Rico a motive for the "fall" Monte took.

"Rico?" Justine asked.

"Scroll back to the fall."

I moved the timeframe back until it was several minutes before the murder. We found Rico talking to Monika. I was starting to see a theme. He wandered off camera for a few minutes before he walked to the glass screen with Monika and Alex. Suzanne appeared, then Monte came barreling into the frame, freshly arrived from his fishing trip.

Monte's body blocked Rico, but I slowed the video to a crawl. Frame by frame, or second by second in the digital world, we watched the security chief's movements. The slow pace hurt my bones to watch and revealed little. There was just no angle to see if Alex fell or was pushed, and how the glass shard came into play.

"Nothing," I said.

"It's never nothing." Justine pushed me out of the way and started working the mouse. "Watch his right arm."

In super-slow motion, I watched as Rico's right arm disappeared from view. A second later Alex fell and I could see the arm again. "That's far from damning," I said.

"Oh yeah? Stand over there like she was."

I got up and moved to an open area of the lobby. Justine stood in front of me, just as Rico had faced Alex. She moved her arm like he had. The second I was in Alex's position, I saw how threatening his body language was, and then Justine jabbed me in the chest.

Even though I knew the strike was coming, I almost fell backwards. Gaining my balance, I rubbed the spot where Justine had hit me. I could only imagine what the real thing must have felt like. Alex was a strong woman, but Rico was a very strong man.

"We need to call Sid," Justine said, moving back to Mariposa's desk to retrieve her phone. She dialed his number and placed the phone in speaker mode. Holding it between us, we waited while it rang.

"Does he ever answer?" I asked.

"For me he will."

I could have been jealous, but I knew their relationship was like a father and daughter. She had called the office number for the medical examiner's office, and since it wasn't a cell phone she let it ring. I lost count after ten and was about to give up when Sid answered.

"Dade ME."

"Hey. I need your help."

"Anything for you," Sid said. "Still got that boyfriend?"

"Stop it. You know we're married. Hey, Is Alex's body still there?"

"No, the funeral home picked it up this afternoon. You should watch the news more. Must have been a dozen reporters here to record it."

I wondered if Reese was one of them.

"Can you shoot me the pictures of her chest before you cut her?"

"Sure. Your work email?"

"No." Justine gave him her private email and said she would explain later.

A few minutes later her phone pinged and we crowded over the screen as she pulled up the pictures.

23

THE ONLY THING THAT STOOD OUT ABOUT ALEX LUNA'S CHEST WAS that she'd had work done. We already knew that. No bruising, though that could easily be explained by her bleeding out seconds later. The purple and blue discoloration of the skin due to bruising are subcutaneous broken blood vessels. No blood, no bruising. The picture was inconclusive.

"Back to the drawing board?" Justine asked.

"No. I think Rico pushed her and Reese cut her."

"Better slow down there, Kemosabe. We've got no evidence."

I sat down and leaned back in the chair. Several deep breaths later, I calmed down enough to realize she was right. There's a lot of water between suspicion and conviction. I needed to slow down and do this right, or we would both be out of jobs.

Without life insurance or unencumbered assets, there was no motive for killing Alex for her money—she didn't have any. It was assumed that stars, celebrities, and athletes were all wealthy, but many spent more than they earned. Chuck Knoll, the coach of the Pittsburgh Steelers, was noted for telling his rookies that the most important thing they could do was to find something to do outside of football—their careers could end in a second. There were some big names who had declared bankruptcy. Several, like Elton John, recovered, while others declared insolvency several times. Poor management, bad spending habits, and back taxes were the common threads.

I didn't suspect Monika of the murder, but still felt that whoever benefited from her as a rising star were the prime suspects. Monte had been my first guess, but since he was now in a coma, he was no help. There was still no evidence whether he was pushed or fell. His status eliminated him as a viable witness, but not as a suspect.

"Who benefits by Monika's success?" I asked.

"Monika, but assuming she didn't do it, I don't know. I'm the evidence chick."

And I was supposed to be the detective. "If this works, they all keep their jobs, the boat, the whole deal stays the same." I wondered where Monte would land in this. I hadn't forgotten about the knife. Realistically, he was the only one who had the opportunity to toss the knife and implicate Chico. "Monte might be the biggest winner. Without the tour, he's bankrupt. Alex just didn't seem into it. She certainly wasn't into maximizing profits."

"Sounds like a pretty good motive to me."

"So, let's follow him now. We know when he appeared at the glass screen, but not what he did before then."

"The murder occurred only a few minutes after he and Chico came aboard."

I moved back to the computer. "The video feed link is here somewhere." I clicked through every open screen and checked the browser history, but didn't find anything. Justine hovered over my shoulder, giving me ideas that I probably shouldn't be having while investigating a murder. I yielded the mouse to her and a few minutes later she gave up too.

I checked the time. It was too late to call Mariposa. We sat there at Mariposa's desk, staring at each other. It only took a few seconds before things naturally progressed.

"Nothing more to be done tonight?" I asked.

She shook her head and winked.

"We can take Susan McLeash's boat out to Adams for a last fling."

"Heck yeah."

I shut down the computer, turned off the lights and, with the keys to the twin of my center console in hand, was out the door. Justine beat me to the boat and had the dock lines in hand before I stepped aboard. I was glad for her eagerness, but knew since this had been Susan's boat we should have made sure the engine started first.

The engine turned over right away and I nodded to Justine, who tossed the lines aboard and stepped onto the gunwale. Once she was snuggled up beside me on the leaning post, I idled out of the slip. It wasn't until I turned into the main channel and saw the fuel dock ahead that I thought to check the gauge. It showed a quarter of a tank, which should be more than enough to get out to the island and back, but analog gas gauges were notoriously inaccurate. I knew whenever the trim of the boat changed that the needle would waver. I only hoped it would be in our favor. I considered checking the cooler in front of the console for beer. With Susan it was possibly stocked, and Ray had bragged that Yamahas could run on beer.

I didn't want to test that theory and, knowing that Ray generally kept several five-gallon fuel jugs by his house, decided to chance it and pushed down on the throttle. Slowly, the boat came up on plane and, thinking about what lay ahead, the smile on my face bloomed into an all-out grin. I was running faster than I usually do and had to admit it felt good. I was nowhere on the case, but with the water flying by and Justine next to me, I was happy.

Typically, I was more cautious about speed and route when running the Park Service boats. Other boaters recognized the forest green T-top and followed my lead. If I cut a corner that I knew was passable at high tide, they would inevitably remember what I had done, except run it at low tide, and ground. They would usually report it as my fault. Tonight, there were no navigation lights in view. There might be some boats hidden in the mangroves out by the barrier islands or inside by Turkey Point, but no one was anywhere near us.

If not for the promised land activities, the ride would have ended too soon. Within a minute of tying off the boat, we were upstairs in bed. Even Zero didn't have time to make it down the stairs of Ray's house to greet Justine.

We woke in a tangled mess. Justine's suspension had aligned our schedules, which had its benefits, as it was another hour before we made it to the kitchen. Over coffee and with phones in hand, the real world encroached on our little hiatus. Talking to Grace seemed the most urgent issue. I had to assume that she'd found out about our incident at the crime lab.

I absorbed her rant, knowing that she was right, and that I also had an ally in Moses. When she finally calmed down, I suggested that we do a joint press conference later today.

Setting a time to meet the press reminded me that I had two days before the tour left for Tampa. I did have the foresight to have Grace put a hold on the yacht. I wasn't worried about losing the crime scene. Miami's subtropical climate and the harsh marine environment already had seen to that. I needed to keep an eye on the people. Once the yacht put to sea, they would be out of our control.

Checking my phone, I saw it was almost eight. "We should go. Mariposa will be in by the time we get there." The weather looked good, though a front threatened later today.

"Roger that," Justine yawned.

"Unless you need to go back to bed?"

"I think you're about spent. Let's go."

It was strange to be a visitor in my old house—all that was left were the boxes under the tarp downstairs. After tossing the sheets and towels in the washer, we left things as we found them. The minute we started down the wooden stairway, I heard Ray's screen door slam and the click clack of Zero's toenails as he lumbered down the adjacent stairs. Zero must have gotten wind that Justine was here. He met us at the bottom of the stairs, already panting from the exertion. I left Zero with Justine and walked down the path to the dock where Ray was working on some crab traps.

"Couldn't stay away?" he asked.

"Needed a little break. You ought to put the house up on Airbnb until they assign someone out here."

"Don't think I haven't thought about it. Kind of like the privacy, though."

"You have any fuel?"

He glanced at the boat. "Susan's? Figures."

"Yeah. Mine's up in Miami." That could lead to a more detailed explanation of the case than I wanted to give. Ray preferred his autonomy out here, but he didn't see many people and loved his gossip.

"Sorry. Gotta run in and fill 'em. We can siphon some if you're desperate."

"Nah, gauge shows about an eighth left."

He gave me the stink eye. We both knew I was cutting it close.

"Give a yell if you get stuck."

"Appreciate it." Justine finally breeched Zero's defenses and made a run for the boat. She hopped aboard and we were soon moving off toward the mainland. The wind had shifted overnight, a prelude to a coming front. Instead of the typical southeasterlies, which the barrier islands did a nice job of blocking, it came from the northwest. With miles of open water, the small wind-waves quickly built and many had whitecaps.

"Gonna be a wet one."

"Need a shower anyway," Justine smiled.

I angled the bow on what appeared to be the best line to headquarters. There'd be one zig and one zag, but running headlong into the building seas was going to be slower and wetter. To make matters worse, as it is before most fronts come through, the air was thick enough to cut with a knife. It was almost a relief when we pulled into the channel.

We'd made it on the fuel we had, but it was nice having the use of both boats. I was pretty much running the enforcement division of the park singlehanded. We were just out of season, which made some of the policing easier, but smugglers and poachers didn't take time off. Susan's boat rarely left its slip, but it would be noticed that I wasn't out and about. Down a Special Agent and a Special Agent in Charge, I had both boats at my disposal.

I would have filled the tank even if Susan were here. Leaving a tank empty invites condensation and water in the fuel is a bad deal. Instead of turning to the right and the entrance to the small marina by headquarters, I pulled up to the gas dock.

The attendant came over with the nozzle. "Bet you that one's empty."

He knew Susan, too. "Yeah." I started to fill the tank. I rarely let mine get below half. Pumping thirty-five gallons took a while, but having to fill the tank with seventy was time enough to drink a coffee. Justine went inside to get two *café Con Leche*. The mixture of espresso brewed with sugar is worth coming to South Florida for—and not available at Starbucks.

She was back a few minutes later, and handed me a Styrofoam cup before climbing aboard and sitting next to me on the gunwale. I figured the tank was about half full. I lifted the cup to my lips, blowing on the surface before taking a sip.

There was little activity at the ramp and when I saw Chico backing his boat down, it caught my eye. I waved, sincerely hoping there were no hard feelings and was relieved when he returned the gesture. But I nearly spat out my coffee when I saw the man who stepped out of a rental car and strode purposefully toward the guide. I was able to hold down the coffee, but the pump suddenly clicked. I had missed the telltale whooshing sound of the tank filling and the fuel spitting from the overflow port. Both me and the boat took a fuel bath before I released the trigger.

I glanced down at my coffee, which now had an oil slick on top, and then looked back at the ramp for confirmation that ruining a good coffee was worth it. It was. I hadn't been mistaken. The man with Chico was the *Diva's* captain, Gerard.

I'd forgotten to follow up on who had booked the trip for Monte, but that was apparent now. I dumped my coffee into the bay, returned the nozzle to the attendant, and walked over to the ramp.

24

I walked directly up to Chico, ignoring the captain for the moment to see how he would react. "Hey. We good?"

Chico held out his hand. "Yeah. Sorry I took off like that. Got spooked."

"No worries. You're in the clear." I glanced over at the captain as I said it. He fought the urge to look down. I caught his eye and held his gaze. He wasn't happy to see me.

"Going fishing?" I couldn't help myself.

"Hopin' for some bones. The tour'll be heading up north and this is my last shot at them," Gerard said.

He thought pretty well on his feet. If I hadn't known he was the captain of a dead woman's boat, I wouldn't have suspected anything unusual.

"Hear anything about Monte?" he asked.

Chico glanced at me with a confused look on his face. Since he was already embroiled in this, I saw no reason to cover up the identity of his client. "Gerard's the captain of the *Diva*." I could tell by his reaction that this was news to him.

"No shit," he muttered. "I gotta get some hooks." Chico took off to the store. I thought about asking him to grab me a coffee to replace the one I had tossed, but decided against it. The captain and I suffered an awkward silence until Chico was out of earshot.

"So, if I did some digging and looked up whose credit card paid for Monte's trip, would I find that it was yours?"

After a brief pause to consider his options, he saved me the work.

"Yeah. Booked myself one too. Nothing wrong with that."

Indeed there wasn't—if no one had died. "The way Monte said it, it was kind of forced on him."

"It was Alex's idea. She was trying to get him to be more active. She knew I liked to fish, so she asked me to set it up. He was pretty excited when he caught that tarpon."

His story could have been true. Unfortunately, it couldn't be confirmed. "You guys know each other before?" I glanced at the boat.

"Chico's a legend. I've fished with him before, yeah. He's the first choice for anyone who wants bonefish on a fly."

He was right about that, too. Chico had been by my side when I had caught my one and only bonefish. My excitement at seeing the captain here started to wane. Maybe it was innocent. But the bait knife still bothered me. There were two pieces of physical evidence—the bait knife and shard of glass. Both had been handled within seconds of each other, but two hundred feet apart. It was conceivable Monte could have tossed the knife, then crossed the deck to where Alex was talking to Monika, Suzanne, and Rico, but it didn't explain the shard—nothing did.

I saw Justine waiting by the boat and said goodbye to Chico. Gerard was clearly excited to get a shot at a bonefish—or get away from me. Leaving them to splash the boat, I walked back to the center console.

"You don't look so happy," Justine said.

"I thought we had him. Maybe there's something, but that accent makes everything he says sound condescending."

"Those French."

That brought something to mind. I had climbed over the transom of the *Diva* several times and had noticed the gold stenciled lettering with her name. In smaller letters below was the port of call.

"The yacht is registered in Malta. Maybe they had to have an EU crew."

I had learned the difference between documented versus registered vessels the hard way. My first few months here, I had stopped several larger boats that I thought were missing registration numbers, thinking it was like driving a car without a license plate. The owners were patient with me and explained their boats were documented with the Coast Guard as well as registered with the state. In Florida, registered boats were required to have numbers on both sides of the bow, along with the current year's registration decal. Documented vessels were identified by their name and hailing port, with the registration decal being placed on the port-side windshield or mast. For commercial vessels and cruisers there were many benefits to documenting a vessel.

To make things more complicated, there were several offshore countries that did a brisk business in registering yachts and commercial vessels. I had looked for the value of the *Diva* in the financial documents that were available to me, and had noticed there was nothing on the yacht. I found it strange at the time, but figured like everything else she and Monte owned, it was on the easy payment plan.

Having the yacht hail from Malta meant that Alex, or more likely Monte, had set up a corporation there that owned the boat, and probably laundered as much cash as he could funnel into it. Panama was the leading country of registry for commercial ships, mostly tankers and container vessels. More vessels flew Panama's flag than the US and China combined. Beside the financial benefits, relaxed labor and safety laws made the small country appealing for commercial vessels.

Malta has one of the larger registries for private yachts. Alex and Monte might not be broke after all. "We gotta get back to headquarters."

"It's right there, relax."

She didn't understand my enthusiasm, which I quickly explained as we idled across the channel and into the small marina. I glanced over and saw Johnny Wells's ICE Interceptor in its slip. He waved to me as we passed, and I asked if he could wait for a minute. I slid Susan's boat up to the dock and helped Justine secure the lines. I usually tilt my engine, flush it with freshwater, and hose down the decks, but with Susan's boat, it would take a mechanic and detail crew to get it right, so I left it.

"Hey." I walked up to the Interceptor.

"What's up, Hunter? Got some new toys to check out if you've got some time," Johnny said.

It was hard to hide my boat envy when looking at the Interceptor. "Not now, but I do have a question."

"About Alex Luna?"

The word had reached ICE. "Yeah. Her yacht is registered in Malta. How do you handle that kind of stuff?" ICE had to deal with situations like this more than occasionally.

"We have the same broad authority as the Coast Guard, which means we don't even need reasonable suspicion to board a vessel in state and federal waters. That gets us to the Bahamas."

"So, registering a boat offshore is more of a tax dodge than an evasion tactic?"

"Yeah. It's all about the money. I worry about some of the

foreign registries because of their crews, but not the pleasure yachts."

"Thanks." Money had been the suspected motive from the start. I had just gotten it backwards. They apparently had more than I thought—much more.

"No worries. Let me know if you wanna go for a ride sometime."

"Yeah." Of course I wanted to, but it was like asking a pretty woman for a date—you didn't want to appear too anxious.

We walked down the dock and entered the headquarters building. I asked Mariposa to go through the surveillance feeds from the store and see if the captain had been around here more than he was letting on. Justine and Mariposa hadn't seen each other for a while, so I left them to catch up. I grabbed an extremely substandard cup of coffee and headed upstairs to my old office. My plan was to crack Malta's ship registry.

For someone used to being outside most of the day, the glare of the fluorescent lights made the windowless office seem like a prison cell. I sat down at the antiquated computer and started my search. The top ten results, aside from the Maltese government's own page touting the benefits of registering a yacht there, were all companies that would assist in registering your vessel. That in itself spoke for the benefits.

It took longer than expected to drill down through the sites, and I never did find an actual listing for vessels registered in Malta, but in Googling the name of the yacht, I found the ownership. As required, it was a Maltese corporation. Finding the officers and registered agent proved to be a problem, and I heard Justine call from downstairs before I could find any names.

"Got 'em."

I was at the top of the stairs looking down at Justine's and Mariposa's triumphant faces. "What?"

"Captain Gerard buying a bait knife. That's what."

The "coincidence" was no longer that. I took the staircase two treads at a time and stood behind Justine and Mariposa. They played the video feed back several times, though there was no need. After the first, it was clear Gerard had bought the exact knife that Chico had. That meant he knew the brand beforehand, and I made a note to ask Chico if today was Gerard's first charter. The evidence was circumstantial, but adding up. The possibility of another murder weapon at large poked holes in my case.

It was almost noon by the time Justine and I were ready to head back to Miami. I had a copy of the video and a sheaf of printouts about the *Diva* and its owners.

We stood next to her car. "Where to, Kemosabe?"

"I need to speak to Grace, but I'm going to have to do it alone."

"Yeah, I get it. What can I do?"

Go home and not get in trouble would be the easy answer, but there was no way she was going to do that. "Can you keep an eye on the yacht?"

"I was wanting to get in a paddle. That'll work."

The paddleboard was a good ruse and would hopefully distance her from the players. I didn't expect anything to come of it, but if Gerard had been spooked by our encounter, he might do something stupid. He acted like the yacht was his, and he wouldn't leave Miami without it.

I followed Justine past the old Homestead Air Force Base. In its heyday during the Cold War, it had been an isolated but vital military location. Homestead had morphed from a military community to a Miami suburb and the base was now a reserve facility.

Once we got onto the Turnpike I started to sort through everything I had learned in the last few hours. This morning I had nothing—now I had yet another prime suspect, as well as the possibility that the glass shard was not the murder weapon. Everything should have been falling into place, but they were round pegs in square holes. Learning that Gerard had booked Monte's trip pretty much excluded Monte as a suspect. There was still the issue of whether Monte had been pushed or fallen. Checking on his condition seemed to be the logical next step.

Justine turned off the Turnpike and onto 836. We exited together, but went our separate ways from there. She was going to her condo to grab a board, and I was headed to Jackson Memorial.

I didn't get past the uniformed guard in front of Monte's room. When I glanced inside, he was hooked up to every imaginable machine, including a breathing tube. The doctors said his condition had improved, but he was a long way from talking to me.

I hadn't expected much, but I knew he could confirm my theory. Whether it was incompetence or some petty interagency thing, Miami-Dade's forensic accountants had been near worthless. I had discovered more in my initial internet search of the Luna's credit history than they had in half a week. Asking them to look into a Maltese company was like me finding a narwhal in Biscayne Bay.

What I needed was someone who could pierce the corporate veil, and the name that came to mind was Daniel J. Viscount. It had been several years since I'd paid his five-figure retainer fee to get Allie back into my life. Since then we had helped each other several times. I wasn't sure if he owed me a favor or if I owed him. At this point, we both knew it was a symbiotic relationship and would even out in the end.

Back at the truck, I called his office. The receptionist placed me on hold, and where a few years ago, I would only be thinking about the meter ticking as I waited, now I was sure he would answer.

"Hunter. Trouble with the Luna case?"

I ignored the barb. "What do you know about Malta?"

25

STEVEN BECKER
A KURT HUNTER MYSTERY
BACKWATER DIVA

THERE WAS A PAUSE AND I WONDERED IF I HAD CROSSED SOME unknown legal boundary. I knew attorneys had them, but wasn't so sure about Daniel J. Viscount.

Suddenly he began spouting a flurry of information he would never have dished out so completely if the clock were running. I grabbed my pad and started taking frantic notes, knowing there was probably a way to record the call, but by the time I figured it out he would be finished.

Finally, he took a breath.

"How do I find out who the corporation officers and registered agent are?" In the US, corporations are registered in each state. When the officers reside elsewhere, a registered agent who lives in the state is required.

"Give me the name."

"The Luna Corporation."

"Original. Hold on."

Apparently, he had a secret lawyer link and was back on the line with the information a few seconds later.

Monte and Alex were the two officers—no surprise. The registered agent was—Gerard.

The captain of the ship now appeared to have control of the company, which I assumed held all the assets the Lunas had shuttled out of the US. Prior to learning this, I'd thought Monika had the most to gain from Alex's death. The former number two could profit, but only by having a chance to succeed—far from a given if she failed to capture the hearts of Alex's fans on her own.

I moved the captain to the top spot on my suspect list.

"You understand how corporations work?" Daniel J. interrupted my thoughts.

"Somewhat." That might have been an overstatement.

"Listen carefully. This is important."

I gripped my pen and prepared.

"Corporations are set up for many reasons. Decreased liability and tax benefits to the stockholders are among the better known. Their existence as an entity, even after the death of a single, or multiple, shareholders are lesser known, but important here."

"Got it. With Monte in a coma and Alex dead, Gerard is running the show."

"For now. Alex Luna probably has a clause in her will giving her shares and voting power to Monte in case of her demise and vice versa. His current situation is interesting. It would seem that as long as Monte's alive, Gerard is making the calls. If Monte doesn't make it, there'll be a will and probate.

"That'll give you something to sink your teeth into. Call me if you need me." He disconnected.

Out of curiosity, I checked the time on the call and saw it was less than four minutes. With his hourly scale, this wouldn't have been free info, but I knew I owed him one.

The evidence implicating Gerard was piling up, but so far all circumstantial. There was no proof that the knife the dive team had found was the same one he'd bought; it was more likely it was Chico's and tossed over by Monte, which brought up the question of whether Gerard, Monte, and Reese were in this together. It was an unlikely trio.

I called Grace to bounce the new information off her, hoping a different perspective would help. We decided that the best thing we could do was to interview Gerard. Talking to him aboard the yacht would be easy, but considering the ongoing IA investigation and Justine's suspension, it made sense to bring him in.

After we disconnected, I texted Chico to ask what time he would have his client back.

His response surprised me.

Now, if I could get away with it.

What's up? I texted back.

Cocky SOB. Hour tops.

I took Gerard's explanation for hiring Chico at face value. He could be a killer and still want to catch a bonefish. I called Grace back to see if she could send a cruiser to pick Gerard up at Bayfront Park. If we were going to do this aboveboard, there was no reason not to use all the resources the department had. There would certainly be a difference in his mindset being picked up and brought in, rather than having Grace and I pay him a visit aboard the yacht. I wondered if it would be worth having Greg Bittle around for effect and texted Grace. Dragging the over-anxious ADA into the fray could only help our cause. Maybe facing three naïve Americans would keep his cockiness at bay. The press conference would coincide nicely with the interview, and if there was a chance we could crack Gerard, I expected Bittle would want to be there.

As usual, my plans went out the window when the unexpected happened. The news vans were already assembled when I reached the police station. I was able to dodge the reporters with a promise to reveal all at the press conference later. They backed off too easily, and I was just about to walk through the glass doors when I saw why.

A cherry-red Porsche had just pulled into the circular driveway in front of the entrance. I knew before the driver's door opened who it was. Daniel J. Viscount stepped out of the car, tossed the keys casually to his short-skirted assistant, and stepped up to the microphones. I caught his eye and he smiled.

"He lawyered up." I tried to keep my emotions in check.

"You've got to be kidding," Grace said, stepping through the doors.

My best hope was to figure out how to turn Viscount's appearance into a conflict of interest, but couldn't find an angle. The onus would be on Daniel J. to recuse himself, and I was sure he'd thought of every angle to dodge that. It was inevitable that law enforcement and attorneys know each other. Conflict of interest specifically referred to the attorney being unable to consider, recommend, or carry out an appropriate course of action for his client. If anything, our relationship might aid him in his client's defense. Viscount would make this work at all costs, as the publicity from a case like this would be worth even more than his fee. It was little consolation that I had wiped my debt off his books.

I now realized my mistake in our phone conversation. There was no super-secret lawyer-only database for corporate information, and if there was, Viscount would have had an underling perform the task. He had responded to my query so quickly because he already knew the answer. Viscount and Associates were the Lunas' attorneys, and as such would be representing the corporation, which Gerard was an integral part of. Viscount had only given me the information because I could have found it anyway.

The law can be as straightforward as a ship's course over deep water, or it can be as twisted as a route through the flats.

Grace and I walked through the interior doors, away from the reporters' prying cameras. Bittle waited outside the interview room. We both knew the deal, and unfortunately, Greg Bittle was our best chance to navigate the treacherous waters ahead. There's a difference between a good detective and a good cop. I was the former, Grace the latter. Usually the combination yielded results. This time, we were both crippled by the law.

"This is going to be a freakin' circus. I hope you have something on him," Bittle said.

"It was supposed to be an interview, not an interrogation," I said.

"That's a fine line when the media and attorneys are involved. This might be your one shot at this guy. I'd make it count."

We talked strategy for a minute. Bittle did have some good advice. It wasn't SOP for two LEO officers and an ADA to attend an interview, but this was a different kind of rodeo. Bittle would handle Viscount—Grace and I would question Gerard.

Viscount chose to bring his assistant into the interview to counter our numbers. An officer was sent for two more chairs, accounting for a slight delay. Finally, everyone had a seat.

Grace stated the attendees, time, date, and other pertinent information for the record.

Viscount added that his client had yet to be charged with a crime. I wasn't sure what additional protections this gave him, but the man knew his business.

"You are the registered agent for The Luna Corp?" I started the questioning.

"Why don't we cut to the chase?" Viscount interrupted. He turned to his assistant, who handed me a sheaf of papers. "Corporate documents."

I handed them to Bittle, hoping he could scan the legalese. Score one for Daniel J. I took a deep breath and continued.

"There is a CCTV camera in the store on the fuel dock at Bayfront Park. Five days ago, you were seen buying a bait knife there."

Gerard glanced at Viscount, who nodded. "I like to fish," he said.

"And it's just a coincidence it is the same knife the divers found?"

Viscount glared at me. "Is that all you have?"

I needed to regroup, and quickly. Stopping the interview would only make things worse. "Monte was the president of the company. He's in a coma, and with Alex deceased, where does that leave you?"

"I just get the mail," Gerard said. "They needed an address in Malta to register the company. It's totally legit."

God, he was smug. This was falling apart in front of my eyes. The image of wrapping this up and declaring victory at the press conference was evaporating. This case was leading me, instead of me leading the case.

"What is your relationship with Monika Ruiz?"

"Relationship, like am I doing her?"

It was my turn to glance at Daniel J., who whispered something in his client's ear.

"I stay away from the dancers. Nothing but trouble on a boat if you get mixed up with the guests."

"And Monte?"

"He was the boss. We got along OK. Since we were outnumbered, we guys kind of stuck together."

"How was his relationship with his wife?"

Gerard glanced at Viscount, who nodded. "Didn't say much about it, I think they got on fine."

"Did she ask you to set up the fishing charter for him that morning?"

"Yeah. I didn't think anything about it."

I can often detect a tell, but his face remained set in stone. It was his word against a dead woman's.

"She paid you back for the trip?"

"Actually, no. I'll send the receipt to the accountants."

"And who might they be?"

Viscount approved the question and gave me the information. Keeping up a yacht was expensive, and I imagined Gerard was in constant contact with Alex's money people. The information was for a firm in Miami. That was a break, making it a lot easier to subpoena records.

As we went back and forth, I found that if I made my questions quick and easy, he would just answer them. But in the end, besides the information on the accountant, I knew little more than when we started. I asked Grace and Bittle if they had any questions, and gave Gerard the "don't leave town" speech.

"The yacht needs to stay here for at least a few more days."

After some discussion it was agreed that the cast would fly to Tampa, and the yacht and crew would remain in Miami. That was a win.

Now I needed to get through the media. The official press conference was not for several hours. Grace, Bittle, and I agreed to meet thirty minutes beforehand in order to devise some strategy that would appease them. We started walking toward the exit together, then realized it was a bad idea. Bittle headed for a side door, and Grace went back inside to her office.

I stopped her. "What's next?"

"I've got the paperwork going to subpoena the corporate file from the accountants," Grace said.

"Do you really think that's going to solve anything?"

"Gotta cover our bases."

I turned back to the exit. Some had taken the bait and were streaming to the side door to catch Bittle. Others hoped they could get a better story from my ineptitude and waited. Taking a deep breath, I crashed through the doors, and with my arm held out like a billfish about to charge a bait ball, pushed through the crowd.

Ignoring the comments, I took off at a jog for my truck. I guessed they were filming me, but it was better than having my answers to their questions sliced and diced like a big tuna being prepared for sushi.

I was in a dismal mood when I left the parking lot. My perspective was gone, and instead of the pieces falling into place, it felt like they had been dumped on the floor.

I thought about checking in with Justine, but didn't want to inflict my mood on her.

In the end, I listened to the voice in my head telling me to go fishing.

26

STEVEN BECKER
A KURT HUNTER MYSTERY
BACKWATER DIVA

On the way out of the lot I caught a glimpse of the media. They had been here several hours, alerted when someone sniffed out that the captain was being brought in for questioning. Their vigil would last until after the press conference later this afternoon. Some would linger even longer to assault anyone they could in search of that unique sound-bite. The crowd included not only the media. A segment of society, apparently with nothing better to do, crowded around the entrance with their cell phones in hand.

The cliché says that everyone gets their fifteen minutes of fame. With social media, it's more like ten seconds and you better hope your post sticks. The playing field has been leveled. In a world where the benchmark for fame is measured by how many likes or followers one has, anyone with a phone and a Twitter, Facebook, or Instagram account can be famous—and too many have tried.

I pulled quickly out of the parking lot. Chico had told me the tarpon were thick under the bridge, which was how the case had started. I didn't expect to find the smoking gun, but I often got perspective when I soaked a line. Right now I wanted to be as far away from here as I could get.

I picked up Justine and headed to the marina to our boat. She was relieved to have a purpose. She might say otherwise, but I knew the suspension was grating on her. Her sightseeing paddle hadn't been nearly hard enough to burn off her pent-up energy and anxiety. Combine that with her internal motor, which rarely lowered to an idle, and it was a recipe for disaster.

Our center console was similar to the Park Service boat, but we owned it. With Internal Affairs probably watching me for anything they could use against Grace, and Justine already in hot water, I decided to leave the Park Service boat.

My intention after I left Grace was just to ditch the press conference. I'd known then I would probably change my mind, but used the opportunity to be petulant and blow off some steam. With the time constraint, I decided to forego bait and use the lures we had onboard. I actually preferred fishing with plastic to bait. Besides the convenience, the lures require an angler to impart action to them. It made things interesting and for many species was just as productive.

Tarpon were more susceptible to live bait like pinfish or crabs, but still took flies. I was anything but a tackle snob and always left two rods in the holders under the gunwales. They were protected well enough there, although anything left in the elements close to the ocean is going to pay the price.

We reached the Intracoastal and I slowed. Justine gave me a questioning look when I turned to port. "I'm gonna take a run past the yacht."

She sidled up next to me. "That's a big surprise. Didn't think this was all for fun."

I think we both knew the fishing trip was a cover to see what was going on aboard the yacht. As we approached the arena, I saw at least fifty boats circling the area around the *Diva*.

Curiosity was the driving force and boating the excuse. We blended in with the other boaters, and despite my khakis, which could pass for fishing clothes, we were invisible.

There were no surprises. The yacht remained tied to the seawall by the dock. I could hear a low mechanical murmur, and seeing water spewing from several ports I figured it was the generator running the air conditioning and not the engines.

Boaters in Miami came in several varieties. There were the divers and fishermen who, giving odd looks to the casual boaters as they passed, headed directly from their docks or boat ramps to the inlets accessing the Atlantic. They avoided the inland waterway at all costs. The sandbar folks thought the same of the Intracoastal people. They gravitated to the shallow bars where they could beach or anchor their boats in a few feet of turquoise water. They were a party crowd, seeking the serenity of the water, but wanting to share it with a hundred other boaters of likewise persuasion.

Last were the Intracoastal cruisers. Surprisingly, they often had larger boats that never saw the blue waters of the Atlantic. Instead, they cruised the inner waterways checking out the numerous bars and restaurants with docks, and lusting after boats that were larger than theirs. Near the arena was a mixture of all three, cruising back and forth past the yacht. To their credit, a Miami police boat moved around them, keeping them at bay.

As we passed the *Diva*, I saw some activity aboard. The reverb of music could be heard across the water and there were dancers on the deck.

"Did you hear how it went for Monika last night?" I asked Justine.

"Heard she rocked it. I guess she's the new Alex Luna."

"Just like someone planned it."

"About that ..."

"Can it keep? I want to get out of here."

We continued traveling north in the Intracoastal, then turned when we were out of sight of the yacht. Coming back, we stayed to the outside of the other boaters and cruised right past the arena. We continued down the main channel to Government Cut and went under the bridge to Dodge Island. The tide was running nicely past the piers, and I wished we had live bait. I could have stopped here, but there was little room between the spans to comfortably fish, and we were too close to the arena and yacht to relax.

South of Dodge Island the bay opens up. Following the more industrial side leads back to Fisher Island and the cut. I steered south to the Rickenbacker Causeway.

The dozen or so boats scattered around the bridge pilings confirmed my guess that the tide was favorable and the fishing would be good. The prime spots on the up-current side were already taken. With the tide running toward the bridge and the fish, these anglers had a distinctive advantage. Though some of the other boats looked familiar, I didn't see Chico. I steered clear of several buoys marking the boats' anchor lines, and idled up to a spot adjacent to one of the piers. Without the aid of the current, we would have to work harder here, as the best we could do would be to cast toward the piling and wait a handful of seconds for the water to take the lure out of the strike zone.

Method didn't matter to me. I was here to clear my head.

Justine dropped the anchor, clipping one of the fenders to the line just in case we got lucky. I had leaned over to grab the rods when I heard my phone. There was little doubt it was Grace.

"Sorry, I know I shouldn't have left like that." I did feel badly and should have stayed. "Can you push the conference back an hour? I did a little recon." At least it wasn't a lie.

"I guess it won't matter. Internal Affairs can't hold that against me."

She gave an awkward laugh that wasn't like her. As we talked, I could tell she was nervous.

"I can make it sooner if you can have someone meet me at the dock by the impound lot." I guess five minutes of fishing was better than none.

That helped, and I could tell she was relieved, though I had no idea how having me stand next to her during a press conference was comforting. I guess she would look good by comparison.

Justine went forward to pull the anchor. "I know. No worries here."

Within a few minutes we were cruising back toward the pair of high-rise condos on the northern point of Brickell Key. I was about to turn into the river when I saw a large yacht on the other side of the bridge that led to the port. It wasn't an unusual sight. Miami was loaded with luxury barges, but there was something familiar about this one.

"That's the *Diva*," Justine said, pointing to the ship.

The yacht had just made the turn to the east that would take it out Government Cut. The manmade channel was the best route to the Atlantic from the arena. Wide and deep enough for cruise ships and tankers, there were also no bridges between the arena and the ocean.

I pushed down on the throttle and accelerated. A small boat like ours would be invisible to the hundreds-foot-long yacht. There are rules of the road on the water. Many call it *right of way*, but that is a misnomer. *Stand-on vessel* is the accurate description. To say a craft has the right of way implies that it is free to maneuver however it wants. Stand-on means that the craft needs to hold course and speed. Small boats have to understand that the larger vessels are restricted in both their turning radius, draft, and ability to stop. Boats have no brakes. The only way to stop is reverse.

I stopped just short of the bridge to the port, silently apologizing to the fishing boats that would have to suffer my wake. There was no chasing down the yacht. I could likely match speed, but the difference in fuel range between our boats was probably a thousand miles. I didn't really have a plan, but wanted to get a better view. Once I knew the yacht was heading for Government Cut, I spun the wheel and turned into the channel running down the south side of Dodge Island.

There was no reason for our twenty-four-foot boat to play possum with a yacht ten times her size, and I wasn't taking chances. We would be invisible to the yacht behind the island, and if I could reach the channel between Dodge and Fisher islands before the yacht, it would give me a clear line of sight to the bridge and be enough to confirm it was Gerard at the helm. After that, the best I could do would be to follow them out of the cut to see which direction the captain was running.

My guess was south or east. A turn to starboard meant he was likely heading down to the Keys, the route that would lead him into the Gulf of Mexico and up to Tampa. Straight ahead meant the Bahamas and international waters.

Fisher Island is as exclusive as it gets. Sitting opposite the tip of South Beach, the island, which is actually a private club, has the highest per capita income of any zip code in the country. Accessible only by private boat or ferry, its exclusivity was only marred by the fifteen large fuel tanks directly ahead of us. Nestled in a corner of the very private golf course is a fuel depot. That was where we lay in wait. With our cameras in hand, we started snapping shots of the yacht as it passed us.

"That's them. What do you want to do?" Justine asked.

"Just see where they go. There's no way to chase him."

"Damn. You know they keep a police boat at the USCG station by the causeway?"

I decided against reinforcements at this point, wanting to be one-hundred-percent certain that Gerard was guilty before calling in the calvary to stop the yacht.

"There are a whole lot of innocent people aboard."

I watched the *Diva* head straight for deep water and knew who to call. Johnny Wells and his Interceptor would keep an eye on things here while I dealt with the press.

27

STEVEN BECKER
A KURT HUNTER MYSTERY
BACKWATER DIVA

"I have to go back," I told Justine.

"Not going rogue on the press conference after all?" she asked. "I'll follow up with Johnny, then."

Stopping her was not an option and I could use the help. She knew as well as I that the best way for her to be reinstated was to solve the case. Everything would be forgiven with her boss. The same result would allow Moses to close his investigation.

We were quiet until we reached the *Slow speed — Minimum wake* zone, where I dropped to an idle as we entered the river. "Johnny Wells has the authority and his boat has the range. He can follow him damned near to Bimini, or around and into the Gulf if Gerard's heading to Tampa—but with one boat can't do both."

"He's not desperate enough to run to the Bahamas."

She was right. I wasn't sure what Gerard's motive in moving the yacht was. In any case, the creative and business gamble to transition the spotlight from Alex to Monika had apparently gone better than expected. Gerard currently was the only able signer on the corporate accounts. No financials would be forthcoming from Malta and I doubted the Miami accounting firm would be willing to hand anything over without a warrant. Even then, they would dribble out information so slowly we'd all be dead before I had any kind of picture of what was going on. Monte's tax evasion scheme seemed to be working. For Gerard's apparent plan—to funnel money out of the Lunas' company—to pay off, they would need to get the crew to Tampa for the next show. Given the newly discovered state of the Lunas' finances, there were likely enough liquid assets to make fraud worthwhile, but it would take time to sell the yacht. The best chance for Gerard's plan to pay off was to keep the ball rolling.

"They can't go the inland route." There was a fixed bridge on the eastern side of Lake Okeechobee that's fifty-five feet tall. The yacht would never clear it. In order to reach Tampa, the Seven Mile Bridge in the Keys was the best bet.

That was my friend Mac Travis's territory. I turned over the wheel to Justine, found his number in my contacts, and pressed connect. I hung up when the call went to voicemail. Mac would see the missed call and return it. He was a boat person. If he were on the water, his phone would either be out of range or ignored.

She must have seen me disconnect without leaving a message and had a suggestion. "Try Mel."

Mac's girlfriend was his opposite in technology and always had her phone with her. I didn't have her number, but knew who did. Two calls later, I reached Alicia Phon in Key Largo, a former CIA operative, investigative wizard, and shared friend, who was happy to give me Mel's number.

Mel answered on the second ring. I gave her a quick explanation, and she immediately agreed to help find Mac and have him on standby.

I tried to map out Gerard's options in my head. "If they're going to Tampa, he's got to go through the Seven Mile Bridge or all the way around Key West to make the Gulf."

"Don't they have some kind of trackers on those ships?" Justine asked.

A ship that size would surely have an AIS transponder aboard. The Automatic Identification System was used by owners, shipping managers, insurers, and lending institutions to track any boat in the world—if the instrument was turned on. Just in case, I opened the Ship Tracking app on my phone and zoomed in on the area just outside Government Cut.

The app identified vessels by name, owner, and speed. There were several in the area. I pressed the icon by each and none were the *Diva*. Without the AIS active, using radar or a helicopter were the next choices.

Radar would be of little use unless you were close enough to confirm the target.

"He's pretty much on a pleasure cruise with Alex's entourage as hostages, though they don't know it," I said.

Justine turned into our marina. "What about Miami-Dade? They've got assets."

I could just imagine the melee a hovering helicopter would cause. I was already heading into a press nightmare. Gerard had proven to be ruthless, and having a gaggle of police boats or a chopper after him would be too dangerous to the dancers.

My phone interrupted my train of thought. A glance at the screen told me it was Johnny Wells.

We were approaching the dock and I needed to help with the lines, so I let the call go to voicemail. I hadn't been paying attention and we were coming in hot. One of the first rules of boating is that if you're going to hit, hit slow. Heading upriver, Justine passed the dock, then suddenly swung the wheel toward starboard and spun the boat. We were still moving at speed with the bow at forty-five degrees to the dock. Even though I trusted her, I braced myself, but just as the bow was about to hit the dock, she dropped into reverse, arresting the forward momentum. She spun the wheel again, this time cutting the engine into the dock, and the boat settled a few inches from the pilings.

"You done, Speed Racer?" I asked her.

"Damn, a little butt-hurt?"

We smiled at each other and I tied off the boat. A short vibration from my phone told me that Johnny Wells had left a voicemail. I didn't bother listening to it and called back. I explained about Gerard taking the yacht. He already knew the rest.

"Damn. If you don't want to spook him, I could use a pair of eyes to make sure we have the correct target."

I wanted to go, but skipping out on the press conference wasn't going to help Justine or Grace. I looked across at Justine. She seemed happy enough in the moment, but she was like me —the boat ride had settled her, but not for long. I knew in a few minutes she would be itching to jump back in the game.

"Hold on." I placed the phone on my knee and turned to Justine. "Want to take a ride with Johnny and the ICE guys?"

Her face lit up. "Oh, heck yeah."

I got back on the phone and arranged a pick-up at the boat ramp in Matheson Hammock Park. Having Justine drive all the way to Homestead would put her squarely in rush hour traffic. The park was located halfway and in the direction I believed Gerard would be traveling. The yacht would be past there by now, but the ICE Interceptor could catch a flying fish.

I told Justine the plan. She wasted no time and pecked me on the cheek in goodbye. Less than a minute later, I heard tires squeal as she pulled onto the road. As much as I wanted to go with her, it was a good thing for her to be involved. Now, I had to play my part and meet the press.

It felt like only seconds later I walked through the doors of the station. This time, there was only the small group of second-tier, cell-phone reporters clustered there. Not wanting to spend the night in jail, they parted to let me through. The real vultures were all waiting inside, where the conference would take place—and they probably smelled blood. A man in street clothes called me over as soon as I was inside the main door. I suspected he was a lurking reporter, but he introduced himself as a Miami-Dade media officer. Key card out, he swiped the doors that allowed us access to the station, and in a few minutes I stood inside the press room.

"Look what the cat dragged in," Grace said.

The smile on her face told me she didn't care what I looked like as long as I was there, but she did take a second with a comb to attempt to civilize my boat head. I followed her to the podium, catching Moses's eye on the way. Seeing him gave a boost to my waning courage as we stepped up to the microphone.

With the lights in my eyes, I had to squint to see the crowd of reporters. Grace told me to quit trying, and I averted my eyes. The glimpse I did get was like seeing snapper feeding on a chum slick. With the patience of a kindergarten teacher, Grace settled them down.

"I have a statement, and then Special Agent Hunter and I will take questions."

My mind wandered as she spewed the neatly organized facts of the case, leaving out anything about the yacht disembarking. While she spoke, I couldn't help but glance around the room, trying to pinpoint which reporter I might face off with. I would have preferred to face a bull shark than anyone in the press room.

The questions came before I was ready.

"Agent Hunter. Any comments on the suspension of your wife from the forensics lab?"

I almost blew up, but felt Grace shift her hand over mine.

She took the question. "We will only answer questions relevant to the case."

"But Ms. Doezinski was suspended for improper collection of evidence in this case. Isn't that correct, Agent Hunter?"

This was not going away. I cleared my throat. I turned the question around like the head of a big fish running from the boat, which brought me to Reese. A little tit-for-tat was in order. It was a gamble, but I took it.

"The photograph by Jake Reese was taken out of context and should not have been distributed." I couldn't help myself and glanced at Moses. He was on his phone, probably confirming the story. It gave me an idea.

"The media's response to this case has shackled us at every step. Our only goal is to determine who killed Alex Luna and serve justice upon them."

The room fell silent. Glancing at Grace, I saw the faintest smile cross her lips. The pause allowed her to pick another reporter and move on. It quickly became evident that the press conference was a dog and pony show. We had nothing of substance we were willing to share with the media. After they'd slung some mud and seen nothing stick, there were no real questions.

As we walked away from the podium, I felt drained and confused. I often had an uneasy feeling after a press conference, mostly because of how the reporters twisted my words. They'd done it before and would do it again. It was a sad state of affairs. I didn't mind investigative journalism. Putting the facts out and letting readers reach their own conclusions was the way this was supposed to work. Weaving stories from loosely collected facts was the realm of fiction writers and, it seemed, entertainment reporters.

My hand was on my phone in my pocket and my mind on

getting an update from Justine when Moses stepped in front of me.

"Got a minute?" he asked.

"I've got nothing but time."

"Celebrity cases are a bitch," he said, sensing my mood.

I shrugged. At least with Moses I didn't have to worry if he was sincere. "Not the first time."

"I remember the case with the Miami football players. That was big, but not Alex Luna big."

I differed. With million-dollar donations and contracts at stake, the murder committed with the famed Turnover Chain had been every bit as difficult.

"If I can offer a suggestion," he started. "I think you can bring the photographer in."

That caught my attention. If I could prove that Reese was guilty of something, it might help Justine's case. "Go ahead."

28

STEVEN BECKER
A KURT HUNTER MYSTERY
BACKWATER DIVA

MOMENTUM WAS EVERYTHING AND I FINALLY FELT I HAD SOME. The reviews on my press conference would probably be mixed, but Moses may have solved the Reese problem, and Gerard running with the yacht was the best thing that had happened since I had boarded it four days ago. I was feeling good about Justine's and Grace's jobs, and was ready for the chase that I hoped would close out the case.

Justine didn't answer my call, but that wasn't surprising. The individual engines on the Interceptor were fairly quiet, but times four they made enough noise that made it hard to hear.

A text came through before I could leave a voicemail.

They had a visual on the yacht. Surprisingly, it was back on one of the mooring balls at Fowey Light. Justine asked for instructions. Gerard hadn't run after all. We had told him not to leave town. The Fowey Lighthouse didn't have a Miami zip code, but it was close enough I didn't think it would bring him trouble. It also had me questioning my conclusions—again.

My intention after leaving the press conference was to find and arrest Reese. Bringing him in would hopefully give Moses enough ammunition to take the heat off Grace and reinstate

Justine. With the yacht stationary, I decided to make a run out to the light.

Johnny Wells probably could have picked me up and taken me to the yacht in the same amount of time it would take me to run out in the Park Service boat. In a move Martinez would surely appreciate, I decided against it. The Interceptor was fast and fun, but those engines were thirsty, and I didn't want any crap over an interagency reimbursement bill.

I risked a glance back on the way to my truck. No dogs were chasing me down—the press was otherwise occupied. Within a few minutes, I turned onto 836, heading to the marina. Brake lights met me as I approached the airport, and I slowed for the inevitable. If one believed in omens, the traffic could be interpreted as a good sign. The universe was trying to keep me from my goal, which obviously meant that I was on the right track.

My mind was working faster than the traffic was moving. Thinking about Moses and Reese, I decided to call Grace. She deserved to know what was happening.

"You bailed on that awful quick," she said, by way of greeting.

I had no counter. "Ran into Moses in the hallway. He seems to be leaning our way, and told me that Reese should be picked up for distributing the picture of Justine and I at the arena. Might clear you guys."

"I'll put out a BOLO for the weasel now." She paused. "And make sure the camera doesn't survive."

The comment could have been construed as in bad taste with all the unrest about police brutality lately, but it was between friends—and I understood exactly what she meant. "Gerard moved the yacht, too. It's back out at Fowey."

"What's his game?"

"I don't know, but I'm headed out there now." There was no

point in telling her that Justine and the ICE crew were babysitting. Plausible deniability and all.

"I'll see what I can do to track down Reese."

I disconnected just as the off-ramp came up. A few minutes later, I reached the marina and hopped aboard the center console. The ride out went almost too quickly, and the tower stood in front of me before I had a plan. Part of the problem fell on the shoulders of my old friend—jurisdiction. The excuse of arresting Reese was my best chance to board the yacht without alerting Gerard that I was on to him, but that posed a problem. Even though the photographer, or at least his fingerprint, was somehow involved in the murder, the statute that Moses had cited meant that Miami-Dade needed to issue a warrant. He had taken the pictures on their turf.

The ICE crew was hanging out a mile away from the light. Sitting on the drop-off just outside the reef, they were close enough to have eyes on the yacht and far enough away that Gerard would probably think they were a fishing boat. If the Interceptor hadn't spooked the captain, I doubted the much smaller Park Service center console would.

I pulled up on the downwind side and received the lines tossed across. Johnny's crew had put out two large fenders, and after I tied off the lines they snugged the boats up. It was a high step from my gunwale to his, and I hopped down to the deck. The engines were idling, making it easy to talk over them.

"I'm going to see if Reese, the photographer, is aboard." I explained how the pictures had been illegally distributed.

"You want backup?" Johnny asked.

"I'm going with him," Justine said.

"No, you're not. Arresting Reese can clear you. Moses is playing ball—hell, he's even pitching. One picture, or even showing up on the surveillance footage while you're suspended, is going to ruin that."

She got that pouty look on her face that usually got me to back down, but I held my ground. I declined Johnny's offer as well. The *Diva* cast and crew were familiar with me. I could board without cause, but I decided to radio Gerard and give him notice that I was on my way. I hoped it would serve two purposes. First, by being "invited" aboard, which I assumed his response was going to be, a sketchy situation would become more tenable for him. Second, if his intentions were bad, I would force his hand.

I started back to my boat, but Johnny stopped me.

"Take this. If you get into trouble press the red button. Otherwise, it's your standard issue radio." He handed me a handheld radio with a coiled cord connected to a remote microphone and speaker. I clipped the larger unit on my belt, routed the wire to my side, and attached the microphone to my lapel. I wasn't used to it and took a second to familiarize myself with the controls. It was a good idea. Even though it was not part of my usual gear, radios with lapel mics were so commonplace I didn't expect it to get a second glance.

I nodded to Justine, who shot me a look that I did my best to ignore. We had been in the shit together before, and I would have actually preferred her to go with me, but in this case it was for the better if she stayed away.

I climbed back up and then down to reach my boat, then tossed the lines across to the crewmen. Once the current opened a gap between the boats, I moved away. Working in a large circle, I ran almost back toward Miami before turning and setting a course directly for the light. When I radioed Gerard, he would instinctively look in the direction he expected me to be coming from. If he saw me heading toward him from the south, he might have a closer look at the Interceptor. Johnny had moved further away, but binoculars would reveal him.

I dropped speed, opened the recorder app on my phone, and

pressed the red button. My ploy was to have him grant me permission to board. If things went badly that might be important.

I took a deep breath and unclipped the mic from the dashboard. Confirming the VHF was on channel 16, I hailed the yacht. Gerard answered and we switched channels. Marine frequencies are public and any interested party could listen in, so I kept things generic.

"I'm heading out your way."

"Problem?" Gerard asked.

"No, just some follow-up questions."

"Roger. We'll be waiting."

I hit the red button again and stopped the recording, then placed the phone in my pocket and pressed down on the throttle. The steel tower and yacht were just visible, and though I couldn't see the bridge, I expected that Gerard had his binoculars trained on me.

As I approached the light, I moved to the north to avoid the shallow water where the reef lurked ever ready to claim another victim, then circled back to the stern of the yacht. Gerard had two crewmen waiting on the swim platform to help me secure the boat. I stepped across.

"Captain's on the bridge. You know the way?" one of the men asked.

"Yes, thanks. I can find it." I gave a quick glance to check the boat was properly secured, moved toward the starboard-side staircase, and climbed two decks to the bridge. Gerard was kicked back in the captain's chair with his feet on the wheel, looking as nonchalant as he could. His little display of arrogance was probably meant to unnerve me, but he had to know that part of my reason for being here was his disobedience.

"Were we not clear that you were not to leave Miami?"

He waved his arms around him dismissively. "And we

haven't. The press was getting out of hand. Paying for security guards on the pier is an unnecessary expense."

"They found you out here before, they'll find you again."

"On that point we agree, though maybe you'll have this murder sorted out before that and we can go. You said you had questions?"

I felt the heat building on my neck and breathed deeply to control my temper. There was nothing else I would rather do than lay into him right now, but it would serve no purpose. All I could do was stare him down, knowing even that could end up in a pissing contest. "Reese aboard?"

"Ah, the detective has done some detecting."

My right hand instinctively went to my holster. It was a habit that many officers had, called indexing your weapon. It was comforting knowing it was there. A typical LEO pose had the gun hand on their holster and the other on their spare magazines or taser. It wasn't meant to be intimidating, but I felt it was. Since I rarely found myself in situations that required force, I tried to avoid it.

I badly wanted to correct him but didn't, though I promised myself that when I did bring him down, it would be a hard fall.

"Is that a yes or no?"

"Thought I saw him earlier." He reached for a mic clipped to the ceiling. "I'll have Rico round him up."

I shook my head. "I'd rather just bump into him."

"Crafty. Try the video room. Saw him down there earlier."

I thanked him and left the bridge. I remembered the pistol he had the other night and was glad that I had Johnny Wells sitting over the horizon. After descending the stairs, I reached the main deck and entered the salon. Several dancers were lounging around, most wearing earbuds and with their phones glued to their faces. Fowey Rocks was within five miles of Miami and still had cell service. If Gerard had intended to hold them captive, he had done so without their knowledge. As long as they were connected to the internet, there would be no questions.

I made my way to the interior stairs, but Monika stopped me before I reached them.

"Any news, Special Agent?"

I tried to hide my smile. It was impossible to know if she realized what she was doing, or if it was just part of her natural charisma. I tended to think it was the latter. "Heard your show went well." I had expected a smile, but her face remained blank.

"Under better circumstances, I would be happy, but I miss her."

"I've got some leads."

"If there's anything I can do to help."

I shook my head as I left her, went for the stairs, dropped to the next level, and made my way to the video room. I stopped short when I saw a body slumped forward on the work table. A pool of blood spread out around the head. Another step forward confirmed it was Jake Reese.

Slowly I approached and checked his jugular vein. There was no pulse, but he was warm. Moving my finger to the pool of blood, I touched the surface, and found it warmer than the air-conditioned room. There was little doubt that his death was a direct result of my coming aboard.

Without a second thought, I pressed the red button.

29

STEVEN BECKER
A KURT HUNTER MYSTERY
BACKWATER DIVA

I WAS A ONE-MAN CRIME-SCENE MACHINE. THE ROOM WAS LOCKED down, and I had all aboard gathered in the salon by the time the ICE cruiser reached the yacht. Johnny Wells came aboard himself with two of his crewmen who, without asking, took positions at the exits. Justine appeared a second later.

I moved toward her. "I don't think you should be here."

"Is that sham of a photographer really dead?"

I wasn't sure if it was her fascination with corpses, or if she truly wished Reese dead. In either case, I wasn't letting her near the scene until she was reinstated.

"Give me a minute." I turned to the door leading to the back deck and whispered to the ICE agent. "Keep an eye on her, please." He nodded, and I continued through to the open deck. I sat on a lounge chair that was worth more than my boat and called Moses.

"Reese is dead." I relayed what information I had to him.

The line went quiet. I leaned back and waited for him to process the information.

"It's a bitch being dead and all. No way to defend yourself. I'll call the major and see if he'll clear Justine."

He sounded relieved. Without the looming threat of the rogue publicist, Moses could write his report the way he really saw it. He'd never said as much, but I figured he had been pressured into his initial stance by his superiors. The high profile of the case was bad enough. Having inflammatory pictures posted all over social media had put his superiors in a corner. I took that as a green light and went back inside.

"You're in the clear, at least with Moses. He's calling your boss right now." I started to think through the implications of this 3D chess game as I spoke. "Although we have a couple of problems." She started to interrupt, but I wanted her to hear what I had to say before she gave the counterargument that I knew was coming. It was going to take more than words to stop her.

"First, you're going to have to explain how you got here, and second, your boss is going to have to accept Moses's call and officially reinstate you."

She pulled out her phone in response and turned away. We had few secrets between us and shared a common password for our devices, but she didn't want me to know who she was calling. A few minutes later, she looked at me and smiled when her phone rang.

"Boom. Reinstated." She flung her fingers out like fireworks. "Lead on, Kemosabe."

I had to admit it was a relief. Grace's superiors were waiting on the IA report before delivering an opinion on her status. I suspected Grace would be relieved as well about Justine, so I called her.

"Hello, crime scene?" Justine snapped as I hung up.

She was in work mode now and there was no stopping her. I took her down to the locked room.

"Can you find a first aid kit?"

It took a second for me to realize that she needed gloves, and

Backwater Diva 205

I left her, to conduct my errand. The last thing she wanted was me breathing down her neck, but she would be limited to taking pictures with her phone until I could find gloves for her.

With the first aid kit in hand, I stopped to check in with Johnny Wells and his team. Before I could reach him, I was accosted by several dancers wanting to know what was going on. To them, it seemed that I was the bad guy. Their thinking was that Gerard had taken them on a pleasure cruise, though it was to a macabre destination. They blamed me for what they now thought was their incarceration.

I dodged the question and asked Johnny to hold on a little longer and told him help was on the way.

He shook his head. "Don't mind helping you out, Kurt, but I'd just as soon be gone before Miami's finest show up. Can you hold down the fort until they get here?"

It wasn't really a question. Johnny and his crew had done us a large favor. We both knew that another four miles offshore and we would be out of state-controlled waters, and he would have had jurisdiction—not that he really wanted the case. I nodded and asked him to hold tight until I delivered the kit to Justine. He agreed, and I headed back down to the room.

"Johnny's going to take off. I have to get back upstairs." I left the first aid kit on the floor by the door. Justine was so engrossed in whatever she was doing that she didn't notice, so I headed back up, thanked him, and returned the radio.

Five minutes later, Johnny and his crew had disappeared over the horizon. I had asked Grace to send the Miami-Dade troops, but they hadn't arrived yet. For once, I was grateful for the help. The salon was becoming unruly and if I started interviewing people, I wouldn't be able to keep an eye on the rest of them.

This time, I knew the perpetrator was someone on board. While I waited for backup, I glanced from face to face. Some hadn't moved from their phones. Others were talking in groups. For now, I had nothing except my gut to go on, but my gaze kept moving back to Suzanne. I still couldn't figure out what she had to gain, though. As the newest member of the cast, it would have benefited her to have Alex alive and prosperous. That would ensure her income.

Planning my interview, I glanced at my phone. It had been almost a half hour since I had discovered Reese's body, and I was starting to feel like the redheaded cousin again. Dade County has got to have a hundred law-enforcement vessels. Ranging from deep-water rescue to air boats, every public entity seemed to have one. In addition to the sheriff, police, FWC, and Coast Guard, many of the smaller municipalities had their own boats. Conditions between the Everglades, canal system, Intracoastal, and open water, as well as the lack of roadways for directions and location, made coordinating even the same department's vessels a daunting task. I was wary to make too many calls. I had little love for Miami-Dade, but considering what was going on, I had no choice but to use their assets.

I was also skeptical when Justine said she was reinstated. It might not have been official yet. Bureaucracies didn't work that quickly. Those kind of decisions needed to run through channels that created an inevitable paper trail. In her eagerness to do what she loved, I was concerned that Justine had started back prematurely.

Interviews were off the table until backup arrived, so I decided to call Moses.

"Figure you're worried about your girl. Don't be. I cleared it myself. They've got two other active scenes, and you don't make major by not being pragmatic. He decided that with the photographer out of the way, there was no longer a case against her, though she'll at least get her hand slapped."

"Gotta say, I'm relieved. What about Grace?"

"This was never about her."

It suddenly made sense. Assigning Moses to the case was a ruse to keep an eye on me. The Park Service and Miami-Dade were in this together. If I went off the rails, it would reflect poorly on them. It went back to something Grace had said. I was a good detective, but a terrible policeman.

"Are you done, then?" I had to ask.

"Not till it's over. Just wanted to let you know that Herrera is fine."

"I could use some backup out here. You seem to have a magic wand." It was good to hear him laugh and I actually felt a smile cross my face. I usually fought two battles, one with the department, the other to solve the crime. Hearing directly from him that Justine and Grace had nothing to worry about was a relief. My mind immediately focused on the case. It felt like I was looking into gin-clear water instead of the murky stuff I had been staring at.

"On their way. Had to wait for the ME."

I glanced out the window, hoping to spot them. The water was empty, and my gaze moved back to the room. I noticed Suzanne was by herself typing something into her phone. Everyone else was in groups, and seeing her as an outcast emphasized how different she was from the rest of the cast.

"If you've got time, can you run a name for me?" I asked Moses before we hung up.

"Sure thing, Text it over."

I pulled the paper Rico had given me yesterday from my pocket, found Suzanne's name, and pecked it into my phone. Just as I finished, I saw the reflection of the sun on something in the water. Another glance told me it was Miami-Dade.

While I waited for them, I planned my next steps.

Justine was all over the crime scene, but I knew it would take time for her to get back to the lab and process any evidence she found. That meant hours, if not days. Gerard's move to bring the *Diva* into open water was troubling. I could understand and even sympathize with getting away from the media. The only problem was that the yacht was poised for a run.

"Hunter." I heard my name called and swiveled around to see Little Willy and a uniformed officer standing in the doorway.

"Yeah, can you keep an eye on this crowd? I'm going to check the crime scene and start interviews."

"They told us to cooperate, so you're the boss. ME should be aboard shortly," the uniform said.

Little Willy didn't seem happy about it, but the men took stations at the two exits. Not sure how long this cooperation was going to last, I quickly headed down the stairway to the lower deck. Instead of checking on Justine, I continued to the electronics closet.

The knob turned and I switched on the light. The array of equipment was as daunting as when I had first seen it, but I had a very specific goal. I already knew the general layout from Gerard's tour and went directly to the helm controls. Even modest outboards are run by computers. The *Diva* was no different, just on a larger scale. Fortunately, each component was clearly labeled, allowing me to pass by the nonessential systems like the autopilot. What I needed was something that could disable the engines—or at least give the illusion that they were malfunctioning.

Much like the check engine light on a car, boats had similar signals that something was wrong. Most were loud buzzers and not as easily ignored as a small icon. I wanted the loudest buzzer, and found it with the engine room fire-suppression system. Fire is one of the biggest fears aboard a vessel, and a notification that there is a malfunction is not likely to be ignored. Reaching for the box, I gently yanked the cables free, being careful to leave them in place so a casual inspection wouldn't easily reveal the cause. Once the fire system was offline, I found the interface for the engine. My intent was to initiate an alarm that the engines were overheating. Coupled with the loss of the fire system, I hoped the combination would create a big enough scare to stop Gerard from fleeing.

Using the flashlight on my phone, I pulled a black unit out and studied the back panel, finally settling on three wires that might work. I unscrewed the terminals on those, as well as the adjacent ones just in case, leaving them looking like they were still attached. Just as I was about to return the box to its position, I saw a glint of metal.

My heart beat loudly in my ears as I pulled out a familiar-looking knife. The sheen of the blood told me it was recent, and I guessed it was Reese's. There were two people who had access to the closet: Reese was dead, making Gerard the obvious killer. Now I needed to divert Justine's attention from the corpse to the evidence.

Confident that I had bought myself some time, I climbed back to the main deck and salon. On the way, I could hear Justine and Sid processing the scene. There was nothing for me to do there. It was time to see what Suzanne was all about.

30

STEVEN BECKER
A KURT HUNTER MYSTERY
BACKWATER DIVA

I WENT DIRECTLY TO THE CHAIR OPPOSITE SUZANNE. SHE LOOKED up from her phone as I sat.

"I've got some questions."

She put her phone down and swung her feet to the deck to face me. "Figured."

"My gut tells me you don't fit in here. I can either go into a whole line of inquiry and waste both of our time, or you can just tell me why."

She didn't even blink. "Not here."

On the surface, that meant that she didn't want to be overheard. It could also implicate her as a snitch. "You sure about that?" I glanced around the room to see who was watching. She caught my eye and nodded. At least she had been warned. I got up and moved to the door, feeling her right behind me. We eased past the officer and stepped toward the stern.

"After I tell you why I'm here, you've got to promise to get me off this boat."

I was going to come back, *That depends on what you have to say*, but she hadn't been specific about where she wanted to go.

Any doubts about what she was about to reveal and I would send her into Miami-Dade's care.

"OK."

She glanced over my shoulder to make sure we were alone. "Alex hired me as a private investigator."

My blank expression told her this wasn't enough explanation.

"She was worried that Monika was having an affair with Monte."

"You're close," I said.

"You know?"

I figured offering up a few tidbits that she might already know wouldn't hurt. "The two people with the most to gain from all this are Monika and Gerard. I thought Monte might be involved, but his 'accident' has pretty much cleared him."

I usually let the interviewee talk, but with one sentence Suzanne had changed from a prime suspect to an ally. Working for Alex meant that she had no motive to see any harm befall her. In her business, referrals were everything and her consulting fee probably dwarfed whatever paycheck she got from the tour. "So, you were about to tell Alex what you suspected?"

"Monika had no idea who I was. She resented me because Alex had hired me for the show. As you've probably figured out, Monika runs the show. She didn't care for me as a dancer, either, and in truth, I shouldn't be on the same floor as these women. I'm not a professional dancer."

"But Gerard figured it out."

"I'm not sure how. This isn't my first rodeo."

I suspected Reese was the missing link but, unsure of their relationship, decided to hold that card. "With Monte incapacitated, Gerard's in charge."

"How?" she asked.

I explained about the offshore company. Once she grasped the concept, she nodded, reaffirming that I was on the right track.

"I figured it was something like that. Gerard tipped off Monika and when she saw me pull Alex aside during the rehearsal break. I guess she felt she had to act."

I let her run with that theory. It still had holes, but they were filling in. With Monika and Monte both rushing toward Alex, she could easily have fallen or been pushed through the glass screen. I had motive, means, and now opportunity. "But who stabbed her?"

"I would guess Gerard or Reese. Neither were accounted for when the incident happened."

I was willing to gamble the forensics would come back with Gerard's prints or DNA on the knife. Once Gerard knew I was coming out to talk to Reese a bullseye had been placed on his back. My radioing ahead was the trigger that caused his death. I now suspected he had either witnessed or had some photographic evidence that Gerard had finished off Alex. I could see why Suzanne wanted off the boat—she was probably next.

Two officers wheeling a gurney past us distracted me. Justine and Sid followed. I'd shared my theory and given the evidence bag to Justine, who had made short work of the crime scene. Sid had apparently been equally as efficient with his preliminary work. Suzanne and I stood back and watched as they loaded Reese's body aboard the police boat.

To do her job, Suzanne had to work like an undercover operative. A stone-cold face was essential to her success. I studied her, looking for any sign of emotion and saw none.

"Can you confirm you were in Alex's employ?" Trust but verify was appropriate here. I believed her, but this wouldn't be the first time I'd been duped. Even though I liked to see the good in people, my experience had more often proved me wrong. I had become cynical, and tried to refine my skills to detect deceit. Most of the time I got it right, but when I was wrong, it was usually because the other person was especially devious. That type of person tended to know they were skilled and often didn't hesitate to use their talent against others.

She frowned. "I can forward you our email correspondence."

"That'll work." I gave her a card, and remembering our arrangement, escorted her to the police boat. She stepped aboard, apparently not at all worried that she was carpooling with a corpse that she may have slept with. I waved to Justine as they pulled away, suddenly doubting my judgment.

I decided that until I received the email verification from her, it would be better if Suzanne remained Miami-Dade's guest. I pulled out my phone and called Grace.

"You want what?" she asked, after my request.

I held the phone away from my ear.

"We're not running a bed and breakfast here."

"OK, I get it." I took a breath, hoping she would do the same. Once the line was quiet, I explained my theory and how Suzanne's presence tied into it.

"Just another pretty face," she said, sarcastically.

The jab landed and I waited for the follow-up punch, but it didn't come.

"Listen, I suspect she was sleeping with Reese, the publicist. She said he was doing some backup work for her. Could you ask her to send me any pictures Reese sent her, along with her emails from Alex?"

"Well, at least you didn't believe her outright. That's progress."

We both knew I trusted my gut too often. Grace disconnected before I could reply, and I found myself staring at the water, wondering if I had enough evidence to bring Gerard in right now. Justine had left without a hint of what she had found, leading me to believe there was nothing to act on yet.

The knife was on its way to Miami, and the boat, hopefully, was disabled. After talking to Suzanne, I didn't feel the need to conduct any more interviews. Confirmation would happen on the other side of the bay.

I walked up to the uniformed officer by the door facing the stern. "I'm heading back to Miami. Can you stay out here for a bit? I'll talk to Captain Herrera when I get back and she'll revise your orders." It was as far as I could go with him, and we both knew it.

"Expecting trouble?" he asked.

"Not sure, but I don't want to lose the yacht or anyone else aboard until I figure this out."

He gave an almost sympathetic nod, which would never have happened if I were talking to Little Willy. I couldn't help but glance at the port-side door, where his partner was leaning against the rail smoking a cigarette and ogling the dancers.

The officer followed my gaze. "I'll talk to him."

"Thanks." I left before he had a chance for his partner to change his mind. My boat was inboard of the police boat, and it took a few minutes to juggle the lines so I could slide free. With the engine idling, I allowed the current to pull the center console away from the police boat and the *Diva*.

With the tide running out and the wind at my back, it was a choppy mess, but once the boat was trimmed properly it skipped over the waves. Had they been any bigger it would have been a slog, but I made decent time and pulled up to the marina about a half-hour later. I checked my phone on the way to the truck, hoping to see a message from Justine, but there was nothing. I didn't want to bother her and an unannounced drop-in was a bad idea, so I sucked it up and called.

"Yo, Kemosabe. I was just about to call."

"Anything? I need something on Gerard."

"Nada. Looks like most of the crew had been through that room recently. I'm on my way to the lab to see what I can pull off the knife."

I realized I had never asked what had killed Reese and could be jumping off a cliff with my conclusion. I needed confirmation. "Murder weapon?"

"Sid thinks it's consistent with a knife."

"The one I found?"

"Patience. We've got to follow procedure."

I had mixed emotions to her newfound commitment to protocol. "Yeah, but without anything solid, and with Viscount as the corporation's attorney, I don't even have enough to bring him in for questioning yet."

The line went quiet for a long second. I knew Justine and I were thinking the same thing. The silence got uncomfortable.

"I gotta go," I said.

"Call me if you need me." She paused. "I love you."

It wasn't a casual goodbye. My grandfather used to say, there's more than one way to skin a cat without getting scratched. I was worried, though, that Gerard was over the edge and I didn't have the luxury of time. Without evidence, there were a few options. A confession would be nice, or an accomplice turning state's evidence. Neither was likely.

That left one more possibility, and from past experience, I knew it could get messy.

Flushing out a suspect led to erratic behavior. Place a murderer into a corner with no apparent exit and bad things can happen. Desperation is dry tinder for trouble, and Gerard had a ship full of innocents.

It was the kind of ploy that I would have to do alone. I knew Justine, Grace, and Moses would probably jump onboard, but this kind of decision is a potential career wrecker. If anyone were going down, it would be me.

I sat aboard the Park Service center console watching the boat traffic going in and out of Government Cut and tried to figure out how to force Gerard into showing his hand—without collateral damage. If I had pulled the right wires, the boat was dead in the water and the Miami-Dade officers aboard would hopefully mitigate any violence. Whatever plan I concocted, I needed to get Gerard off the ship.

There was at least one acceptable means. The "dinghy" was a twenty-seven-foot, twin-engine center console. If full of fuel, which I expected was its normal state, he had enough boat to get to the Bahamas if he wanted. Now, I needed a lure to get him off the *Diva*.

Twilight in subtropical latitudes is a short-lived affair. Darkness doesn't linger like it does further north. In the time I had taken to formulate a plan, daylight had waned. Gerard was a captain and, though capable, would know the disadvantages of traveling at night. The pros and cons didn't apply to covert activity. Smugglers had been using the dark as cover for their activities for centuries.

Under normal conditions, boats and ships of all sizes are required to illuminate their vessels with running lights. On a clear night, the lights can be seen at great distances. Turn those lights off and stay near the coast, and a boat could be virtually invisible to see or distinguish by radar. Knowing the waters was an advantage, but chartplotters had leveled the field in recent years. Gerard would be comfortable and have no hesitation to make a nighttime run.

That left me little time. For my idea to work, I needed the prime-time window when everyone was glued to their phones.

31

STEVEN BECKER
A KURT HUNTER MYSTERY
BACKWATER DIVA

SAYING THE MEDIA HAD NOT BEEN KIND TO ME WAS AN understatement. I dreaded any encounter and avoided them at all costs. Those tables were about to turn. If I was going to catch Gerard, for a change I needed them. In order to do that, I had to shake up the status quo and befriend them.

On the way into the marina, I wracked my brain for anyone who might help me. That went nowhere. I'd made no friends in the press.

After securing the boat, I started walking toward the truck, carelessly spinning my phone in my hand. Of course I dropped it and had that *OMG* moment that it might be broken, but it landed softly. As I picked it up, I saw a notification from my Facebook feed.

The answer came to me.

I didn't need the media. I had the power to do this myself—or sort of. I could post something on social media that would go viral, and quickly. As I sat in my truck, trying to figure out how that unknown and invisible world worked, I had another idea.

Writing the message was easy. How to get it to Gerard was the hard part. Needing a computer, I started the truck and drove to Justine's place. Once there, I sat down to see if my social media skills were up to the task. It took only a few minutes for me to admit I needed help. Fortunately, I had a teenager only a phone call away who was ready to assist me.

In less time than I had stared at the blank screen, with Allie's guidance I created a secondary email account. That was easily accomplished, and as I waited for the confirmations to come, we worked out a message and, more importantly, which hashtags to use to get the paparazzi's attention.

Finally, she asked the question I had been waiting for.

"Is this legal?"

She was majoring in criminal studies and probably knew more than me. It wasn't the first time I had flexed the law during this case, and I was wondering myself where the invisible line was. The one that, once you crossed it, there was no looking back. It had felt far away, but her question made me think.

"People make fake profiles all the time."

"What if you just started real Twitter and Instagram accounts? You can get way more exposure that way. I bet @agentkurthunter is open."

She explained how hashtags worked. What do you say when your daughter is smarter than you? I let her continue. "Go on."

"I guess the actual message is correct. You do think the captain did it." She paused. "Probably a good thing Martinez is gone, though."

The tension broke as we both laughed at the mention of Mr. Paranoid. I'm sure he had a firm grasp on the Twitterverse, and I wondered if he would see these posts.

"If Gerard didn't do it, he won't react. If he did, I'll be there to deal with it," I told Allie.

"What about all the people aboard the yacht?"

I wondered if she shouldn't be looking at law school after her undergrad degree. She was every bit as astute as Daniel J.

Viscount. "They'll be OK," I reassured her, and steered the subject away with questions about the social media landscape.

The account needed to be real, or at least pass a quick inspection. Most entertainment reporters' idea of investigative work had been reduced to online creeping. They search online for a person and browse their accounts. I knew because I often used the same methods. Without a mountain of patience and the desire for the truth, it was impossible to sniff out the real from the fake. From my experience, these kind of fake "journalists" had neither.

The days of having two verifiable and independent sources were long gone. I didn't like the idea of using my own photo, but Allie insisted and texted one over. We created a few posts—most about fishing, but the next-to-last post was about going to the Alex Luna memorial show. At least that wasn't a lie. And then the big one—that we had a suspect.

A few minutes later, I was on Twitter and Instagram. I was already marginally on Facebook, mostly to see what Allie had been up to when she was younger. Now she posted elsewhere, and I rarely checked my page. She went into my account and added a few pictures and posts to at least make it look like someone lived there. Satisfied the Facebook account looked authentic enough, we did the same with my other new accounts. The message would be cross-posted to each.

I could only hope the reporters would be eager enough to scoop each other that they would skip any deep dive and discover there were only a few posts, though my devious daughter had instructed me how to back-date them. The worst case was that I had wasted an hour, but even then, I would have planted a seed. If the reporters didn't outright retweet what I wanted, they would have a social media treasure map to follow. In either case, it was good father-daughter time.

Staying under 280 characters on Twitter sounded daunting, but in my last tweet I said what I wanted in half that:

This Special Agent believes Alex Luna's yacht captain responsible for murders

Allie helped add the hashtags #AlexLuna, #Diva, #Luna, and a dozen others, and we hit send. My original thought was to tag several notoriously unethical reporters in my other posts, but by the time I got them finished, alarm bells were already going off on my Twitter account. Within seconds of posting, I had forty likes and several retweets. As I sat back and watched even more notifications pour in, I couldn't help but wonder about the integrity of the platform. A minuscule percentage of the population was actually engaged on Twitter. I had heard something that only ten percent of users posted eighty percent of the content. The eagerness of these folks to forget about any kind of verification process and like or retweet the post so quickly was evident.

Now, it had to reach Gerard, and my plan for that was simple.

"I think I have it now. Thanks." We did a bit of catching up, then she asked the second question I had been expecting.

"Does Justine know about this?"

There was no dodging her. The two were close. Allie would have no issue calling her. "No. It's better for her if she doesn't."

"Does anyone know? It'd be nice if someone had your back."

I thought about who I might tell and came up with Moses. He wasn't my boss, and I felt I could predict his reaction to my strategy. She was right. Having someone know what I was up to before I charged in firing bullets was probably a good idea.

"There's an officer I can tell."

"OK, Dad. Be careful."

We said goodbye, and I glanced at my notifications again.

Monika Diaz's accounts were easy to locate. As a public

figure, she had no interest in privacy. Her overnight fame after last night's show had her trending everywhere. I quickly jumped on board and followed her on Twitter and Instagram, then liked her Facebook page. I added her handle and name to my posts and tweets.

After observing her for the past few days, I knew how often she checked her phone. With her career riding the crest of a wave, if she wasn't addicted to her feeds before, she was now. My aim was for her to see the posts and bring both to Gerard's attention. Then I'd see how it played out.

Gerard had to be nervous with the police camped out aboard the *Diva*. Whether he'd discovered my sabotage I would probably find out shortly. The Twitter notifications continued to pour in. I had figured it would take hours for the post to reach the right people and go viral. With over a thousand likes in less than twenty minutes, I had grossly underestimated the platform.

I raced to the marina, left the truck, and hopped about the center console. There was no need for discretion, and I cruised out the river at a good clip. I wished I had a light bar to pacify the angry comments thrown from other boats, but I turned a deaf ear and continued out to the Intracoastal. Once in open water, I ignored the *Slow speed* signs and brought the boat up on plane. It wasn't until I was two miles from the Fowey Rocks Light and could see the lights of the yacht that I relaxed and slowed.

There were two ways to play this. I could race toward the yacht with my navigation lights on, or come in dark. I chose the former. Even if Gerard hadn't already made an escape plan, he was certainly paranoid. He would likely scrutinize any boat coming toward them at night. Binoculars would give him plenty of notice that it was me.

Gritting my teeth, I continued at speed toward the light. About a mile away, I slowed. I wanted to give some time to Gerard to get off the yacht. Once I was in binocular range, I slowed further. While I waited for the bow wake to recede, I took the binoculars from the electronics box. Once the boat settled, I focused them on the yacht and panned across the deck.

Nothing seemed to be amiss. I could see people in the salon, and the officers remained at their posts. The center console sat on its supports. Fearing that I had blown it, I stopped.

The sea floor between Miami and the main reef is covered with smaller patch reefs. I was in the area where they were common and decided that if I was going to stop and wait, I might as well look like I was fishing. Turning off the running lights, I left the white all-around-light on to show that I was at anchor. The current was slight, and someone would really have to be watching to realize that I was adrift.

Training the binoculars back on the *Diva*, I hoped that if Gerard were looking back, from this distance the Park Service boat would look like a small fishing boat. The only distinguishing features were the forest green T-top, which wouldn't reveal its color in the dark, and the Park Service insignia on the bow. With the only light above the T-top, I felt confident that Gerard wouldn't be able to figure out who I was.

With nothing to do and feeling like a crack whore about to get a fix, I checked my Twitter feed. The likes and retweets were still pouring in. It had to be just a matter of time before Gerard found out about it.

Sitting on the leaning post, my phone vibrated. Apparently, my intended audience was larger than I expected and included Justine.

"What the hell are you doing?"

My first thought was that Allie had ratted me out. "You know half the world has Twitter, right?"

While Justine continued her rant, I got two calls, which I ignored. One from Grace and the other from Moses.

"I'm just watching. No harm done."

"I'll have to talk to Allie about parenting her father."

That broke the tension. "I couldn't involve you. You understand, right?"

She finally gave in with a stern warning to not go cowboy. Grace and Moses had both left voicemails in the meantime. I ignored the messages and, bracing myself for a similar tongue lashing, returned their calls. It took some talking to bring Grace around, and she agreed to call the officers aboard the *Diva* and ask them not to stop Gerard from leaving.

As I was explaining my plan to Moses, I finally saw action on the deck.

I couldn't see if it was Gerard, but I did see the davits start to swing the center console over the water.

32

STEVEN BECKER
A KURT HUNTER MYSTERY
BACKWATER DIVA

THE DAVITS MADE SHORT WORK OF LIFTING THE BOAT FROM THE supports. Within a few seconds it was above the rail and swinging toward the water. I needed to close the gap before Gerard had a chance to take off. With twin 250s, he was much faster than my single engine. I explained to Moses what was happening, and he agreed to send help.

The boat was in the water now. Moses could dial up Miami-Dade, but I had Johnny Wells. Once underway, it would be too loud and bumpy to manage a call. Dialing his number, I waited a few long seconds for him to answer. The call went to voicemail and I left a quick, but detailed, message.

Several figures appeared and led the "dinghy" down the length of the *Diva* to the swim platform, where the center console could easily be accessed. I figured they were part of the security team. What surprised me was that two figures appeared to exit the salon doors—not one. Gerard had an arm around a woman. I would need my binoculars to see who it was for sure, but my guess was Monika. Whether she was an accomplice to his escape plan or a hostage was yet to be determined.

I knew from boarding the yacht the other night that Gerard

would be armed, so before heading toward the yacht, I checked my sidearm and unlocked the clips securing the shotgun in the center console. Just as the two figures reached the swim platform and were about to board the center console, I accelerated.

The center console moved away quickly. I was expecting him to run toward open water, but found the green and red bow lights coming directly toward me. He wasn't running dark, and he wasn't heading for the Bahamas. It appeared Gerard's destination was Miami. I spun the boat ninety degrees to port on a heading that ran perpendicular to Gerard's course. If he was heading for Miami, I had time to call in a road block of sorts.

It was too early, though. The water has no marked lanes or exits. Even heading toward land, Gerard had the ability to turn on a dime and change course. The Rickenbacker Causeway, Government Cut, or a handful of other inlets further north were all still open to him. His course toward the mainland did give me the advantage of observing from a distance and letting the big boys do the heavy lifting.

Communications was a problem, though. Had Gerard committed to an offshore destination, using the VHF wouldn't be a problem. The microphone would pick up my end of the conversation even at speed, and the speaker was loud enough to hear any response. I had to assume Gerard was at least monitoring the VHF, and if he heard any police chatter, he had the ability to avoid the trap. Using my cell phone required that I slow considerably.

I turned back to parallel Gerard's course and followed from about a mile away. As he approached Cape Florida, he continued to hold a course toward the causeway and the Intracoastal. It appeared his decision had been made and I stopped to call in the cavalry.

Moses was a kick-the-tires, wear-out-your-shoes kind of guy. Herrera was a manager. That made Grace the logical first call.

We agreed to cordon off the causeway. If Gerard got past the bridge, the water opened up with several routes he could choose. Bear and Government Cuts ran toward open water. If he chose to escape by land, he could head up the river or into the Intracoastal. Either of the latter choices offered a multitude of places to ditch the boat and head inland.

Within minutes I saw the blinking lights of a chopper. I hoped the police boats used a bit more discretion, or Gerard would turn around and head out to sea. I hadn't heard back from Johnny yet, leaving that angle undefended.

Thankfully, the chopper veered off before spooking Gerard. I guessed the maneuver was meant to get eyes on the target. In the tight confines of the area we were heading, the only aerial advantage was observation. There were too many bridges, stories-high cruise ships and tankers, and condos for the pilot to safely fly low.

Gerard was past Cape Florida and heading toward the causeway. With land on his eastern and western flanks, I felt safer closing the gap between the boats. Thinking he was in the clear, Gerard had been running at an efficient speed, rather than with a wide-open throttle, which would have sucked precious fuel. He had several options, and running low on gas would take half of them off the table.

His speed allowed me to get closer, and he was still well away from the bridge when I rounded the point and accelerated after him. I could see the causeway clearly now. It was a dark night, and the shadows cast by the bridge above concealed any boats sitting below the span. There was no sign of a blockade. It was so quiet, I began to doubt anyone was there.

Just in case it was all up to me, I pushed the throttle to the stop. I got another five-thousand RPMs, but I could hear cavitation from the propeller and backed the throttle slightly. The engine evened out, and I studied the water ahead. The bridge was about a quarter-mile away, and it appeared that Gerard was just about to cross under the main span. He slowed slightly to navigate the dark water.

I was less than two hundred yards behind him when the scene lit up.

The darkness came to light as the flashing red and blue lights of three police boats illuminated the scene. Though it was the best choke-point within miles, it was far from easy to block off. To block the entire span of the bridge would have taken a dozen or more boats. Whoever designed the blockade had counted on Gerard heading for the center span. During the day, he could have veered left or right, but those spans were unlit at night. Initiating the lights even a minute earlier would have given Gerard enough notice to cross under an unguarded span.

Gerard was close. I cringed, waiting for the sound of the inevitable. It didn't happen. A less-experienced boater would have fallen quickly into police hands, but Gerard was a NASCAR driver compared to a casual boater. The visual and audio cues told me the story of what he did.

The sound of the transmission grinding indicated he had crashed the throttles from forward into reverse. The boat suddenly jerked backward. The wash behind the boat told me that he had left one engine in reverse and slammed the other into forward. The boat spun ninety degrees before the police boats knew what he was doing. The momentum of the turn spun the bow of the center console toward an open span, and Gerard pushed both throttles down hard. The twin engines propelled the boat under the bridge and into the clear.

The maneuver had taken all of ten seconds, during which I had continued my approach. I was close enough to see the surprised looks of the police officers. They had obviously been preparing for a crash. It took them a long minute to respond. While they regrouped, I cleared the bridge through the same span Gerard had. I could hear the roar of his engines, but he had turned off his nav lights, leaving his wake the only visible sign of his course.

Seconds later, I could feel the police boats right behind me, and I could see the search lights of the helicopter panning the water in front of us. Gerard had a good minute's lead and, since he was running dark, the chopper would have to find him with their spotlight.

Even with my throttle wide open I fell behind, and the police boats quickly passed me. I suffered their wakes and followed in the wash. The officers' determined looks told me they intended to use brute force to catch Gerard. He had already proven he was craftier than them. They might get lucky, but I felt a different approach was in order.

With the chopper and the more evenly matched police boats after Gerard, I slowed and considered his options. We were in a square-shaped area. About a mile ahead was the southwest-facing side of Dodge Island where I often docked. On my port side, or to the west, lay Brickell Key and the entrance to the river. To starboard were the flats leading up to Virginia Key.

I suspected the police boats weren't Gerard's first concern. It was the helicopter. He could reach land and make a run for it, but the chopper could follow him on land or sea. That took the river out of play as a destination. I also ruled out the surrounding islands. Heading straight into the Intracoastal was not an option either. The waterway was wide, but Miami Beach would lock him into a straight run that would eventually lead to another bridge and another blockade.

Even if he didn't plan on escaping to open water, running out of Government Cut gave him the most leeway of any of the choices. He could circle back or run up on miles-long Miami Beach. If that didn't appeal to him, to the north, east, and south lay open water.

My plan was to take the same route I had taken when I followed the *Diva*, and follow Fisherman's Channel past the south-facing side of Dodge Island to Government Cut. Running Norris Cut was another option, which I had all but ruled out. The flats surrounding Virginia Key and Fisher Island were tricky during the day. I didn't expect him to try them at night.

The scene in front of me was like a night club. The brilliant white of the helicopter's searchlight and the flashing lights of the police boat created a strobe effect, where the action seemed to start and stop. Suddenly, like a special effect from the light show, I saw a huge rooster tail of white foam shoot skyward. Gerard had chosen the flats. Accelerating and trimming up his engines allowed the boat another few feet of draft.

I had no reason to chase him across water I wasn't familiar with, so I stayed to the channel, but the police boats followed. Whether that was a good decision was yet to be seen. From my perspective, with three boats they could have stayed in deep water and cornered him, but the adrenaline-fueled captains had chosen to chase him.

I waited for the inevitable brown mud to shoot up from one of the rooster tails, telling me that one of the boats had grounded. While the other boats chased Gerard across the flats, I moved into the space between Dodge and Fisher islands and waited. Downwind, I was able to hear the high pitch of the engines as the propellers fought to grab water.

The sound from Gerard's engines suddenly changed. The boat slowed, then stopped. My first thought was that the engines had overheated. Running wide open with the motors trimmed up would increase the RPMs, causing the engines to redline. At the same time, the angle of the engines reduced the water intake. Together they were perfect conditions to blow an engine.

The first police boat came close but avoided Gerard's boat. The other boats, their line of sight restricted by the lead boat, followed its course blindly. They hadn't seen Gerard stop, and with a crash, the trailing two boats collided with the first. One flipped and crashed a hundred feet away. The second ran straight into the transom of the first. Just as they realized what had happened, rooster tails shot from Gerard's engines, and he took off toward the channel.

33

STEVEN BECKER

A KURT HUNTER MYSTERY

BACKWATER DIVA

My Park Service center console was no match for the twin engine "dinghy." The larger boat's wake slammed against my hull, forcing me to grab onto the T-top's tubing. He had reached deeper water about a hundred yards ahead of my position. Even if I hadn't seen him, I could tell from the pitch of the engines that he had made it to the channel and trimmed them down. My guess was he was going forty knots, a good dozen more than I could get out of the Park Service boat on a good day. If he ran with his lights on, that would give me about a half hour before he faded from sight. If he ran dark, I had half that time at the most. With open water ahead and his choice of running north, south, or east, I needed help.

The disparity between our boats was evident in the time it took the underpowered Park Service boat to get up on plane. The throttle was jammed against its stop, but the bow remained high in the air. I jammed my index fingers into the down rocker on the trim tabs controls. The bow came down slightly, then in a hurry. Still dealing with the remnants of Gerard's wake, I was forced to drop speed until I hit clean water, where I jammed the lever down again.

Running at wide-open throttle is an uncomfortable feeling for me. The RPMs maxed out at 5600, just below the redline, but it was the sound of the engines running all-out that worried me. My father had taught me that when you force things they break. I guessed this applied to more than construction. The engine being overdue for its hundred-hour service didn't help.

The *thump thump* of the chopper's rotors eased my anxiety slightly. I could hear the pilot approaching, his searchlight flashing over my boat for a hot second, then it was gone, flashing back and forth over the dark water. The light had blacked out my night vision, forcing me to squint to allow my eyes to readjust to the dark. The bright lights of South Beach passing on my port side and Fisher Island on my starboard extended the process.

By the time I passed the fishing pier and jetty marking the end of Government Cut, my vision had acclimated, but with the exception of the chopper's searchlight fanning out in the distance and the blinking red and green strobes of the lighted buoys marking the channel, the ocean was pitch black. Gerard was running dark.

I couldn't see him, and I knew I was falling behind the escaping boat. There was nothing I could do to catch him. I needed to step outside my box and organize the effort. The VHF radio was set to channel 16, the standard call-and-receive channel. I reached over and pressed the transmit button and broadcast my name and position.

My handheld radio was in the console and worthless in this situation. One of the issues when coordinating a joint effort was communications. With each agency having their own frequencies, I needed a dedicated radio operator to reach them. Even then, the frequencies were public and offered only slightly more security than the marine radio.

The pilot responded immediately. With the chopper out

ahead, there was no reason for me to risk damage to my boat or myself. I slowed to 4400 RPMs and trimmed the nose down to stop the boat from porpoising. The ride and noise level both benefited.

"Metro Police Chopper Four Mike Papa. Vessel is in sight. Pursuing from a distance. Over."

Helicopter pursuit was more art than science. The success rate, especially in traffic scenarios like chases and stolen cars, was near perfect. On the water, their effectiveness was limited to observation. Right now, I needed a pursuit craft. The Coast Guard was an option, as was the FWC. I preferred Johnny Wells.

To reach him this time of night, I had no choice but to call or text. That meant I had to stop, but with the chopper pilot keeping an eye on the fleeing Gerard, I was comfortable falling further behind.

My call again went to voicemail. I left another message, then texted him. I had to face the reality that there was every chance neither would be received until it was too late. Biting back my ego, I accelerated. Once I reached speed, I set course for the helicopter, picked up the microphone, and hailed the Coast Guard. Their response, probably since they had been listening to Miami-Dade's radio chatter, was immediate, though their reaction was measured.

The Coasties are damned good at rescue operations, as well as boarding known targets and patrolling. This chase was outside their wheelhouse. They promised to move a cutter that was lurking further offshore onto an intercept course, and would ready several RHIB vessels once a destination had been established. The FWC was even less help. The officer on duty was on land, working several of the local boat ramps. It had proven more efficient for them to have the fishermen come to them than to go after them on the water.

Knowing that the intercept might come down to me, I accelerated. Zooming out the chartplotter, I established that if Gerard maintained his present course he was heading back to Fowey Light and the *Diva*. That made sense. Even with his fast boat, once the Coasties reached his position, he knew he was outmatched.

Escaping on the yacht, assuming he didn't know I had sabotaged it, would lead to the same result. The answer was the worst-case scenario.

He needed hostages.

A glance at my position on the screen and noting the location of the search lights, now at least a mile ahead, told me that he was going to reach the yacht before help arrived. To make matters worse, someone at Miami-Dade had authorized the police boat that had been stationed at the yacht to follow the center console. That boat, along with two others, were now stuck on a flat by Virginia Key.

I wondered how the Coast Guard handled hostage situations, and was not sure I wanted to find out. As my center console skipped over the waves, I tried to put myself in Gerard's position.

The first thing I would do would be to pull anchor. Gerard would believe he had more options that way, and the yacht would be harder to board if he were underway. Maybe my sabotage effort would pay off. That was my best bet—as long as the wires I had pulled crippled the ship.

In my mind's eye, I imagined the anchor coming up, and with the direction of the wind, the boat would quickly be blown onto the reef. At this point, no one was going to stop that from happening. The insight gave me time to prepare.

I radioed the Coast Guard, explained the situation, and asked them to send the RHIBs out to the light with a hostage negotiator. They were ready to roll and gave an ETA of thirty minutes. By then, the cutter would be in range to help as well.

Again I was waiting for Gerard to make his next move. The last time I was out to the yacht I had wanted him to see me coming. This time I preferred to stay invisible. I cut my nav lights and turned off the chartplotter. Both the *Diva* and the Fowey Light were visible now. I knew these waters and had no need of the electronic guide. I searched the horizon for any sign of the Coast Guard cutter, but the circling helicopter was the only thing in sight. Clouds drifted over the moon and darkness surrounded me, giving a surreal feeling to the ride.

From a half-mile away I could clearly see the outline of the yacht, but not what was going on aboard. I closed the gap by half and observed two men hoisting the center console onto its supports. Another man was on the foredeck, where I assumed he was releasing the mooring ball. Standard procedure before leaving an anchorage would be to start the engines, so I figured my sabotage was still undetected—or had failed.

I saw the line drop into the water, but the yacht sat in place. The only wake came from the water blasting out of several ports from the water-cooled air conditioning system. A couple of hundred yards away, I stopped completely and let the motor idle.

The Park Service center console bobbed just outside of the lights flooding from the larger ship. I figured Gerard would have to be night blind to some extent with the extraneous lights everywhere. I was confident I hadn't been observed. The sound of an alarm and two men yelling wafted over the water.

Gerard must have figured out he had engine trouble.

Just as I heard them, I saw the boat begin to drift toward the light. The sound of a door slamming came across the water. Gerard had left the bridge and was running down the stairs, presumably to the engine room. Watching the gap between the lighthouse and the yacht close, I might have been more concerned about dropping the anchor than starting the engines.

It was the first boatmanship mistake he made, and I wondered if he wasn't close to cracking.

Bad decision-making was a sure sign of stress. It also meant he was volatile. I needed to proceed with caution. For now I could do nothing but watch as the yacht drifted closer toward the shallow section of the reef.

The southwest side of the light guarded the shallowest water. Charts marked the shoal at six feet, but I remember seeing water breaking over a section of it at low tide. The *Diva* was heading directly for the platform on that side of the lighthouse. Gerard hadn't reappeared from the lower decks, not that it mattered. The fate of the yacht was out of his hands.

The light from the 130-foot tower illuminated the surrounding area. It pierced the veil of darkness that hid me, but I wasn't worried. For the first time, I had the upper hand.

The telltale sound was probably much worse aboard the multimillion-dollar yacht. As the collision happened underwater, it was inaudible from my location, but I had a clear line of sight to see the boat suddenly stop and shudder as it struck the shallow portion of the reef.

The salon emptied and I could see and hear the cast and crew as they gathered outside to witness the destruction of the *Diva*. My concern was now twofold, and rescue became the first priority.

Turning in the direction of Miami, I scanned the water, but the light flooding from the tower again limited my night vision. I assumed the two promised RHIBs were closing. A call to the Coast Guard station confirmed they were inbound and that the cutter should be on-site in a matter of minutes. Another helicopter would be dispatched as well.

With that situation in hand, I studied the wreck. The yacht was listing but didn't appear to be taking on water. It was more common than not for boats striking the reef to remain above water until the next storm took them under. The situation for those aboard wasn't urgent.

That left me to focus on Gerard.

34

STEVEN BECKER
A KURT HUNTER MYSTERY
BACKWATER DIVA

It was a long few minutes before the Coast Guard arrived. Sitting on the inshore side of the light, I watched the water for the promised support and the *Diva* for any sign of Gerard. I planned on boarding with the Coasties and apprehending Gerard with their help. Surely he would see the foolishness of a standoff with the fifth branch of the military at my back.

Apparently he did. The cutter was in clear view now, as were the RHIBs from Miami. Even if he didn't see them, he had to hear the loud hailer advising them to stand by for a boarding party to inspect the damage. I heard the message and picked up the mic to notify the captain of my intentions. Just as I clicked the button to transmit, I saw Gerard leave the cabin.

He half-dragged Monika behind him. It didn't appear to be against her will—she was just moving slower than he wanted. Sensing he was about to make his move, I idled closer to the yacht. As I rounded the bow, I saw where he was headed.

The six lighthouses standing sentinel over the reef were all steel structures. Otherwise, they were all different sizes and construction. The Fowey Rocks Lighthouse, known as the "Eye of Miami was the last one built. A two-story keeper's house was built into the frame with a platform off the southwest side. The yacht hovered just inches away from the steel loading dock.

Gerard had one leg over the bow rail when I saw him. Monika was right behind him, but the situation appeared to have changed. Once he reached the dock, he turned back to her with his pistol extended in her direction. She complied, taking her time as she climbed the rail. At first I worried that she wasn't going to make it, but she was athletic and easily crossed over to the tower. She appeared to slip, but recovered her footing.

In my estimation, she now hovered somewhere between being a hostage and a murderer. I would have to decide how to deal with her when the time came. The pair quickly crossed the platform to the main tower and started up a vertical steel ladder that led to the two-story keeper's house. It appeared that Gerard intended to hide out there and escape later. If I hadn't been watching he might have gotten away with it. His presence would be missed aboard the *Diva*, but the Coasties priority would be the evacuation of the people aboard.

I kept the center console behind the bow of the *Diva* until Gerard was out of sight, then idled toward the platform. The height of the yacht's deck made it possible for him and Monika to just step off to the dock. Many feet lower, my situation was much different. I reached one of the supports for the platform and tied off the bow of the center console to the barnacle-clad steel. Hoping it wouldn't cut through the line, I pushed down on my pistol to insure it was snug in its holster and half-stepped, half-jumped onto the steel leg.

The octagon-shaped tower was constructed with large, steel screw-piles at each of the eight corners. These were braced with smaller beams running at different angles, crisscrossing the structure like a spider web. The low tide made the first few feet of the climb difficult—and bloody—but after that I was able to move back and forth between the braces and the main support to climb to the platform. The barnacles and rough steel cut my hands, but I continued on until I pulled myself over the edge. Glancing up, I saw no sign of Gerard. He must have gained access to the keeper's quarters.

I slipped and found myself standing in an inch of guano. Moving into Gerard's footsteps, I made it to the cover of the main structure and scurried up the ladder, knowing how vulnerable I was if he saw me. I found myself on a catwalk that circled the first floor of the keeper's quarters. The solid wood shutters were closed and secured, allowing me to walk around the structure undetected. I supposed I could camp out here until Gerard decided the coast was clear.

At least I had him cornered. With my back against the old wood siding, I reached into my pocket for my phone, figuring Grace would have the resources to help flush him out, but my phone was gone. Whether it had fallen out on the climb, or I had left it aboard the center console didn't matter. I figured there was no harm in climbing back down and started toward the ladder.

A woman's scream stopped me at the top rung. It had to be Monika. Her potential guilt didn't enter into my decision to help, and I quickly climbed back to the catwalk. A single door was the only access. But even if it was open, I wasn't going to wander into a bullet.

Over the years, I had seen the lighthouse from every conceivable angle. One of its unique features was the enclosed, fifty-foot spiral staircase that went from the second floor of the keeper's quarters to the light itself. Originally, it had housed a first-order Fresnel lens. That now sat in a museum somewhere after being replaced by a solar-powered LED light.

There was nothing to do but climb the outside of the structure and hope I could gain access to the quarters from above. At least I would have the element of surprise. The steel web was just outside the exterior of the quarters, making the first twenty feet an easy climb. After that, I was exposed.

Swinging from beam to brace, I started my ascent.

Halfway up, I'd no problems, but heard the rotors of a chopper moving toward me. My first thought was that I hadn't notified anyone of my intentions and had been spotted. That changed to anger when I saw a man leaning out the side door of a news helicopter taking video of me.

Gerard was blind to my approach, but I assumed he had his phone, and the livestream would be spread across the internet any second. I waved the chopper off, but it was too late. The clock was ticking. With twenty-five feet to go, I climbed as fast as I could and reached the top platform. At the lower level, the catwalk had seemed wide and, though there was no railing, it felt safe. Here, the walkway was much narrower and the railing a necessity.

I circled the light and found an access hatch in the floor. Moving toward it, I pulled my pistol from the holster and, with one hand on the gun, reached for the handle. A loud creak came from the hinge, and I froze for a long second before slowly raising the lid.

I stopped again and listened for any sign that Gerard had heard me. It was quiet, though I thought I could detect the sound of a woman crying. Holding the pistol in a low, ready position, I started down the spiral staircase.

I was halfway down when a gunshot startled me. The bullet ricocheted off the railing nearby and echoed loudly as it struck the iron skin of the walls. I dropped to a squat and was about to continue down when I heard the sound of footsteps coming up the stairs. I peered carefully into the center of the well but couldn't see anything. The treads were spaced about a foot apart, so there were probably between fifty and sixty of them.

That meant there was a lot of steel between me and Gerard, which gave me some comfort and time.

If he were coming up, my best move would be to retreat and find a place I could ambush him in the light tower. I reached the platform of what appeared to be a workroom. Another set of stairs led up, and as I heard the sound of footfalls on the steel stairs echo louder, I climbed to the next level.

I heard Gerard gasping for breath on the level below me. On my belly, I peered over the edge of the landing. I found myself staring into the barrel of Gerard's pistol. I jerked away just as the shot fired.

The concussion did as much damage as the bullet might have. My eardrums felt like they had burst. I was disoriented and my head screamed in pain. I was barely able to think, but knew I couldn't stay here. I rose to my feet, wobbled, and almost fell down the stairs. Shaking my head to clear it, I grabbed the railing that led to the lantern room and pulled myself up the stairs.

I had no doubt that Gerard would follow. The best I could do was be ready. I knew the brilliant LED light was beside me. I moved behind it, but failed to register that it was rotating. Just as the light hit my face, I looked down to see Gerard's gun hand clear the landing.

A shot fired, but went harmlessly through one of the window openings. I kicked at his hand and readied to fire just as the light beam hit me. As painful as the concussion from the shot on the lower level had been, the light had the same effect on my eyes. Feeling like I had been shot through with an electrical charge, I dropped to the floor. It was probably what saved me, as the next shot passed where my head had just been.

My moment of incapacitation had given Gerard the advantage. When my vision somewhat returned, I found him standing above me with the gun pointed directly at my head. I could see the muscles in his forearm tense as I tried to figure a way out.

Monika yelling something from below might have saved me. Gerard's attention wavered for a split second, which allowed me to sweep his feet out from under him. He grasped for the light housing, and just as he was about to gain his balance, the beam hit him in the face.

I knew exactly what he was going through and pressed my advantage home. Before he could move, I jumped to my feet and slammed his head against the protective frame. The beam was pointing the other way, but I held him there until it returned. Even looking away with my eyes closed, the LED light, which was made to be visible twenty-five miles away, blinded me. With Gerard's face pinned to the glass, I could only imagine what it was doing to him. His body slumped as if he had been hit by a taser, and I grabbed his gun.

The fight wasn't out of him, though, and he swung around to face me. Fortunately, the light saved me again as it caught him off-guard with its next rotation. Blinded, he thrashed around. I avoided his desperate blows and slid behind him. A second later I had locked his arm behind his back. Raising it toward his head, I reached behind my back for the zip ties in my belt and secured his wrists.

Breathless, I rolled off him, only to have another light blind me. With it came the sound of a helicopter.

35

STEVEN BECKER
A KURT HUNTER MYSTERY
BACKWATER DIVA

THE NEWS VIDEO MIGHT HAVE ALERTED GERARD TO MY PRESENCE, but the clip of me climbing the tower had been seen by Grace—and a million other people. The first thing I saw—after my vision cleared enough to see around the floaters in my eyes—was her head popping through the access hole. Two more officers followed and took Gerard down.

"You OK?" Grace asked.

I saw the light spinning toward me and ducked. "Yeah. What happened to Monika?"

"Coast Guard is running her in. She'll live."

I'd already seen that Gerard had survived. Hopefully, that meant that both would receive justice. I started to rise, grasping the railing around the light for assistance. It was a struggle, but once on my feet I felt better, not that it mattered. I was determined to get out of the light room before the beam swung around again.

Grace came over to help me, but I shrugged her off and made my way to the ladder. *One rung at a time* became my mantra as I descended to the workroom. The spiral staircase was easier, but I had to regroup again before I attempted the vertical ladder to the main level.

I flinched when I stepped onto the platform, but my eyes acclimated quickly. Around me was a circus. Searchlights panned across the water, revealing what appeared to be twice as many boats and a half-dozen helicopters jockeying for position. The boaters weren't interested in the beauty of the reef and largely ignored the mooring balls. Each one had at least one phone pointed at either the *Diva* or me. With the exception of the police helicopter, the other choppers all had a cameraman attempting to defy gravity in order to get "the shot."

The *Diva* remained where she had struck the reef. The Coast Guard was evacuating the ship from the other side of the yacht, where there was deeper water to maneuver. The rail on this side was empty, except for a lone figure. Justine vaulted across the small gap, landing squarely on the inch of guano coating the platform's deck. She had what looked like a cane in her hand and used it to regain her balance. Even with the aid, she hovered for a long second before gingerly walking toward me.

I smiled and reached for her, but she stepped back and raised the cane. With a pop, it revealed itself as an umbrella. Justine reached around me with her free hand and hugged me tightly, using the fabric dome to hide us from the cameras. I felt a surge of relief spread through me.

"Thought you could use a break from the publicity."

"You have no idea. I guess the videos saved my life, though." I shuddered to think what the outcome would have been if Grace hadn't seen the livestream of me climbing the outside of the tower.

"I'd keep that to yourself. We don't want the vultures to get any bigger heads than they already have."

"No worries there."

"If you're up to it, Grace said there was a press conference scheduled for later."

I thought about it for a second and realized I was no longer in fear of the questions or cameras. From my manipulation of social media to flush out Gerard to the livestream that saved me at the light, I realized that the posts, videos, and reporters were merely tools. It was good to know—but I would still dodge them when possible.

"Maybe I should get an agent first," I said.

We both laughed.

As we walked toward the edge of the platform, I realized we had nowhere to be. In addition to the increasing stream of recreational boaters, the Coast Guard was on the scene, but they were more interested in evacuating the yacht and providing medical attention. There was one Miami-Dade boat trying to keep order, but most of their fleet was incapacitated on the flat by Virginia Key.

I don't remember ever being happier than when I looked down and saw the center console still tethered to the support below.

Justine followed my gaze. "You OK for that?"

I nodded and started the descent. The bulk of the *Diva* concealed us as we climbed down, and I finally landed on the deck. Justine was right behind me.

"Where to, Kemosabe?"

"I know a nice, new little condo with both our names on it. Think it's time to break it in."

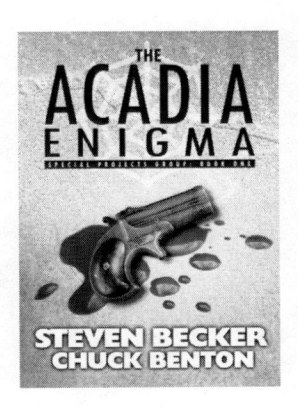

A rash of killings threatens "The Way Life Should be" in Downeast Maine

The Downeast region of the Maine coast is known for its independent, hard-working people, its picturesque settings — and its seafood. But behind the thousand islands, the countless miles of coastline, and the postcard scenery, bad things are happening in Acadia National Park.

GET IT NOW

https://www.amazon.com/dp/B08L8H933C

ABOUT THE AUTHOR

Always looking for a new location or adventure to write about, Steven Becker can usually be found on or near the water. He splits his time between Tampa and the Florida Keys - paddling, sailing, diving, fishing or exploring.

Find out more by visiting www.stevenbeckerauthor.com or contact me directly at booksbybecker@gmail.com.

facebook.com/stevenbecker.books
instagram.com/stevenbeckerauthor

Mac Travis Adventures: The Wood's Series

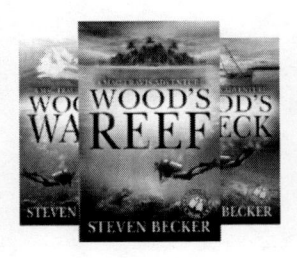

It's easy to become invisible in the Florida Keys. Mac Travis is laying low: Fishing, Diving and doing enough salvage work to pay his bills. Staying under the radar is another matter altogether. An action-packed thriller series featuring plenty of boating, SCUBA diving, fishing and flavored with a generous dose of Conch Republic counterculture.

Check Out The Series Here

★★★★★ *Becker is one of those, unfortunately too rare, writers who very obviously knows and can make you feel, even smell, the places he writes about. If you love the Keys, or if you just want to escape there for a few enjoyable hours, get any of the Mac Travis books - and a strong drink*

★★★★★ *This is a terrific series with outstanding details of Florida, especially the Keys. I can imagine myself riding alone with Mac through every turn. Whether it's out on a boat or on an island....I'm there*

Kurt Hunter Mysteries: The Backwater Series

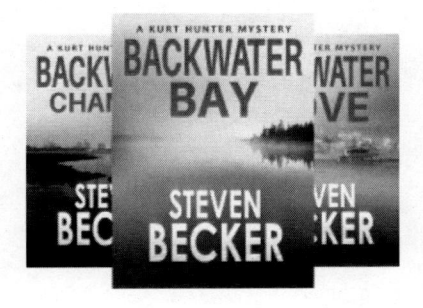

Biscayne Bay is a pristine wildness on top of the Florida Keys. It is also a stones throw from Miami and an area notorious for smuggling. If there's nefarious activity in the park, special agent Kurt Hunter is sure to stumble across it as he patrols the backwaters of Miami.

Check it out the series here

★★★★★ *This series is one of my favorites. Steven Becker is a genius when it comes to weaving a plot and local color with great characters. It's like dessert, I eat it first*

★★★★★ *Great latest and greatest in the series or as a stand alone. I don't want to give up the plot. The characters are more "fleshed out" and have become "real." A truly believable story in and about Florida and Floridians.*

Tides of Fortune

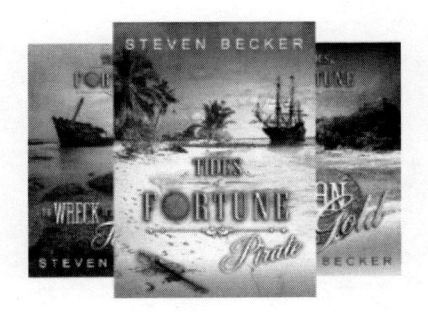

What do you do when you're labeled a pirate in the nineteenth century Caribbean

Follow the adventures of young Captain Van Doren as he and his crew try to avoid the hangman's noose. With their unique mix of skills, Nick and company roam the waters of the Caribbean looking for a safe haven to spend their wealth. But, the call "Sail on the horizon" often changes the best laid plans.

Check out the series here

★★★★★ *This is a great book for those who like me enjoy "factional" books. This is a book that has characters that actually existed and took place in a real place(s). So even though it isn't a true story, it certainly could be. Steven Becker is a terrific writer and it certainly shows in this book of action of piracy, treasure hunting, ship racing etc*

The Storm Series

Meet contract agents John and Mako Storm. The father and son duo are as incompatible as water and oil, but necessity often forces them to work together. This thriller series has plenty of international locations, action, and adventure.

Check out the series here

★★★★★ *Steven Becker's best book written to date. Great plot and very believable characters. The action is non-stop and the book is hard to put down. Enough plot twists exist for an exciting read. I highly recommend this great action thriller.*

★★★★★ *A thriller of mega proportions! Plenty of action on the high seas and in the Caribbean islands. The characters ran from high tech to divers to agents in the field. If you are looking for an adrenaline rush by all means get Steven Beckers new E Book*

The Will Service Series

If you can build it, sail it, dive it, and fish it—what's left. Will Service: carpenter, sailor, and fishing guide can do all that. But trouble seems to find him and it takes all his skill and more to extricate himself from it.

Check out the series here

★★★★★ *I am a sucker for anything that reminds me of the great John D. MacDonald and Travis McGee. I really enjoyed this book. I hope the new Will Service adventure is out soon, and I hope Will is living on a boat. It sounds as if he will be. I am now an official Will Service fan. Now, Steven Becker needs to ignore everything else and get to work on the next Will Service novel*

★★★★★ *If you like Cussler you will like Becker! A great read and an action packed thrill ride through the Florida Keys!*

Made in United States
Cleveland, OH
29 August 2025